CANCER SHIPS AQUARIUS

Signs of Love #5

ANYTA SUNDAY

First published in 2020 by Anyta Sunday,
Contact at Bürogemeinschaft ATP24, Am Treptower Park 24, 12435 Berlin, Germany

An Anyta Sunday publication
http://www.anytasunday.com

Second edition

ISBN 978-3-947909-64-3

Cover Design: Natasha Snow
Cancer and Aquarius Art Design: Maria Gandolfo (Renflowergrapx)

Content Editor: Deborah Nemeth
Line Editor: HJ's Editing
Proof Editor: Lynda Lamb

Warning: This book contains sexual content.

Cancer Ships Aquarius

Cancer Ships Aquarius. Forever and always, if Cancer would just open his damn eyes.

Reid Glover—loyal, emotional, **Cancer**—has a *slight* aversion to the ocean. So becoming a live-in manny aboard the *Aquarian* should be fun.

Sullivan Bell—blunt, humanitarian, **Aquarius**—seems to find Reid ridiculous. *Ridiculously distracting*. And that goes two ways.

Reid can't stop looking at the tough, gorgeous widower. Can't stop trying to repair his broken heart.

Well, crap. These tender feelings can't be happening. There's no way Sullivan can return them.

Right?

Mis-adventure prone Cancer will need a sure-footed Aquarius to figure it out.

"Love is what I had. Heartbreak was its price. I won't buy into it again."

-James
Second Time Around

Chapter One

Reid Glover dunked his fingers into his latte and dabbed the scent of coffee on his *Feminist Is My Favorite F-Word* T-shirt. A shirt he'd loved yesterday, beautifully rumpled on a sleepy Toni, but today it smelled too strongly of her and the putrid stench of rejection.

Laughter twittered around him, and framed Elvis pictures winked at him from the walls. Hopefully the cheerful environment would reenergize his spirits before his nanny interview with the Bell family.

He sank low on the café sofa and shut his eyes, refusing to re-live every line Toni had delivered. Refusing to dissect it. Refusing to drown in inadequacy.

"It's not you, it's me."

A groan escaped him.

That damned line, delivered by his last four girlfriends. It *was* Reid. Had to be.

Footsteps clapped over tile, followed by the familiar hushed voices of his ever-dueling friends—loveable egomaniac Loretta, and steady-as-a-rock Natalie.

"It's your best friend," Natalie narrated to Loretta, "and he's as green as his shirt."

Loretta poked his cheek. "What's wrong with him?"

Reid opened his eyes, swatting at their fingers. "Stop prodding my cheeks. I'm deep in despair, not dead."

Loretta tucked wavy brown locks behind her shoulders. "What 'fuck you' did the universe bestow on our Reid?"

Reid grimaced. "A lover's disagreement."

"Disagreement?" Natalie queried.

"Toni dumped me."

Loretta smirked. "Knew it! You owe me ten bucks, Natty." Natalie nudged her ribs, and Loretta *oof*ed, then aimed for genuine concern. "I mean . . . so sorry, what happened?"

Reid scrubbed his face. "I wanted us to move in together. The feeling was not mutual. I thought it was our dream, but . . . apparently it was just mine."

"Not gonna lie," Loretta said, "that's a stinger."

Reid drowned his self-pity in a gulp of his latte. He kept her parting line to himself.

The words hurt too much to toss around.

Loretta sank onto the couch. "I'm sure there's someone, somewhere who could love—"

Natalie gave Loretta a filthy shake of her head and sat on Reid's other side. "Don't listen to her. Look, you're hot. For a guy. I think."

"Sooo much more helpful," Loretta said sarcastically.

Natalie's eyes sparkled with the promise Loretta would pay for that later. "You're also crazy clever and thoughtful, Reid. And your hair is better than anyone's—"

"—Except mine." Loretta patted Reid's wrist comfortingly. "What we're saying is, there is someone out there who won't mind that you work as a manny, or cry at commercials, or are horrendously misadventure-prone."

"I'm *not* misadventure-prone."

"Last weekend you locked yourself in a toilet cubicle."

Reid flushed. "It didn't have a handle. I didn't see the out-of-order sign, and I totally climbed out on my own—even if I did collapse on a Viking using the urinals, and fuck God I will be single forever."

"Yes," Loretta agreed.

Natalie reached around him and tugged Loretta's hair.

Even down in the dumps, his friends made him laugh. "I haven't told you the worst part."

"It gets worse?" Loretta skedaddled out of Natalie's reach.

Heat scorched up Reid's neck. "Toni mentioned wanting to be . . . to be dominated. In the bedroom. And I said I was a twenty-eight-year-old dog you could teach new tricks."

"Not in those words, I hope."

Reid tucked his mortification into another sip of coffee. "I tried to sexy-growl. And I might have spluttered the word bitch."

Loretta palmed her forehead. "Reeeeid."

"Then buckled under the wrongness of it all and called myself the bitch."

"Oh, please stop."

"I mean, I love sex as much as the next horny man, but I have to admit, I love it most when I get to lie there. When I'm told what to do and how to do it."

"You've killed me—and possibly half the customers here."

Reid gazed around clumps of conversing friends, landing on a stunning guy sitting across from them. Dark crew-cut, broad shoulders, sleeves scrunched up hairy forearms, and piercing eyes stuck on Reid.

Reid's posture stuttered for an embarrassed second and the demigod before him dropped his gaze to his laptop.

"Anyway," Reid said, laughing at himself. "At least you guys will never leave me."

Unnatural silence passed between his friends, and Reid had the prickly feeling he shouldn't have tempted fate.

A silent conversation passed between Loretta and Natalie that Reid wasn't privy to. "What?"

Natalie shook her head. "Nothing."

Reid was depressed, not stupid. He knew something was happening. "Tell me."

"Don't you have an interview to rush off to?" Loretta stonewalled.

Reid checked the time, cursed, and propelled himself to his feet. "Spit it out, ladies. You know my imagination makes mountains out of molehills."

With a sigh, Natalie palmed Loretta's thigh and looked Reid in the eye. "There's something we haven't told you."

He left his sunny-side marina, sailed as far north as he could, and hoped his habit of falling for the wrong guys hadn't followed him.

-David
Second Time Around

Chapter Two

They were in love. His always-bickering friends. In love. With each other.

They were planning a six-month round the world trip.

Leaving in a week.

Loretta and Natalie had skirted around telling Reid for *three weeks*, uncomfortable at the idea they were leaving him behind.

Reid left Kings Café feeling throat-achingly empty.

He thought his breakup was bad, but it was nothing compared to the prospect of half a year without his friends.

The entire bus ride to the neighboring town, Reid couldn't stop picturing how Loretta had folded into Natalie the moment Natalie told him their news. The love and adoration in Loretta's gaze was staggering. Deep happiness pulled at Reid's heart. He was . . . thrilled for them. Absolutely.

He shot off a message to Loretta.

Reid: I expect gifts from every country you visit.

Loretta: We'll miss you, Reid.

Reid totally didn't sniff. Nor did the words on his phone screen blur.

Reid: Wish me luck in this interview. Definitely need a win today.

Loretta: You're the best manny. You'll land the job, no sweat.

REID WAS SWEATING.

A port? A *yacht*?

This was the location of the live-in manny position?

Reid paced Dock J, glancing longingly past the boat lifts toward the marina boardwalk.

Some might call Waverly, this little seaside town, idyllic with its brightly painted historic buildings, golden-leaf trees, and bustling café fare. Some might call the *Aquarian*, the superyacht before him, a classic.

Reid would call it classically outside his comfort zone.

He double-checked the email his cousin Callaghan had sent.

Absolutely no mention of the Bell family residing on water. Just endless gushing about Sullivan Bell's intelligence and parenting skills with his daughter Joanna. Oh, and a single line stating Sullivan is an inventor and four years widowed.

Sullivan's emails hadn't said much either, save a date, time, and an address that had led him to the Marina Service Center, where an attractive, sparkly-eyed Puerto Rican woman named Alanis had asked how she could assist him.

Reid had barely dropped Sullivan's name before Alanis towed him outside the center and jerked a finger toward Dock J and the *Aquarian*.

God, if he didn't need this job so bad. So urgently . . .

But he did. He'd recently paid off his student debt. Hadn't thought he'd need his savings for a rental deposit. Loretta would let him crash on her floor, but only until her lease ended in a week. He was straddling homelessness.

Yeah, he needed this job.

"Reid Glover?" A pondering—quirkily British-sounding—

female voice sailed toward him from the boat. Reid shoved his phone in his back pocket.

A red-haired girl appeared at the gangplank. Tall and gangly—teetering between child and teenager—and freckled like Reid. Her freckles weren't confined to the bridge of her nose like his, rather swept across both cheeks. He liked her instantly.

She smiled widely. "Here for the nanny interview?"

"That depends," Reid said, eyeing the boat suspiciously. "Is the interview held on board?"

"The interview doesn't have to be. The job? Just a bit."

"How much is a bit?"

"Your bedroom overlooks the ocean."

"As I feared." He sighed. "Are you Joanna, then?" Reid inched to the gangplank. He could do this.

He could.

He *would.*

He had to.

"That's me," Joanna said.

"Lovely to meet you. Say, you wouldn't have a life vest at hand?"

Giggling, Joanna tossed him one. The bright yellow vest not only fit, not only promised to keep him alive, it also smelled strongly of bleach, better covering Toni's scent from his T-shirt.

Straps tight, he strode with shaky legs up the gangplank.

He hit the wooden deck and resisted the overwhelming urge to adopt a surfer's pose at the gentle sway underfoot.

"Lead me to your dad?" he begged, an octave too high.

Joanna curled her finger, and he followed her inside the yacht.

It looked like an apartment squeezed in by a third. A small open-plan kitchen with cupboards and benches, an oven, and spices strapped into shelves. A four-person dining table bolted to the floor and cornered by a built-in booth-bench, one long wall with partially open cupboards revealing books, and a large L-shaped couch with blue-and-white striped cushions.

He palmed the cupboard wall like a lifeline—when would the bobbing stop?

Joanna picked up a copy of Reid's three-page resume and a box-filled checklist from the table. "Nice, isn't it? This is the saloon." She pointed to the kitchen. "That's the galley, upstairs leads to the cockpit." She pointed down the ship behind Reid. "My twin cabin and the head—toilet—is behind the dividing wall. Dad's cabin, studio, and second head is downstairs. Along with the nanny nook."

"It's bigger than it appears from outside," he murmured, then panicked. "How does it float?"

She chuckled. "Sit wherever you're comfy. We'll start before Dad comes back from afternoon coffee."

"I thought he knew I'd be here at four?"

"I told him you called and changed it to four thirty."

Meddlesome.

Curiosity piqued, Reid sidled to the couch, bracing against furniture the whole way.

Pen in hand, Joanna studied him over her checklist. "Have you been crying?"

"Er, no?" Reid dabbed his puffy eyes and deflated. "Yeah. Sorry about that."

"Don't be, I love it." Joanna ticked her checklist. "You're blond, which is a definite bonus. Are you married? Single?"

The questions were unorthodox, but he'd never been a stickler for rules. "Single, as of two hours ago."

Her eyes lit up. "Excellent."

"Is it?"

She nodded. "I need someone who'll stick. This year I'm searching for permanence."

This kid was something else. A mature, clever something else.

Reid angled his head, trying to decipher the questions on her checklist. The print was too small. "Why are you running this interview without your dad?"

Joanna scoffed. "Come on. I'm almost thirteen. Do you think I need a manny?"

"So why am I here?"

Joanna sat on the couch, checklist pinched between her fingers. "Dad thinks I want someone who knows the town and can explore it with me. Someone who can help me navigate school and relationship stuff. I told him a nanny would be perfect. Also to help cook and clean and shop and run the household. He loves me—and hates dishes—so he reluctantly agreed."

"So your dad thinks you need a nanny, but . . ."

Joanna smirked and light danced in her eyes. "But what I need is a manny for *him*."

His brows rocketed to his hairline. "Come again?"

"Dad is still broken from . . ." She couldn't finish, but she didn't need to. Reid recognized the loss in her voice. She cleared her throat. "He loves me. But he finds it hard playing 'home'."

"He ignores you?"

"Nothing like that. He's always around. We usually eat together, just never at the dining table. Never with guests like we used to. Life is . . . functional. Mostly he busies himself downstairs in his studio and hopes money will solve my problems." Joanna glanced toward a blue-rimmed window. "But it won't, because my problem is I want a family. A happy one."

Emotion lumped Reid's throat and he swallowed hard.

Joanna continued, "Do you know how many times we've based ourselves in a new marina in the last four years? Four times. At the end of every school year we up and leave. He can't settle. It's like . . . whenever we start settling, getting to know people, building connections, whenever we vaguely resemble a normal family, he can't handle it." Sadness lurked behind Joanna's big, shiny eyes. "I don't want to keep driving off."

Joanna's need clawed at Reid's heart, because it echoed his own thirteen-year-old heart. If Reid had known his dad would leave him, he'd have fought, he'd have changed, he'd have done anything to be enough.

"Have you told him this?" Reid asked.

"He hears me, but he doesn't *listen*."

"So you want a nanny for your dad."

"But under the guise that it's for me. We'd be working on my dad together. Project Anchor the Storm."

"Storm?"

"Dad is an Aquarius. An air sign, you know? But his inner life is in turmoil, hence storm. Not that you'd see it on the outside. Dad doesn't know how to show his emotions—but that doesn't mean they're not there. They're swirling under the surface, and I think they need to be unleashed. Maybe then we'll stay in one place."

The sad yearning in Joanna's voice felt like a hiccup in his own chest. He needed to take this opportunity to help keep a family together. "How do you imagine . . . unleashing them?"

"First and foremost he needs a friend. Someone to show him all this town has to offer. Show him what a new home could look like. Maybe even to encourage him fall in love again." Her eyes darted around the room, and back to him. "That's what this interview is for. Sussing out your compatibility."

Reid beheld the strong young woman, nodded, and answered her hypothetical queries. If he found a book that told his life story, would he finish reading it, knowing he couldn't change anything?

"I'd stop reading and hope for a happy ending." Even if he feared he couldn't manage one. "Any other questions for me?"

"What's your star sign?"

Reid didn't believe in zodiacs or horoscopes, but he found it charming that Joanna seemed so serious about it. "Cancer."

A wonderful smile crested her face. "A homemaker. Perfect." Her posture deflated. "Ugh, not the greatest match with Aquarius, but you and I should get along like two fish in the sea. Or two fish and a crab."

A throat cleared, and Joanna whirled off the couch. "Dad!"

Reid jerked with recognition. Holy shit, the demigod from the café was standing at the door.

His whole body goosebumped at the coincidence. Crazy, synapses-frying goosebumps. This felt bigger than coincidence—like the stars had lined up. Like something in his life was about to change.

Reid shook off the eeriness, silently laughing. It was all this talk of star signs that did it. Nothing more.

Sullivan wore a faded brown jacket and casual jeans. A scuffed bike bag hung from a strap over his shoulder, and his eyes were riveted on Reid.

Sullivan recognized him too, then.

Joanna threw wiry arms around her dad, and Sullivan's bag plonked to the slat floor. He wrapped his big arms around his daughter and kissed her cheek. "Started without me, I see."

More Britishy accent. Even more Britishy than Joanna's.

"Oh, Dad, Reid is *perfect.*"

"Perfect? High praise indeed."

"Not in all areas," Reid said. Not even in most. "But I make an excellent manny."

Joanna set down Reid's resume on the counter. "See for yourself." She ducked behind the half island. "I'll make us all elderflower tea."

Sullivan busied himself slotting his bag in a cubbyhole and

hanging his jacket in a hidden closet. Shirt sleeves shoved to his elbows, he picked up Reid's truncated life story.

Expression undecipherable, Sullivan read every line, strolling nearer.

Milky light washed over him from the overhead hatch, and Reid was hit with Sullivan's full . . . magnitude. His hair was mostly mahogany, a darker shade of the ship's wooden interior, with silver kissing the top of one ear. He was also tall—topping Reid by six inches—and his presence flooded the saloon. Maybe it was the way he moved. Easy. Comfortably in control. *Balanced.*

The boat rocked and Reid clutched the couch.

Sullivan side-eyed him. "Two pages of extra-curricular activities?"

"What can I say? I used to be interesting."

Sullivan read aloud, drily. "Economics club."

"I can file any finances. Blindfolded."

"History club."

"War is bad." Sullivan looked at him, unimpressed. Reid amended, "Sorry. War is *very* bad."

Sullivan's gaze scrolled down the list. "Gay-Straight Alliance."

Reid stiffened. He and most of his friends were gay or bisexual. His last job had been working for married couple Theo and Jamie Wallace, babysitting their adorable twins Atticus and Darcy a few afternoons a week, living for free in their attic. While Reid was inexperienced with men, he sat happily between gay and straight. "If you have a problem with that, I am not the manny for you."

He'd stand to emphasize his point, but the floor was moving, and he wasn't sure he actually could.

"That won't be what I'd have a problem with." Sullivan continued scanning the list. "International Thespian Society, Red Cross Club, Civil War reenactor?"

"History buff, remember?"

Sullivan turned the page and then dropped the resume with a snort. "National Spelling Bee?"

Reid rolled his shoulders and projected his voice. "Uptight. U.P.T.I.G.H.T. Uptight. Origin: possibly staring at it."

Their gazes clashed and Reid detected a faint glimmer in Sullivan's eye. "Boss," Sullivan replied. "B.O.S.S. Definition: I choose whether to hire and when to fire."

Reid shivered. A pleasant, very inappropriate shiver. *Boss: One in charge. One Reid shouldn't become attracted to.* "Touché."

"Stop intimidating him, Dad," Joanna snickered from the kitchen.

Sullivan's gaze frisked Reid from his ruddy sneakers to his ruby-red lips. Sullivan took in his high cheekbones and stubborn chin, lingering on his styled blond hair. Reid fought the impulse to thread his fingers through it.

Was Sullivan calculating how much authority Reid projected? Or was he judging his protective qualities?

Well, Reid could fight. He could fight like a pro.

As long as the opponent wasn't armed with anything sharper than a silver tongue.

He rolled his shoulders back and held his chin high. Sullivan landed on Reid's eyes, mouth curved into a grimace.

Did Reid's tear-splotched face make the man uncomfortable? Or did something else bother him?

"Look," Reid said, "I love working with families, and I have references that will convince you I'm experienced—"

"—to care for babies. My daughter, as you can see, is not a baby. How qualified are you at providing teenagers with appropriate developmental experiences?"

"Well, I'm not *academically* qualified . . ."

Sullivan clasped his hands behind his back and paced the living room. "Nannies are not a decision to make lightly. Your influence may leave long-lasting impressions."

"I certainly hope so."

"You must have a great deal of patience."

"So I'm beginning to see."

"And be safety conscious"—Sullivan eyed his vest—"though I don't think there'll be any issue there. Sound judgement, on the other hand . . ."

A laugh tumbled out of Reid—this man! He'd never met anyone so . . . tightly wound? Overprotective? Uninterested in a nanny?

All of the above?

Sullivan slid open a cupboard wall and drew out a fat book with a glossy black cover. "It's a live-in position with every other weekend off. I like to start work early and Joanna needs breakfast and a ride to school. A good portion of the day would be spent on this boat."

"Yay." Reid tried for enthusiastic but his sudden couch-gripping didn't lend him much credibility.

Sullivan handed him the book.

Reid gaped at the title. "*The Titanic*?"

Sullivan's brow quivered into an arch. "As a history buff, I thought you might enjoy it."

An incredulous laugh jostled out of Reid. "Are you against the idea of Joanna having a manny? Or against the idea *I* might be that manny?"

Sullivan stilled, unfocused gaze lingering on Reid's face. His Adam's apple bobbed and he pivoted sharply toward the kitchen, but not before Reid glimpsed pain in his eyes. "I think this is a bad idea."

Joanna calmly slid a mug over the kitchen counter toward him. "Please, Dad? I need this."

Sullivan's voice came out thin, stretched, exhausted. "Joanna . . ."

"Callaghan said Reid was as good as they come. You trust Callaghan's judgement."

Sullivan grunted.

"One-month trial," Joanna said. "If you're not convinced Reid is the perfect man, we'll let him go."

"Fine, okay," Sullivan gave in. "Maybe he'll fall overboard before that."

"Dad," Joanna warned.

"I won't push him over." Sullivan blinked toward Reid, who crawled off the couch and pulled himself up using the table leg. "God, I won't need to."

Reid managed not to wave a merry middle finger at his new boss. "I'm very partial to this vest. May I keep it?"

The new neighbor was perpetually neon, noisy, dramatic; he was everything I tried not to be, and I couldn't look away.

-James
Second Time Around

Chapter Three

Not five minutes on the *Aquarian*—Joanna curiously absent —and Sullivan was already angling for Reid to give up and go home.

Like last week at the café, Sullivan was ridiculously mouth-watering wearing jeans and a navy button-down, sleeves pushed mid-forearm. Unlike last week, his jaw hadn't seen a shave, and a black-and-orange whistle hung from a lanyard around his neck. It all added to his sex appeal—*and Reid would not go there.*

He was a professional.

Steady blue eyes absorbed Reid from his shoes to his bag to his coiffured hair. Reid ignored his tightening skin, and the way his breathing shallowed when Sullivan grunted.

An absolute professional.

"It's not exactly five-star accommodations," Sullivan warned.

"My other option is sleeping under a bridge." A swell had Reid smartly hugging the life vest he'd toted into the belly of the vessel.

Sullivan raised a brow, as if he knew how Reid's stomach

somersaulted.

Reid loosened his hold on the vest, adjusted the weight of his backpack, and flashed Sullivan his most dazzling smile.

Sullivan jerked his gaze away and opened a glossy wooden door. "This will be your cabin—the nanny nook."

Reid peered past Sullivan into a cozy room that smelled like waxy polish and fabric softener. A tall, single bed with cupboards beneath filled most of the space. A wooden board was hinged and roped to the wall. Presumably it transformed into a desk. A bookshelf basin was built into the bed's headboard, and as Joanna had promised, a porthole looked onto the sea.

Reid squeezed inside, dropped his bag and vest onto the mattress, and lifted *The Titanic* off the shelf. "I like the attention to detail. The bed is missing a pillow, though."

"Right." Sullivan retreated to the hallway.

"Wait."

Sullivan paused, jaw square, eyes pinned to the wall above Reid's head. "Yes?"

Reid hopped a few inches to sit on the bed. Firm, comfy. He toed off his shoes. "So, are you, like, related to Alexander Graham Bell?"

Sullivan was positively nonplussed. "Pardon?"

"Cal mentioned you being an inventor, and with a surname like Bell . . ."

"So if A equals B, and B equals C, then A must equal C?"

Cue Reid's dumbfounded surprise. "Huh?"

Sullivan leaned against the doorframe. "I am a Bell and a scientist. Alexander Graham Bell was a Bell and a scientist. Therefore all Bells are scientists?"

"And related to each other."

Reid loved the exasperation Sullivan speared him with. It quite . . . flurried about in his stomach. This job might be fun after all.

"Your logic astounds me."

Reid tapped his temple. "My mind is full of it."

"Full of it, all right. Much like your resume, I suspect."

He suspected correctly. Not that Reid had *lied* on his resume, per se. He'd merely . . . embellished.

Loretta's idea. She thought it showed Reid as energetic, creative, and highly capable.

Who cared his participation in soccer league had been during kindergarten?

Maybe it was a good thing that Loretta and her questionable influence wouldn't be around for a while . . .

A small hiccup of loss climbed to the base of his throat, and Reid pushed it down, like he'd been doing since Loretta and Natalie's last hug this morning.

He swung his legs, heels bumping the drawers. "I really am into history."

Sullivan re-entered with a whiff of wood and rope and salt. He scooped Reid's shoes off the floor and set them in an overhead cupboard, tucking in the laces and locking the latch. "I'd like to work a couple more hours before Joanna gets home. We can discuss the upcoming week over dinner."

"Should I, er, cook?" Totally not one of the skills he'd embellished . . .

Sullivan eyed Reid and the vest trapped under Reid's palm. "In your state, I don't think it's wise to play with knives."

Reid feigned hurt. "How cutting. So takeout it is. What's Joanna's favorite food, great-grandson of Alexander Graham Bell?"

Sullivan sighed. "Pizza, and I am not related to the inventor. I lecture part-time at universities around the country and spend the rest of my time tinkering with solutions to ocean waste."

"Ah, a humanitarian." Reid liked what he was hearing. "You want to protect the world and all the people in it."

Sullivan harrumphed. "The ones I like."

With a flash of inspiration, Reid stood. This was the perfect opportunity to forge a first connection. They'd be friends before he knew it. "Watch this, Captain."

"*Sullivan.*"

"Yes, sir." Grinning wickedly, Reid pinched the zipper of his hoodie and pulled.

Sullivan visibly stiffened—more with every tooth the zipper popped open. Maybe it was Reid's angle or the light catching on Sullivan's face, but Sullivan looked like he'd been carved out of the wall, one wooden hand at his side, the other clutching the doorframe, his legs crossed.

Sullivan's eyes flashed. "What are you doing?"

"Convincing you that you like me."

"Keep your clothes on, I beg you."

Reid laughed, prowling forward. Sullivan still didn't move.

"Magic!" Reid opened his hoodie with a final flourish. He pushed out his chest and bared his bright yellow *Recycling Rules* T-shirt.

Relief hit Sullivan's expression and Reid rolled his eyes. Sullivan might not be homophobic, but he was clearly uneasy about men joking around.

"See? Recycling," Reid said, flattening the T-shirt across his not-quite-so-broad, but not shabby chest. "We have things in common."

"*Things* might be a stretch."

Sullivan walked off.

Reid grabbed his vest and hurried after him. "What about that pillow?"

He followed Sullivan into a wide room—three times the size of his nook—filled with a table, computers, lamps, long metal pipes and mesh netting, boards with blueprints, a wall with tools latched to it, and a low shelf filled with plastic trash.

Sullivan's studio.

Reid breathed in, tasting metal, sweat, and salt. He felt the prickle of Sullivan observing him from where he leaned against the table, arms crossed.

Reid studied the blueprints and traced a square-tipped finger around the penciled stern of a ship. He paused at a triangular attachment.

Sullivan cleared his throat. "It's to filter and collect plastic waste. I'm working on a prototype that can be adjusted to all stern shapes. If private yachts used it . . ."

"They'd be doing an environmental service while cruising for entertainment?"

"That's the idea."

This man spent his days designing inventions to protect dolphins, whales, fish . . . crabs. Huh.

Reid peeked at Sullivan from the corner of his eye. "Are you working on this alone?"

"Collaborating with the university."

Reid investigated the room. Every piece of furniture and equipment felt weighted with importance. "I was expecting your studio to be all nonsensical, but this is . . . very sensical." He ripped his trailing hand off the shelf of trash. "Ugh, this part is for experimenting, right? You're not a secret hoarder of trash or whatever?"

"The Cheetos packets and yoghurt containers?" Sullivan moved behind the large table, voice sarcastically dry. "Dear to my heart."

Reid startled. "Sullivan."

Sullivan looked over. "What?"

"Was that joke on purpose?"

That earned Reid an unamused look. Sullivan plucked a pillow from a low pull-out bed, partially hidden behind the table.

He tossed it and Reid caught it against his laughing face. "I have to say, I thought I'd follow you into your bedroom to score this."

Sullivan spoke quickly, voice weary. "My cabin is out of bounds. There will be no following me in there. Okay?"

The strain in his voice twisted sympathy in Reid's belly. He nodded, eyeing the pull-out bed. How often did Sullivan sleep in here? Did it hurt too much being in his bedroom?

As if reading his mind, Sullivan shook his head. "The cot is solely for naps."

"How old *are* you?" Reid asked, earning an admonishing look. "Hey, history connoisseur here. Old things make me happy."

"*Creative* naps," Sullivan said. "I'm thirty-seven. Call me old again, you'll eat dinner on deck with a nice view of the sharks."

Sharks in the harbor? Sullivan was pulling his leg, right? "That's young to have a thirteen-year-old." One should never mess with the possibility of sharks. "Really young."

"I adopted Joanna when I married ten years ago."

Oh. Joanna had come from a previous relationship? Did she have other family around? "Cool," he managed. "I, ah, wondered why you look so different."

"She's a spitting image of her grandmother and . . . Riley."

Did Sullivan see his late wife every time he looked at Joanna?

A lump swelled in Reid's throat, and he clutched the pillow hard against his chest. God, it smelled of Sullivan. How many tearless naps had he rested on it?

Day one, and the man made Reid want to cry.

So fucking sorry she died. All the hugs, man. All of them. "So Riley was your—"

"Yes." Sullivan whisked toward his desk, chin tipped. "I need to work. Explore the marina. Introduce yourself to Alanis at the main office." He paused. "Find your sea legs."

He moved like a stallion, solid and straight like a proud worshipper of Odin, had a handsome face, a furrowed brow over a sharp nose, and grey eyes like an ocean of unshed tears.

-David
Second Time Around

Chapter Four

Alanis sat behind a messy desk of paperwork, swiveling her chair toward Reid as he entered trailing his life vest beside him like a pet.

Her smile twitched as she took it in.

"You're Joanna's nanny, aren't you?" At Reid's nod, she stood and shook his hand, "Excellent. She's excited, and Sullivan—well, he'll come around to the idea."

A loud, vibrant laughed escaped her. So big for such a tiny woman. Reid felt like he'd known her forever. Her friendliness echoed into him. She was pretty too, and his age—maybe a few years older. Not his type, though. He'd always gone for women taller and broader than him. Woman who were assertive, possibly a little controlling.

"Have you known Sullivan long?" he asked.

"They moved here at the beginning of summer. Leased their slip for a year. I like what I know of them."

Reid hoped he could soon say the same.

She showed him around the marina, including the restrooms and showers that boaters preferred to use in the winter months due to plumbing difficulties. The pool bar and snack shack, the onsite store, the fuel dock, and waterfront pavilion. Practical and pretty.

If it weren't for the whole water part, Reid would call the place perfect.

BACK INSIDE THE *AQUARIAN*, REID FLUNG HIMSELF ONTO THE cushioned table bench and stared at the brass clock above the cockpit staircase. He'd been here less than an hour, but it felt like an eon.

Joanna arrived home exactly fifty-five seconds later, hair a windswept nest around her rosy face.

"Reeeeeid," she said, trotting into the saloon. "All settled in the nanny nook?"

"For the most part. Where were you?"

She paused at the table. "Oh, um, doing homework in the marina rec room?"

"You were forcing Sullivan and me to bond, weren't you?"

She grinned. "And? Is he charming? Funny? Think you'll be a match made in heaven?"

Hilarious, this girl.

"Charming? A Disney prince. Funny? Bring the defibrillator, I might die from all this laughing. Match made in heaven? Rename the ship to *Cancaquarian*."

Aquariancer?

She punched him lightly in the arm and bounded toward her room, and he boiled down his core responsibilities for Project Anchor the Storm:

1. Encourage Sullivan to spend more time participating in home life
2. Show him awesome places around the area
3. Encourage him to date

4. Become his friend and confidant and help him unleash his bottled emotions

All the while, it should appear to Sullivan as though Reid was merely organizing the household and educating Joanna.

He let out a worried groan and stared at gray clouds through the hatch.

A plane passed overhead. Loretta and Natalie's?

A jolt of loss sliced through him—and right on time, a craving for coffee.

He eyed the kitchen, a good dozen feet away. It'd only taken him a million minutes to climb up here (possibly including some over-reactive clutching of the banister rail).

He could do this . . .

He stood, jabbed his thigh against the table, fell over while hopping in pain, and resumed his seat with a panicked curse.

He would do this another time.

"What's all the racket?"

Sullivan burst into the living area with knitted brows over concerned blue eyes.

"Joanna's home," Reid said brightly.

Sullivan, not seeing any blood, calmed. But his chest heaved like he was catching his breath. "Did she fall through the hatch?"

Reid laughed nervously, eying Sullivan from behind as he passed into the kitchen. "Oh, the clatter?" he asked.

"The crash, rattle, bang—and 'fuck my life.' Yes, that."

Sullivan disappeared behind the counter and Reid jerked his gaze up to find Sullivan watching him apprehensively.

Reid grinned. "Sorry. I'm, ah, contemplating making coffee."

"With my ass?"

Heat rushed to his cheeks. "Sorry, Captain. You've got a great one, though." Nicely curved and firm, not flat like Reid's.

"Um, anyway . . . sea legs. Look,"—Reid patted the chest of his *Recycling Rules* T-shirt—"no life vest in sight."

"You're sitting on it."

Reid winced, readjusting the floatable cushion under him. "I hoped you wouldn't notice."

Within minutes, the scent of percolating coffee filled the saloon, and Joanna bounced back into the room wearing bright fish slippers and a fleece robe over her jeans and shirt.

She slung herself on the bench diagonal to Reid, and spoke to her dad. "Project's starting well."

"Glad to hear it," Sullivan said. "Your partner doesn't make you do all the work?"

"Pretty sure I lucked out there."

Sullivan set a cup of hot coffee before Reid, pausing behind him. A block of warmth fritzed Reid's side. "How much does it count for?"

"Everything," she said.

"The entire grade?" Sullivan was totally clueless his daughter was a cunning mastermind.

Joanna's gaze ping-ponged between them. "The most important part."

Sullivan's warmth shifted to his other side, more intense. Reid busied himself dragging his coffee closer. "Don't worry, Sullivan. I'll do everything I can to help Joanna."

"Oat milk?" Sullivan asked, bringing a container into view.

"Oat?" A weird thought occurred to Reid. No, that couldn't . . . ridiculous. He eyed the milk suspiciously. "*Oat?*"

"We're vegan," Sullivan and Joanna said together.

Reid whirled around on the bench and stared up at Sullivan. That *whole lot of* Sullivan. "No way."

"Since I was twenty."

Reid dragged his gaze over every damn inch. The hard jaw, that corded neck, those arms that flexed as he folded his arms over his whistle, the hint of defined abs denting his shirt, those solid thighs. He prodded a finger against Sullivan's stomach—yep, definitely washboard. "Nope. You're meat lovers, through and through."

A curious flush speckled the base of Sullivan's neck. "This will be a meat-lover free year." Sullivan's blue gaze tickled over Reid's face in earnest. "No matter the temptation."

Reid held his gaze. "I'll try but what if I'm weak?"

Sullivan shifted, hand clamping the carton, spurting creamy milk from the nozzle.

Reid continued, "Maybe I can smuggle meat into my nook?"

Sullivan hesitated. "Anything you do off-board is your decision, but I'd prefer you didn't bring any home."

"Fair enough." Reid swiveled on his seat and caught Joanna's glittery gaze. "And don't worry, cooking will still be a breeze."

The fuck did vegans eat?

"Is that a yes to oat milk?" Sullivan asked.

Reid lifted his coffee. Sullivan, contrary to his calm manner in the kitchen, poured jerkily. This sure would be a year of new adventures. For both of them.

If he didn't get fired in the first month.

Scratch that, the first *week*.

Sullivan retreated to his studio and Joanna stole his coffee and drank from it. "Dad will fire you the first chance he has. You'll have to ignore him or resist his attempts. A flash of your crooked smile should do it."

"He doesn't seem keen on having me around."

"You pose a threat."

Reid frowned. "I'm not taking you away from him."

"Yeah, that's not the threat he's worried about."

"What then?"

Joanna sighed, her hair bouncing over her shoulders as she

shook her head. "You're interrupting the status quo—and Dad thinks the status quo doesn't need interrupting."

Reid stared at Joanna in admiration and fear. "You skipped a grade, didn't you?'

"Seventh."

He knew it. "What project does Sullivan think you were talking about?"

"Biology."

"I'm happy we're on the same side, Joanna Bell."

"Thank you."

He grinned. "So what's Sullivan's favorite pizza topping?"

"Vegan salami."

"Of course."

"Any other questions?"

"Just one."

She beckoned him to spit it out.

Reid leaned in. "What's with his whistle?"

Joanna pulled a similar orange whistle from her pocket. "You mean these?"

"You have one too?"

"Yep. Dad likes knowing I always have it on me."

"What for?"

"Oh, you know. Emergencies. Like when you fall overboard."

Reid lurched to his feet. "Why didn't he give me one?"

The brave idiot kept trying to talk to me.

-James
Second Time Around

Chapter Five

Reid buried his head under his soft pillow. Wood groaned and for a fleeting second, he groped for his life vest, just in case the boat was sinking.

But sleep had a way of calming Reid's daylight anxieties like nothing else.

A thumping knock sounded on his cabin door with a sharp, "Up you get."

Reid tied himself into a knot of limbs and blanket, trying to return to that pleasant dream he'd been having . . .

The door opened, admitting a cool draft and the scent of cedarwood and salt. Reid cracked open his eyes.

Sullivan loomed a careful distance away just outside the door, dressed for the day in jeans and an open shirt over a white tank top. The safety whistle hung at his sternum.

Reid stirred, yawning, pillow still half covering his face. "What torture is this?"

"Morning."

Seemed a bit dark for it. He stretched his torso with one arm crooked behind his head. "Is it already time for you to disappear into your studio?"

"Disappear?"

"I mean, time for me to take Joanna to school."

"You bet. It's six-fifteen."

Reid laughed, stuffing the pillow under his head. He took in Sullivan, all business, framed by the hallway light. "For a second there I thought you said six-fifteen."

"That's exactly what I said. You should've been up half an hour ago."

Yeah, nope. Reid lifted the blanket over his head and curled into a deeper fetal position.

"What are you doing?" Sullivan said, sounding adorably confused.

"You must be a very muscular figment of my imagination. Must be. No one in their right mind wakes up before sunrise."

"Sunrise was at five-thirty—and a much prettier sight than what I'm currently seeing."

Reid folded the blanket off his face and glared at Sullivan. "Hey, I'm pretty." He raised his head enough to scope Sullivan's whole package. "I might not look like a demigod, but I have a delightful smile and a decent nose—and eyelashes that have caused their fair share of resentment."

Eyelashes that have seen a tear or three too, but that was a challenge for another day.

Sullivan crossed his arms in an authoritative pose. Sneaky goosebumps shivered down Reid's torso. "Out of bed, sleeping beauty."

"Aye-aye captain."

In the end, Reid would struggle through the early-hour wake up. He'd do everything the job entailed. Hell, he'd even wake up with a musical number if that's what Sullivan wanted.

"Six twenty," Sullivan said, eyeing his phone.

Yep, Reid would do everything.

But first he needed his ridiculously hard morning wood to subside.

"Six twenty-one," Sullivan said, eyeing his phone.

Reid laughed and groaned.

"Six twenty-two."

"Come here."

Sullivan eyed him suspiciously. "Why?"

"Please come here?"

Sullivan moved hesitantly to the side of the bed.

Reid curled a finger for him to bend nearer, and Sullivan reluctantly did so. Propping himself on one arm, Reid hooked a finger around Sullivan's whistle and whipped it off his head. "You can swim. I need this. Especially right now."

Sullivan blinked at the whistle, then sighed. "Why especially now?" he asked, checking the damn time. "Six twenty-three."

"Because I'm afraid you'll throw me overboard."

"Get up and I won't have to."

"But that's the problem. I can't get up yet."

Confusion crossed Sullivan's face. "It's not that early."

"That is not my only problem." Reid pointed to his sheet-covered crotch, revealing his predicament. Sullivan's gaze sank down Reid's wrinkled tank-top to the tented sheet.

Sullivan's breath stuttered and he hurriedly jerked back. "You're fired."

Reid pushed into a sitting position and pulled the safety whistle over his head. "No way. I was just spelling out my predicament."

"The only word you're spelling is trouble."

"Well S-O-R-R-Y, S-I-R."

Sullivan moved out of sight muttering, "I'll fire him. By the end of the week, I really will fire him."

~

THIS DAY. THIS *WEEK.*

The boat bobbed on turbulent waters and Reid shuffled through it, knees bent—always bent—ready to land on his ass. He stroked Sullivan's safety whistle through the thin material of his pocket and stumbled to the couch. Two days, he'd barely touched his life vest.

Reid slung himself lengthwise over the cushions, fished out his phone, and ground it against his forehead.

He was beyond his comfortable depth. Drowning in every area.

He might be up and rearing to go at Sullivan's first tap at his door, but the rest of the day turned into Unresolved Sullivan Tension.

Reid wanted to find Sullivan's "on" switch and flick it. Light the guy up. Show him what fun they could have together.

Reid re-read his three unanswered messages to Sullivan.

Reid jabbed the screen and called.

Straight to voicemail.

"Ugh, you suck, Sullivan," he yelled, hand cupped to his mouth, falling half off the couch.

There might have been a responding snort, but Reid couldn't be sure.

He rolled back onto the couch, this time tapping his phone against a grin.

Rain drummed against the roof and a rush of wind tunneled into the saloon.

"Wet, wet, wet," Joanna cried.

The door slammed shut and she scurried inside, dripping water across the floor, hair plastered to her neck and face, a storm-tossed mermaid.

Reid pushed onto his elbows. "You poor thing. I'll make you warm cocoa."

She paused at his feet. "Next time, Elijah studies here."

Elijah, the boy she'd been paired with for her biology assignment. A boy who also lived in the marina, in Dock AA.

A boy Joanna *liked.*

"I'm jumping in the shower," she said. "No cocoa, Elijah bought me one at the snack shack."

"Sounds like Elijah likes you."

She blushed. "It was hot chocolate. Although . . . he mentioned seeing a Marvel movie sometime." Ah, young love. So innocent, so all-consuming, so oblivious. "You really think?"

"I really think."

With a radiant smile that made Reid grin, she disappeared.

Reid's phone vibrated. He dropped it onto his face and scrambled to read the incoming message—

Oh. Not from Sullivan.

Loretta.

Loretta! God, finally. She'd written more than a simple *Landed in London.*

Loretta: Missing you. How's it going?

He dove into a reply.

Reid: This is the last time I take on a job because it tugs at the heartstrings!

Loretta: You took it because without it you'd be homeless.

Well! This was true.

Reid: This is the last time I take on a job because I'll be homeless.

Loretta: That bad, is it?

Reid: Frustrating.

Reid told her about his week, not skimping on any of the UST.

Loretta: Let me get this straight . . .

Loretta: You're all worked up because you don't see Sullivan enough?

Reid: Yes! Also, he doesn't have a car.

Loretta: You don't have a car.

Reid: Yes, but the school's bus stop is a mile away. Sometimes Joanna and I run late, and Alanis isn't around to borrow her car . . . you want to know Sullivan's solution?

Loretta: Yes?

Reid: Biking.

Loretta: Great. Good for the environment.

Reid: Tandem biking. He has no consideration what this does to one's popularity.

Loretta: Joanna sounds like a strong young woman who can handle it.

Reid: But I can't.

Loretta: LOL. I totally feel you.

Reid: And I swear, he stands at the stern and watches us with wild, Britishy amusement as we wobble off.

Loretta: Britishy?

Reid: His father was an American ambassador from Florida, and he grew up in London and moved here after finishing an environmental science degree at Cambridge. Somewhere he learned to sail and drive a yacht, earned his Captain's license, and now looks down on the rest of us mere mortals.

Loretta: Sounds fascinating.

Fascinating. Infuriating. Reid hadn't quite decided.

Loretta: Can't Joanna bike on her own?

Reid: There's nowhere to lock up the bike, I need to ride it back again. Joanna often gets a ride home with one of her school friends.

Loretta: Anything else you want to tell me about your Sullivan?

Reid: Well, I would, if I could pull more out of him.

There was one other tidbit Reid had gleaned about Sullivan. He loved audiobooks. Played them every day.

He'd mention it to Loretta, except . . . he couldn't put his finger on it. Something felt extremely private about it. Maybe because Sullivan always turned off the books whenever Reid got close. Maybe because the air felt heavy every time Sullivan caught Reid trying to listen in.

Something about Sullivan's love of audiobooks felt . . . intimate. Not something he understood and certainly nothing he wanted to share with his best friend.

Loretta: Don't expect to unearth all his secrets in a week. It took me a long time to figure Natalie out.

Reid: I still want to hear that story—the whole sordid story and not just the end result.

Loretta: A decade of dating men, and I could never put my finger on why it didn't feel right. The moment Natalie kissed me it slammed into place, I liked every touch better. Every lingering look. Every snarky conversation.

Reid: Sounds perfect.

Loretta: She is.

Reid smiled, longing for the same, and promptly swore. What was that smell?

Oh fuck, dinner was burning.

Reid dashed to the oven and winced as billows of black smoke puffed in his face.

He crooked an arm over his nose and coughed. He grabbed gloves and withdrew the vegan lasagna that looked nothing like the one on YouTube.

The pumpkin. The fucking pumpkin was on fire.

He threw a dishtowel over it and snuffed it out.

Fuck.

Rain, sea. So much water all around them, yet Reid had managed to make things burn.

He peeled back the dishtowel. How could dinner burn and still be under-freaking-cooked?

Smoke stubbornly plumed through the saloon, so Reid opened the deck door. The boat bobbed sharply, and puddled water seeped over the door rim and soaked his socks.

"What happened?" Joanna asked.

A pajama-clad Joanna fanned her face. She spotted the lasagna on the kitchen bench. "How much of your resume would you say you exaggerated?"

Reid groaned and sank against the opened door, scrubbing his hair. He shivered too, because the wind had an icy bite. He was dressed in a thin pair of tight jeans and a loose, striped T-shirt that may or may not look like the couch cushions, because he may or may not have spotted the shirt in a thrift store and wondered if Sullivan would notice him if he sat still.

Joanna leaned beside him.

"He's going to fire me," Reid said.

"He's fired you three times this week."

"For real, this time."

"So what, you can't cook? You're still a great nanny."

"You barely need a nanny. Cooking made up most of the job."

She elbowed his side. "That was never the job, remember?"

He wasn't making headway on that, either. "Not sure you hired the right guy."

She cocked her head and eyed him, and Reid hid his suddenly stinging eyes behind a fake laugh. "I'd better clean up."

Joanna hooked his arm. "Wait. Dad used to love cooking. Before."

"That right?"

"The galley was his second studio. Recipe inventions left, right, and citrus." Joanna knocked the door behind Reid. "Perhaps we close this, and open the oven wide, and—"

"Smoke him out of the studio?" Reid asked, brow arching.

She giggled and acted scandalized. "Your mind is so devious, Reid."

Reid snorted, and shut the door with a solid thud. "There will be fallout for this."

"I have faith you'll handle it," Joanna said. "If he gets too grumpy, toss your hair about."

Reid opened the oven, holding his breath. Christ, that's bad. "Do dumb blonds get free passes or something?"

"Or something." Joanna bypassed the couch and headed out the room.

"Where are you going?"

"Out of the line of . . . fire. Later."

Reid sank into the couch with an arm braced over his nose.

As if on cue, Sullivan swept into the room. Tendrils of black smoke wisped around him like a demonic halo. The half-opened white shirt he was wearing revealed an unnecessary amount of silky chest hair. His glowering gaze had Reid fighting a nervous inner tickle—and he froze against the couch cushions.

Maybe Sullivan wouldn't see him? Maybe?

Sullivan's eyes latched onto him.

"Dammit. I was hoping you wouldn't notice me."

"You're impossible not to notice," Sullivan said incredulously, crossing to the stairs. "As impossible as this smoke." Sullivan opened the deck door and paused on his return, soaking Reid in. "Are you wearing a cushion cover?'

"T-shirt. Do you like it?"

"Well of course I like it, or I wouldn't have chosen it for my cushions."

Reid beamed. "That's the closest you've come to admitting you like me. I'm just as cuddly, in case you're wondering."

How fast can a man's gaze move away? Jesus. Sullivan strode toward the kitchen. "What burned?"

That *look*. "Dinner."

Sullivan surveyed the casserole dish for a long time. When he looked over at Reid, clarity burned in his eyes. He knew for certain now that Reid's resume sparkled a little too brightly. He had finally landed on something he could legitimately fire him for.

Guilt climbed its hot fingers up Reid's neck, because Sullivan would be well within his rights. But . . . Joanna needed him here. Something else urged him to stay, too.

Something deeper than feeling emotionally moved to help. Reid needed to prove he could knit a family together. Maybe it stemmed from loneliness, from everyone leaving his life. Maybe there was no maybe about it.

"We all have bad cooking days," Reid blurted.

Sullivan's brow quivered. "Are you calling this an anomaly?"

"Yes. Anomaly can cook anything." Did he just butcher the word anomaly for "I normally?" Yep, he did.

Reid felt stupidly happy about it.

Sullivan combed his accidental smile with his palm and hoofed across the room.

"Hold up." Reid hurried after him. "You're not heading downstairs are you?"

Sullivan pivoted, and Reid slammed into him. It was like bashing against rock. Reid bounced off him and stumbled to balance himself. Hands instinctively closed around Reid's waist, warm fingers leaking through his thin T-shirt.

Reid caught tenderness in Sullivan's expression.

Tenderness Sullivan quickly masked when their eyes met. His hands slid over Reid's hips and he quickly folded his arms, setting a buffer between them. He cleared his throat. "You seem confident enough not to need my interference. I'll let you return to"—he glanced over Reid's head at the mess in the kitchen—"cooking."

Oh, Sullivan knew. He *knew.*

Reid could admit he sucked at vegan cooking and flip his hair about for that free pass. But.

The energy between their exchanged words made this feel like a game.

Reid had never cared about winning games. Not with Natalie nor Loretta. But clearly it mattered which opponent he faced. Sullivan made him want to score.

"I mean," Reid said, floundering. "I burned my hand. I'd fix dinner, but . . . *ouch.* I'm so sorry, you'll have to take over tonight."

Sullivan's brow quirked. "You burned yourself?"

"Yes, see?" Reid turned his hand palm up and presented it to Sullivan.

Sullivan glanced down. "I don't see anything."

Reid folded all but one of his fingers and lifted it between his eyes. Warm, slightly callused fingers cuffed Reid's wrist and Reid felt the gentle pressure like a pulse.

Sullivan inspected his finger. "I still don't see anything."

"See that red spot?"

"Yes."

"That's it."

Sullivan's fingers loosened but they didn't slide off him. "Pack your bags, we better race to the ER."

Sullivan stroked Reid's finger absently. "Did you put it under cold water?"

"I put it in my mouth. A little sucking does wonders for relief."

Sullivan dropped Reid's fingers and desperately eyed the exit.

Thunder cracked in the distance, and a violent swell underfoot shot uneasiness through Reid. He lunged for support. Namely Sullivan. Reid clasped Sullivan's firm bicep through the soft sleeve. "So, gonna help me out?"

Sullivan stepped back, shaking his head.

Reid moved with him. "All right, forget about dinner. How about we spend time together? We could invent an exciting game where we crawl off the boat onto firm ground. It could double as yoga."

Sullivan flexed under Reid's tightly gripping fingers.

"Whoa, forget yoga," Reid said, rubbing Sullivan's arms admiringly. "What do you do to grow those?"

Sullivan grunted, then unwound Reid's hands and offered him the table ledge.

Okay, Reid may have overdone it with the rubbing. He grinned, slightly flushed, and pointed at Sullivan's arms, torso, his whole damn body. "Seriously, though. How do you look so good?"

Sullivan scrubbed his jaw. "Swim. Bike. Sail."

From years of habit, Reid spat back, "Fuck, marry, kill."

Sullivan's gaze sizzled into him. "Pardon?"

Erm . . . "Fuck while swimming in shallow waters, marry anyone that worships firm ground, stab anything with sails? You don't know the game?"

"I know the version played with celebrities."

"Loretta and I adapted it for shits and giggles. Whistle. Jacket. Cushion. Go."

Sullivan blinked. "With conversations like these, I could be in real danger of liking you. How about you disappear into the galley and we ignore this out-of-control magnetic force between us?"

Such dry witty sarcasm. Reid gaped, speechless. "You're . . . funny."

"If you say so."

"You make me want to laugh."

Sullivan spun from him and escaped the room. "Laugh while you cook."

The sad Viking God kept looking at him.

-David
Second Time Around

Chapter Six

In the end he salvaged scraps of lasagna and served the Bells dinner with lettuce on the side. The next couple of days he ordered takeout, plated it, and hid the evidence. Not a long-term plan, but maybe he could find workarounds until his trial month ended?

Hopefully.

In the meantime, hanging with Joanna was a breeze. Despite barely seeing Sullivan in the flesh, he overheard him chatting with Joanna in his studio every evening. She did her homework down there, and Reid loved the mental picture of Sullivan patiently answering her wildly smart questions.

The captain might have issues, but loving his daughter wasn't one of them.

Reid slumped into the saloon. A dewy, salty evening breeze funneled in from the partially opened hatch.

He wasn't sure if he was shivering from the cold, the fact he had to make dinner after his credit card was declined while ordering takeout, or the message he'd received from Toni.

All three, probably.

Joanna eyed him from the couch over the magazine she

was reading, elbow resting atop her overnight bag. She wore jeans and a clashing pink pullover that Reid was sure she'd chosen on purpose. Her hair was tightly braided and her freckled cheeks were rosy from the draft.

Reid moped into the kitchen. Blindly, he slid open cupboards, pulling out anything that appeared edible.

Joanna cleared her throat. "You look green."

It wasn't solely seasickness. "Ugh, matters of the heart."

She leapt off the couch and trundled toward him, still holding her magazine. "Tell me more."

Joanna's eagerness tugged at a grin. It didn't last long, though. He groaned. "Toni messaged about picking up my stuff. I mean, I knew it was coming. But it still stings."

She jumped onto the counter next to him, and casually resumed perusing the weekly horoscopes. "Dad needs help with his love life. You need help with yours. I can provide the answers. I think I should quit school and become a matchmaker."

Reid pointed a carrot at her. "No quitting school. But I'll take all the help I can find in the romance department."

Light sparked in her eye. "I'm off for a sleepover tonight. You have no obvious manny obligations."

"Suggesting I put myself out there again?"

"Yeah. Take Dad out and have some fun."

Fun. Good idea. The Unresolved Sullivan Tension was killing Reid. He'd complained to Loretta about Sullivan's countless disappearing acts so much this week, she had threatened to block him unless he took action.

"You're right, Joanna," Reid said. "I need a night with your dad."

~

After a cringeworthy dinner of soup, Reid freshened up. He palmed his ass, admiring his skin-hugging jeans and his favorite black T-shirt with the artistic hole at his hip that had landed him a few numbers.

Bars and clubs weren't his favorite pastime—he preferred curling up with a movie at home—but tonight he was filled with sparkly energy to do something fun with Sullivan.

He snuck to Sullivan's bedroom door. Voices from Sullivan's audiobook droned in his ear, and Reid grinned.

Every night, the same.

Like Sullivan couldn't sleep without it.

He pressed an ear against the door. The male narrator described a surprise kiss—quite the passionate kiss, too. The heroine was getting off on the guy's steady, demanding need to consume her mouth.

"Please, my knees might give way," I said, weakly protesting with the barest turn of my head. He pressed me hard against the galley door, propping me up with his thigh between mine. His breath was hot in my ear and his words trembled, yanking at my chest.

"I want your knees to give way. I want you to know what I feel every time I look at you."

The captain listened to romance books?

Reid *liked* it.

It meant Sullivan was ready to find true romance again, right?

He raised his hand to knock, when a sniff cut through the air. It cut Reid like a jagged rock to the heart.

He froze, fist poised an inch from the wood paneling.

Or maybe it meant Sullivan longed for the love of his life.

Reid dropped his hand. Maybe it was too soon to push Sullivan into the dating scene.

He swiftly backed up.

The door swung open and Sullivan appeared, fully dressed down to the whistle, face wretched with emotion.

Reid's focus suctioned onto Sullivan's deeply pained expression. Not the first time he'd seen this look. But that didn't stop the glimpse into the storm wrecking Reid's fragile emotions. It dumped him in a land far away, where he didn't know how to orient himself.

Sullivan halted, catching Reid in his path. Sullivan schooled his expression and grew another inch as he straightened his shoulders and laid glistening blue eyes on him. "What are you doing outside my door?"

"Aren't I always outside your door?" Reid's gaze fell to the bowl Sullivan balanced in one hand. The soup Reid had attempted to make for dinner. The liquid still sloshed around, barely touched. Like his own bowl had looked. "I mean . . . we should go out. Have a heart to heart. We can save dancing for another time."

Sullivan eyed him warily.

Reid reached out and patted his arm, thumb rubbing across Sullivan's hand. He hoped it said: *sorry man. It's okay to feel the pain. Let it out, okay?*

Sullivan shifted in the doorway, and Reid glanced over his shoulder into the master cabin. The bed was easily twice the size of Reid's, though not as tall, with scrunched sheets and a heavy-looking blue comforter.

Sullivan closed the door behind him, and a flush climbed Reid's neck.

"I was debating heading out for something edible," Sullivan said, moving past him.

Reid's stomach lurched in agreement. "Not the best dinner I could have made."

"Vegan cheese isn't normally a good fit with carrot and—pasta, was it?"

"Pea pasta. Disintegrated a bit. Too much water, I guess. Shall we get dinner together?"

Sullivan headed upstairs and toward the kitchen.

Reid trotted after him. "You won't leave a hungry man without food, will you?"

"Yes."

"Oh my God. You're killing me with your compassion and generosity."

"You're right." Sullivan turned, a twinkle in his eye, and handed Reid his soup. "A minute in the microwave should suffice."

Reid dumped it into the sink. "Don't make me beg. Or do," Reid started dropping to his knees.

Sullivan's nostril's flared and his eyes darkened. He cuffed Reid's wrist and hauled him to his feet. They stood close, five seconds of shared air. Of Sullivan debating whether to let him come along or not. Until, finally, huskily, "Okay. Let's go."

Reid followed Sullivan to the deck door. "Will we eat in? Or takeout?"

Sullivan chuckled. "I'm quite done with takeout. Aren't you?"

Reid grinned and flushed with guilt. "No idea what you're talking about?"

"No idea, hmm?" Sullivan unhooked Reid's coat from the closet and passed it to him.

Reid avoided direct eye contact and struggled to stuff his arm through the sleeve. "So, eating out. What do you think about paying for both of us? Next time on me?"

"This is not a date, Reid."

Reid thought about the dire state of his bank account. He sighed. "I wish it was."

He might squeeze ten dollars out of his card.

He'd have to try.

Sullivan zipped up his own coat, quietly deliberating. Like the idea of dating another guy was outside his comfort zone. Sullivan's vaguely homophobic behavior was the only quality Reid disliked about the guy.

Reid sighed. "Okay, here's another idea. We hit Target and you make food here."

"Or I watch you cook," Sullivan suggested.

Reid inwardly cursed the smugness overtaking Sullivan's face. "I'm off the nanny clock. But you can show me what you love to eat. We'll call it research."

Sullivan opened the door and a wash of sleeting rain hit his boots. "I never pegged Cancer for being this stubborn."

"It's surprising me as well."

THEY SHOPPED FOR AGES. LOTS OF VEGETABLES FILLED THE cart, along with oat milk and muesli, and the whole time Reid chatted, warming up to the meaningful stuff.

". . . because these last weeks, it's felt like I'm doing something wrong." Reid eyed the shelf of chocolate mini muffins longingly.

"Just felt like it?" Sullivan asked, close behind him. "You nearly burned my yacht down."

Reid flashed him an apologetic grin.

"Have you always charmed your way out of misadventures?" Sullivan asked curiously.

Reid studied the desserts. If he were sure his card wouldn't decline, he'd buy those delicious-looking vegan muffins.

Full of sugar, of course. And ridiculously priced. "You're the only person who has ever put my name alongside charm."

He reluctantly shelved his first choice of dessert. Sullivan plucked it off the shelf. He eyed Reid softly, making Reid want to question who the man standing before him was, and what happened to Sullivan.

Sullivan hummed. "I can't believe that."

"Huh?"

Sullivan dropped the muffins into the cart, and Reid couldn't figure out if a compliment lurked in there.

He shook it off and sauntered ahead. "Tell me more about yourself."

"Whatever for?" Sullivan said, sounding like himself again.

"Because I'm curious." Reid turned around, walking backward. "I want to get to know you. Don't you want to get to know me?"

"Yes," Sullivan said absently, and then snapped his mouth closed. "I mean . . . better not."

Delight jumped around in Reid's chest. "You said yes." He grinned. "You want to know me."

"A little."

"You want to know *all* about me," Reid teased. "You want to know me inside out and backward."

The flash of warning in Sullivan's eye halted Reid. Reid might be pushing too far. Being in Sullivan's company longer than half an hour was growth. He had the rest of the school year for Sullivan to warm to him.

If he made it through this trial. Which he *needed* to happen.

Like, *really* needed to happen.

"It's been two weeks," Reid blurted as they headed toward the checkout. "I'm feeling my purpose with your family."

He realized the moment it left his mouth that he'd said too much. Anxiety whistled through him. The true weight of what he and Joanna were trying to do with Project Anchor the Storm settled in his bones.

Also, his nape was sweating from that intense look in Sullivan's eye. Some tension had to give, and that tension would be part of his secret. Enough that he wasn't deceiving Sullivan; not enough to give Joanna away.

Sullivan halted the cart before a stand of bestseller books. "Your purpose?"

Reid gulped and nodded.

Reid felt Sullivan studying him like a beam of sunshine against his temple. He quickly picked up a romance book and skimmed it. "Want to buddy-read this book?" He waggled his eyes. "Or I could read it to you if you prefer."

Sullivan readjusted his grip on the cart, frowning. "A book about a woman smothering an airbrushed man?"

"They're all about women smothering airbrushed men. Not much diversity here. But . . . it could be a laugh?"

Sullivan was supremely disinterested. Surely he was faking it? "I know you listen to romance."

"Sam Baton's books. Only his. What did you mean, your purpose with Joanna and me?"

Reid returned the book to its place, stored Sam Baton's name away for later investigation, and fumbled over his words. "You're a daddy, Sullivan. I need to help you act like one."

"Pardon?" Sullivan sounded genuinely confused. He let one hand go of the cart, twisting to face Reid directly. "Come again?"

Reid clasped Sullivan's upper arms. He couldn't help it. Something about this storm sucked him in. "A daddy, Sullivan. Daddy, daddy, daddy. Let me ride the pony, Daddy."

Shoppers side-eyed them. Sullivan closed his eyes. "Could you perhaps stop calling me daddy?"

"But that's what you are. A good daddy, too. So loving. You've shown me that in glimpses." A shopper shot them a dirty look and muttered something about leaving kink in the bedroom. Reid frowned. Realization had him casting Sullivan a horrified look. "Oh. Did it sound like I was calling you Daddy? Like, spank me and kiss me better, Daddy?"

Sullivan took a calming breath.

Reid had the urge to laugh-cry but it was trapped under a ton of heat crushing his chest. He wasn't sure what made it worse, publicly announcing Sullivan was his daddy, or imagining Sullivan crushing him against the wall, pinning him with enough desire to weaken his knees.

Reid rubbed his forehead like he could erase the unbidden thought and the stirring of his cock. He was fully aware of Sullivan's effect on him, but he'd managed to temper those feelings.

What about poor Sullivan? Of all the kinks Reid could have cast on the guy, "daddy" wasn't the most flattering. Not when he disliked any mention of his age.

Reid whispered apologetically, "This won't get me dinner with a view of the sharks, will it?"

Sullivan continued to stare at Reid like he was an anchor that just wouldn't sink.

A deep laugh toppled out of Sullivan. His shoulders shook, his eyes creased at the edges, and his chin thrust upward. "You're trouble, Reid. So much goddamn trouble I'm in no way ready for. Whatever am I going to do with you?"

"You could . . ." Reid's eye caught on a familiar figure behind Sullivan and the blood drained from his face.

Sullivan noticed too. His laughter choked to a stop. "Reid?"

Reid couldn't answer from the sudden swelling in his throat. He clenched his hands into fists, eyes pinging from his long-legged, graceful ex to the gym-rat specimen she was wrapped around. She wore three-inch heels and a snug crimson dress that barely hit mid-thigh. Gym-rat's jacket hung from her shoulders.

Gym-rat sniffed Toni's dark wavy hair, and the hope that he was a clingy relative disappeared.

Not that Reid cared if Toni had moved on.

But did she have to move on so quickly?

Sullivan followed Reid's pinched gaze. "Ah," he said under his breath. "Your ex?"

Reid nodded, transfixed on Gym-rat. He resembled

Sullivan with all that muscle and rugged handsomeness. A man who knew how to give Toni what she wanted in the bedroom. "Damn him."

And damn again. "They're heading our way."

Panicked, Reid grabbed two fistfuls of Sullivan's opened coat and yanked the man against him. He buried his head against the crook of Sullivan's neck and hid inside a tight hug. Sullivan's surprised breath fizzled through Reid's hair and down his nape.

"Tell me when they're gone." Reid's soft words bounced against Sullivan's clavicle, returning to him dewy and tasting of Sullivan's fresh salty scent.

Sullivan curved an arm around him and pressed his lips against Reid's head, holding there. Passersby must think they were sharing an emotional moment. Good improvising, Sullivan!

His warm lips felt like a massage. No question. Sullivan was the most comfortable person he'd ever wrapped himself around. Warm and stable, with an addicting scent Reid wanted to rub on himself. A pity the guy was so standoffish. Reid would do this all the time.

He capitalized on his current predicament and shifted his arms under Sullivan's jacket around his firm planes of his back. A sigh bubbled up his chest.

Sullivan's lips dragged to the top of his ear. "They're at the checkout in front of us."

Right. Toni. "I suppose hobbling away with you like this would cause her to look over?"

"Among a few raised eyebrows. Wait, *her*?"

"My ex. Toni." Reid whispered back.

"She is *Toni*?"

Reid angled his head to throw him a puzzled look. "I don't remember telling you about any other ex."

Sullivan's arms loosened around him, but he didn't pull

away. "I thought you were gay."

"Bisexual. Even if I've never been with a guy before."

"Could've fooled me."

Reid's nose combed Sullivan's collar as he peeked over his shoulder. Toni and Gym-rat were still there. He ducked his head against Sullivan again. "What does that mean?"

"You're . . . very comfortable flirting."

A nervous *yip* escaped Reid. Sullivan had realized he was into him? Well, this was a fun conversation to have in hushed tones, cocooned in a necessary embrace. "I think the word you're searching for is *unintentionally*. Comfortable? You think?"

"You told me you wished this was a date."

"Because I'm broke and I wanted you to buy me dinner."

"You rub my biceps like you might make a wish."

"But . . . that's . . . true. Huh." He growled. "Is that why you haven't wanted to spend much time with me? Why I put you on edge? Because you think I'm into you?"

Sullivan whispered an emphatic, "Yes."

Reid pinched his side and glowered at Sullivan's chest. "Here I thought you were struggling with the loss of your wife and couldn't bear living without her."

Sullivan stiffened. "My wife . . ." His voice pinched like he couldn't believe Reid had said that.

Guilt sucker-punched Reid. He was still upset at Sullivan for disliking him because he might be gay, but he'd gone too far with that comment. Reid swallowed. "I'm sorry, Sullivan. I shouldn't have mentioned . . ."

"My . . . *wife*?" Sullivan finished, disbelieving.

"Yeah."

Sullivan groaned, crushing Reid in a hug. "There's nothing to worry about."

Sullivan let him off too easily with that, but Reid accepted it. He reluctantly forgave Sullivan for his behavior, too.

"Nothing to worry about." Sullivan murmured into Reid's hair. "Except for how utterly oblivious . . ."

Obliviously Reid had stung Sullivan with that comment.

Sullivan huffed a laugh. "I'm very, very straight. And you're *unintentionally* flirting. This can work. We can be on the straight and narrow together."

Reid's patience evaporated, and he trod hard on Sullivan's foot. "I gotta stop the homophobic-sounding shit escaping your mouth."

"Me? Homophobic?"

"Yeah. I mean, granted you're doing me a solid with this hug right now. But you act like my touch sullies your straight virtue. Well, it's bullshit."

"That is not—" Sullivan halted. Warm breath tickled over Reid's temple. "Yes, okay. I hear you. Nobody is falling for anybody, and all touches between us are friendly ones."

Reid sighed. Another quick peek revealed a checkout line free of Toni and Gym-rat.

He pulled back from Sullivan and gazed up at his thought-absorbed face. "They're gone. Can we start over, Sullivan?"

Sullivan released him, hands skating off his hips. Those shockingly blue eyes pierced Reid. "Let's."

Reid held out his hand. "I'm Reid. I like cuddling. I'm prone to misadventure. And for no traumatic reason, I'm deathly afraid of the ocean."

Sullivan's cheek twitched. "Sullivan. I haven't made the best first impression, but I'd like to get to know you."

"A little," Reid amended for him. He pinched two fingers an inch apart.

Sullivan's chivalrous grin appeared between them. "Maybe a little more than that."

~

Back at the yacht, Reid and Sullivan unloaded their reusable produce bags. Reid couldn't stop biting his lip on the constant urge to grin. The entire walk, Sullivan had fired curious questions at him. Reid had given Sullivan a breakdown of his life, dwelling mostly on his grams, who raised him. Somehow Sullivan steered the conversation back to Toni.

"She might need me to pick up my belongings, and I might not have answered her texts."

Sullivan shut the fridge. "When?"

"She messaged this morning. She wanted me to come today or wait until she returns from Hawaii."

"I'm guessing you're procrastinating?"

"Ugh. I was feeling good, but you seeing how pathetic I am ruined it."

Sullivan laughed. He'd laughed more freely since the supermarket. He was still blunt as hell, but his laughter tempered it. A bit.

"When she's back," Sullivan said. "I'll borrow Alanis's car and drive you."

"Okay, seriously. Who are you and where's Sullivan?"

Still grinning, Sullivan pulled out a package of pasta, onion, garlic, crushed tomatoes, and an eggplant. He procured two wooden boards and knives and handed Reid one of each. "Let's see you cook."

"There he is."

A glint hit Sullivan's eye as he surveyed the vegetables between them and set the eggplant on Reid's board. "You prepare that for the sauce and I'll cut the onions."

Of course Sullivan had chosen the most difficult vegetable. The one Reid had the least experience with. He'd never bought the vegetable before. Had once eaten it at a restaurant —and that was ordered by mistake.

Reid scowled at Sullivan's smug delight. "Stop looking at me like you know everything."

"I do know everything. All the time. Like right now," Sullivan said, leaning toward him, lowering his voice conspiratorially. "You are sweating behind that counter, clueless how to prepare the nightshade before you."

"Pssht. I totally know what to do with it. You focus on your onions. Practice crying."

Sullivan began chopping onion like a pro, and Reid surreptitiously angled his phone under the lip of the counter. He kept his posture casual, tapping out a message to Loretta. He prayed she would answer.

Reid: Help!

He muted the volume, and smiled innocently at Sullivan. "Just deciding how I want to cook it. Too many options, you know?"

Sullivan's lips quirked.

Reid glanced at his phone.

Loretta: What's wrong?

Reid: Sullivan presented me this fat 🍆. What do I do with it?

Loretta: I never expected to hear this from you. Okay, that's a lie, I might have wondered if you'd come to me for this kind of advice.

Reid: Instructions!

Loretta: Why don't you ask Sullivan for instructions?

Reid: Because I don't want him to know I'm inexperienced with 🍆🍆🍆

Loretta: Don't you think he'll guess, since you're texting me?

Reid: Just tell me what to do.

Loretta: Do what feels right. Hold it firmly but tenderly, and use protection. Anything else, consult YouTube.

Protection? Were eggplants poisonous until cooked?

Reid was about to search that, but Sullivan shook his head. "Had enough Googling?"

Reid snuck his phone to his pocket with an innocent bat of his eyelashes. "I need some gloves."

Sullivan stopped midway through cutting a slice of onion. “Gloves?”

Reid rolled his eyes. “For protection, duh.”

Heavy laughter and kitchen gloves flew toward Reid. He caught the latter against his chest and snapped into them. Wriggling his fingers, he looked from the eggplant to Sullivan, who stood, onions forgotten, with folded arms, attention rapt on Reid.

“Stop looking. I’m getting performance anxiety.”

“Would you rather watch me have at it?”

“Oh hell yes,” Reid breathed out in relief. “I know how I like it. But not how you want it, so showing me precisely what you’d have me do . . . would help.”

Sullivan grasped the eggplant without protection. His fingers wrapped around the base and he positioned it before him. “Tell me the truth. You’ve never done this before, have you?”

Reid bowed his head. Sullivan had won. Reid sighed and mumbled, “No.”

Sullivan released the eggplant and rounded the counter to Reid. He curved a finger under Reid’s chin and steered him up until Reid had no choice but to meet his eye.

“You could have told me from the beginning.”

“Maybe, but I didn’t want you to fire me. And . . . I liked playing along. With you. It was fun.”

Sullivan dropped his fingers and scrubbed his jaw. “I might have liked it too.”

“Does that mean you won’t fire me?”

Sullivan glanced at their cutting boards. “Because you’re inexperienced in the kitchen? No. Maybe I can teach you a few skills.”

Did that mean Sullivan would spend more time in the kitchen, the heart of the family home? Reid eyed him with cautious hope. “Really?”

"Yeah." Sullivan grinned and backed toward the counter. "I enjoy telling people what to do and how to do it."

"What shall I do first?"

Sullivan smirked. "Tonight, just watch."

Reid sighed with relief and sagged onto the counter with his forearms over the wood.

"I didn't lie on my resume. I *did* prepare dinner for my last charges." Sullivan raised a brow, waiting for more, and Reid reluctantly gave it to him. "The fare was . . . simpler, that's all."

"How simple?"

Reid watched Sullivan's fingers gliding up and down the eggplant under the faucet with rabid fascination. "I'd put the contents of a box into a bottle, and add water."

"That is not cooking, Reid." Sullivan winked at him. "Prepare to experience a whole new world."

A storm was coming, and if I didn't say something, my neon neighbor might break at the first blow.

-James
Second Time Around

Chapter Seven

Joanna sneaked off the *Aquarian* on the day of their Sunday picnic. Reid had bravely roped Sullivan in with the promise of a healthy family outing.

Joanna was crucial to that promise.

Reid left Sullivan preparing picnic snacks, and raced after Joanna. Her perfectly pinned hair glowed in the mid-morning sun, and the zipper of her backpack winked in the light.

"Sullivan will kill me if you bail on this trip," Reid said, catching up to her on Dock AA, a stone's throw from the small yacht where Elijah lived with his brother. "If he does, I will come back as a ghost and haunt you."

Joanna laughed dismissively. "We had five dinners together this week. Dad sat at the table with us debating the pros and cons of tossing you overboard."

"I may have weaseled under his skin a little."

"*A lot.* I loved it. Didn't love his interrogation into my day, though. Made me question this whole eating together shenanigans."

"He's trying to up his Daddy—*Dad*—game."

She hitched her bag up her shoulder, biting her lip. "I'm

happy with his progress. I think today you should work on developing your friendship further."

"That's the reason you're sneaking off?"

Her cheeks pinked, and her gaze darted to Elijah's boat. Those freckly cheeks darkened and she waved behind Reid.

Reid turned to find Elijah hunched over the side of his boat, *Glinda*, his disheveled mop of dark hair flopping in the wind. His dark eyes, however, were dreamily pinned on Joanna.

Mason, his older brother and sole guardian, tightened something on the dinghy then stood beside him. A spitting image of Elijah aged another fifteen years.

Mason waved at them. "We're heading north to Wingerham Bay. Is it my lucky day and both of you are coming?"

"Reid isn't," Joanna said, scowling at Mason. Funny how she crushed on Elijah, but always appeared to dislike his brother. "He's spending the day with my dad."

"Pity."

Elijah disembarked and took Joanna's backpack with a shy smile.

Joanna started after him but Reid grabbed a fistful of her jacket and held her back.

"Reid!"

"Joanna!"

She flopped back against his chest and made puppy-dog eyes at him. "*Please* let me go?"

Reid looked from her to Mason and Elijah. "She has to explain to Sullivan first."

"Won't leave without you, Jo," Elijah said as Reid steered Joanna down the dock and past the snack shack.

He detoured to pick up keys to the car Alanis was letting them borrow. No matter how hard Sullivan tried to convince him, he was not tandem cycling to this picnic.

"Hey, Alanis," Joanna greeted, rushing into a hug. "Can

you tell the crab to stop pinching me?"

Alanis laughed. "What?"

Reid snorted. "That's me. I'm the crab. She escaped and I'm dragging her back home."

"Right. Well, on your way . . ." She ducked behind the counter and re-emerged with a white envelope. "Sullivan got mail."

Joanna snapped it up, eyes widening with glee as she inspected it. She murmured "later" and drifted outside.

Alanis grinned and eyed him. "Two weeks without toting a life vest around the marina. You're well on your way to becoming one of us."

Reid leaned against the counter and whispered his secret. "I haven't driven over water anywhere, ever. And won't, if I can help it." He shivered.

She laughed. "A nervous virgin, eh? Sullivan will look after you. A nice slow glide your first time. Nothing too extreme. He could take you out at sunset. He could show you the stars."

Reid's mind flew to sensual places and heat swirled in his gut. He fought a rising flush. Silently chastised himself. "About borrowing your car . . ."

She dangled her keys. "Fill her up when you're done, I need her at six tonight."

"Thanks, Alanis. Need anything from Redwood while we're there?"

Reid could make the offer with ease now that he'd been paid—and paid more than originally agreed upon. It had surprised Reid, but Sullivan had shrugged it off, saying he didn't expect Reid to do his bookkeeping without extra compensation, and if Reid wanted more he should tell him so.

It was more than enough.

Reid gripped Alanis's keys, and Alanis shook her head. "I don't need anything. But make Sullivan return those keys. I need my fix of ahhhhhh."

Reid backed out of the office. “He does have that effect, doesn’t he?”

Alanis mimicked a pounding heart, and Reid grinned.

REID FOUND JOANNA LOITERING OUTSIDE, GRINNING DREAMILY at a hopeful message from Elijah. The boy had it bad for her. With a fond shake of his head, he trotted back to the *Aquarian* with Joanna.

Onboard, Reid beelined to the wicker basket filled with handmade sandwiches, crackers, mandarins, and . . . muffins!

“Where did you two disappear?” Sullivan asked, glancing between them suspiciously. “Not devising more surprises for the day, I hope.”

Joanna pranced into the kitchen. “I’m going to Wingerham Bay on *Glinda* with Elijah and Mason.”

Sullivan paused mid-peel of a carrot. “You’re what?”

Joanna thrust up the envelope she held. “You got mail, and I know what it is.”

Sullivan pinched it from her, glanced over the envelope, and paled.

Reid bit into a muffin. “Getting audited, Sullivan? Don’t worry, you’ll be fine.”

Sullivan slung a berating look his way. “That was for the picnic, and of course I’ll be fine. I’ve followed the law to the letter.”

“Well . . .” Reid grimaced, mostly in jest. One oversight in last year’s numbers had Sullivan underpaying taxes by ten dollars. “Don’t worry, I’ve got your back. Now about that letter,” Reid said playfully, eying the envelope that had a stamped emblem in the corner. “What’s in it?”

“It’s an—”

Sullivan fervently shook his head. “Not another word.”

If that didn't make Reid all kinds of curious!

"Send me off to Elijah's yacht for the day," Joanna said, grinning, "and I won't ever speak of it."

Sullivan shook his head in disbelief. "You're a master negotiator."

"I'd say minxy manipulator," Reid said over a full mouth of sweet, chocolatey muffin.

Joanna grinned broadly, freckled cheeks bunching. "Either way, I won't say anything. But," she lowered her voice, "you'll attend, right, Dad?"

"Funny girl," Sullivan said drily. He tugged her against his chest and kissed her forehead. "Wingerham Bay?"

"It's not far. You said you thought Mason was a good guy."

"He's raising his kid brother. There's no question he's a good guy. Whether he's a good enough skipper—"

"He helps Alanis run training programs for beginners. He knows what he's doing."

"Take your phone. Hourly updates out there."

Joanna stood on her tiptoes and kissed her dad's cheek. With a gleeful glance at Reid, she skedaddled off ship.

Reid rounded into the kitchen and rinsed his hands. He leaned against the sink when Sullivan opened a cupboard near his head. In the cramped kitchen space, Reid felt the heat of Sullivan's body as he reached for a glass bottle stacked in the shelf.

Reid's skin tightened as all that *ahhhhh* leaned toward him. He gulped and shot his gaze to Sullivan's. "What are, um, all those bottles for?" Sauces, Reid had guessed.

"Elderflower cordials and liqueurs."

Sullivan spun back to the picnic basket, sliding a bottle inside.

"And the letter?" Reid asked, waggling his eyebrows. "What's in that?"

Sullivan scrunched the envelope into a ball. “Never you mind.”

He tossed the paper into the trash and Reid dove in after it.

Sullivan blinked in surprise, and then crowded Reid against the counter, hips pressed to Reid’s as Sullivan wrestled the envelope free from his grasp.

Reid couldn’t stop laughing—his whole body felt alight with laughter. Sullivan pulled back and straightened out the envelope. He slid it into his pocket. “Don’t even think about it.”

Oh, Reid was thinking about it.

Not about *opening* it—it was Sullivan’s business after all—but he was definitely thinking about pinching it. Teasing the guy.

It’d be his second goal today after compelling Sullivan to fall in love with the beauty of the area.

“It’s sweet,” Reid said.

“What is?” Sullivan went back to preparing his carrot sticks.

“Crushes.”

Sullivan hissed, dropped his knife, and sucked his thumb. “Who are you crushing on?”

“Not you, calm down. I meant Joanna and Elijah.”

“No, Elijah is Joanna’s biology partner. She’s keen to earn an A on her project.”

“Yeah, sure. She also wants to kiss him.”

Sullivan resumed chopping. And how.

“Destroy, obliterate, pulverize.” Reid sidled beside him, glowering at the roughly chopped veggies, then met Sullivan’s eye. “You’re really taking it out on those carrots there.”

“You’re not wrong.”

“Care to explain the mass vege-murder?”

“Joanna is dating a boy?”

“I think it wise not to invite him over here.” Reid picked up a wedge of carrot and staked Sullivan against the heart. "Come on, it's a crush. Maybe a first boyfriend. You remember your first, right?"

"I was sixteen, and we used an eight pack of condoms in one night."

"She won't have sex with him—*eight* times? Jesus, that's serious stamina." What would Sullivan look like all sweaty as he pounded—Reid snapped out of the divergent thought. "Joanna is a smart girl. I think it's sweet she likes a boy."

"Sweet, until . . ." Sullivan stacked the carrots in a container and dropped them into the picnic basket. The silence between them grew heavy. He cleared his throat. "Let's hit the road."

Reid hefted the basket off the counter. "So eager."

Sullivan grunted. "The sooner we leave, the sooner we return."

"SOLID, UNMOVING GROUND." REID THRUMMED WITH ENERGY as he led the way through the woods over rocky terrain. A burbling creek snaked to their left, and Sullivan's heavy gait smacked over fallen leaves.

He breathed in the fresh air and relished the firmness of packed dirt. "It doesn't get better than this."

"Even the ground moves, Reid."

"Not every half-sentence."

Reid paused at a fork in the path and gestured for Sullivan to swing a right along a damp, rocky incline. Sullivan climbed effortlessly, ass flexing with every step. The letter in his pocket winked at Reid.

"You're afraid of water?" Sullivan asked, smacking Reid's extended hand away from the letter.

"Ow. Not water. The ocean. Specifically falling into its icy grip and drowning. Or being eaten by sharks."

Smirking, Sullivan steered Reid beside him, probably to keep a better eye on Reid's wandering hands. They puffed side by side. Well, *Reid* puffed.

Lack of fitness aside, the golden-leaf woods majestically screening the sky made the hike worth it. And Sullivan was here. Joanna had bailed, but he was still here.

Judging by the glitter in Sullivan's eyes and the way he soaked in their surrounds with deep inhalations, he wasn't hating it.

Reid led him down a narrow path against a cliff face and followed it to a craggy entrance. "In here."

"A cave? If I'd known, I'd have packed candles."

A candle-lit picnic? That sounded more romantic than Sullivan intended. "I have a candlelight setting on my phone." He shook his phone and a beacon of light appeared. "Stay close."

The sound of running water grew stronger the farther in they moved, and Sullivan stayed within breathing distance of him. Reid felt every stir along the back of his head. The shivers were more intense in the narrow cave, illuminated with the soft light from his phone.

They turned a bend, and daylight filtered by a trickling waterfall shafted into the cave.

"Here we are."

The cave rose into a ledge where they unloaded their picnic. Reid sat on one end of the checkered blanket and Sullivan the other, angled toward him. "Unexpected." Sullivan commented as they picked at their vegan feast, a sideways glance at Reid. "Breathtaking."

A strong current of elation hit Reid. He angled his phone light toward the ceiling. "Something for you. See those darker lines in the wall?"

Sullivan leaned back and cast his face toward the cave's

ceiling. "Yeah."

"Sedimentary rock. Three hundred million years old. That's old. Before the age of the dinosaurs old. Everything around us used to be at the bottom of the sea. At some point, we'll all be rock and fossils too." Reid flashed his light to different sections of the cave and shared all the factoids he knew, until he was breathless and still babbling.

He glanced at Sullivan, surprised to find the captain's concentration soldered to Reid. Reid shut his mouth on another useless piece of information.

"You know a lot about geology."

Reid flushed, glad their dark setting masked it. "It's history. I love history. It deepens one's connection to a place. And"—Reid side-eyed him—"to a person."

Sullivan packed the remainder of their food into the basket and shuffled until they were sleeve to sleeve, their backs pressed against the reddish rock. Reid's phone was half under his thigh, muting the light to a golden glow around his jeans. Water splashed against pebbles outside and sunlight danced in thin threads before them. "What would you like to know, Reid?"

"What are you willing to share? Could you tell me about your wife? If that's asking too much, whatever is in your back pocket?"

Sullivan chuckled. "You are relentless. Riley was like that, too. Bright and energetic and always seeking adventure." He paused. "Riley was an interior designer for houseboats and an artist. Lots of projects happening all the time. Nineteen when Joanna was born. Not a planned pregnancy, but took responsibility when everyone else wanted to adopt Joanna out."

"You married ten years ago. You must have met her when . . ."

"I was twenty-five. Riley, twenty-one."

"What was your Meet Cute?"

Sullivan smiled nostalgically. "Boating accident. Riley was a fantastic skipper, but too many sleepless nights resulted in inaccurate mooring and the subsequent collision of our vessels. My yacht needed repairs and during that time Riley, genuinely upset to have caused me grievance, volunteered for me to stay with them."

"I love this." Reid sighed. "Keep going."

Sullivan's smile broadened. "Within two weeks living with them, I knew I never wanted anything more than this family. Every time I saw Riley, my knees wobbled. But I didn't know if the feelings were mutual. I waited for signs, but Riley was guarded. The minute one clue slipped, though, I grabbed it. We kissed and the rest was history. We sold our vessels and bought the *Aquarian*."

"Did you name the yacht together?"

Sullivan chuckled. "No. The yacht's name convinced Riley we should buy it, though. We were both Aquarians."

"Your story sounds special, Sullivan."

"It was."

"You were lucky."

"Until I wasn't."

"You don't have to tell me if you don't want to."

"I never *want* to tell anyone."

"I understand."

Sullivan touched the rock beside him as if absorbing its steadiness. "Riley had a heart condition that no one knew about until it was too late. The heart attack happened suddenly. No prolonged suffering."

Except for the people who survived. Reid's throat constricted and heat tickled behind his eyes. "I'm sorry."

"It's been four years. I've made my peace with it."

But a man who upped and left marinas every year didn't seem like someone who was entirely at peace.

Reid stood, took Sullivan's hand and propelled him to his

feet. Their chests bumped and Sullivan gazed down at him.

Reid squeezed their fingers. "Can I . . . give you a hug?"

A wry grin twitched at Sullivan's lips. "I don't recall you asking the last time."

"I should have. Uh, sorry." Reid should be more respectful and sympathize in a less touchy way.

He stepped back, but Sullivan didn't release his grip. "Where are you going?"

"You don't want to be hugged."

"I never said that."

Reid frowned grumpily. "I can't get a good read on you."

"Believe me, I've noticed."

"Sometimes I think you're a robot and I'm constantly pushing your buttons."

"You are doing that."

"Particularly the ones labeled unapologetically blunt and accidentally amused. I want more options."

Sullivan had an almost tender look in his eye. "I want that hug."

"Really?"

Reid's pulse stuttered at Sullivan's exasperated chuckle. "Just step closer."

"Then what?" Reid asked cautiously.

"You sound like you've never hugged a person in your life. Was our last one a fluke?"

With the hiccupy, sweaty way Reid was feeling, he was beginning to think so. "A fluke?" Reid scoffed. "Between the two of us, I'm the experienced hugger. Now, let's try this again."

The outside light dulled suddenly, as though the clouds passed the sun. The effect inside the cave was like switching off a bedroom light. Reid knew Sullivan wore dark jeans and a gray pullover under his opened jacket. Knew that his whistle—like Reid's—was tucked into his inner pocket, but all he could make out was the form of the man, and the darkness of his eyes.

Sullivan's hand shifted around his and Reid's pulse hammered against Sullivan's palm.

"Is this a telepathic hug, Reid?"

Reid scowled, barely making out the rise of Sullivan's challenging brow. "I suddenly don't want to curl my arms and good wishes around you."

Sullivan hummed, gently tugging Reid forward. Reid steadied himself with splayed fingers over Sullivan's chest, the knit of his pullover bumpy but soft.

Reid shivered, despite the block of Sullivan's heat against him, bumping his thighs, radiating against his torso.

This time when Reid looked into Sullivan's eyes, something heavier weighed them.

Like, between them, there was something more. Something meaningful. The start of a deep friendship.

Sullivan's breath shuttled over Reid's forehead. "It's just a hug. Nothing else."

Reid huffed quietly. "You're stealing my lines. Good to know I'm rubbing off on you though. I might be able to introduce you to my gay friends when they return from Europe." Reid stopped. "I mean, if I'm still your manny. You know what? We don't have time for this hug. Too many things in Redwood for you to experience. To fall in love with."

Sullivan crushed Reid against him, pullover muffling Reid's surprised grunt. Reid gripped Sullivan, slinking his arms around his waist, cheek pressed to Sullivan's chest.

Butterflies flapped about in his stomach as Sullivan sighed through his hair. "Thank you."

"Any time," Reid said softly.

The hug grew warmer, heavier. Thrummed around and between them.

Sullivan tightened his embrace.

Reid's breath hitched as his cock hardened. This felt good. A little too good.

Sullivan was off limits. His *boss*. Reid's purpose was to offer friendship and emotional education, not imagine Sullivan's hands tightening elsewhere . . .

He laughed nervously. "Okay, now you're going over-the-top to prove you're not homophobic."

"Is that a complaint?"

Reid should pull away. Put some distance between them. "No. Keep going." Maybe he wasn't the *most* professional manny. He inhaled Sullivan's scent. "Maybe we can override your system."

The shrill ring of Sullivan's phone sliced through the connection. Not enough to let go, but enough for reality to seep between them. Sullivan, one arm locked around Reid, answered Joanna's hourly update.

"She good?" Reid asked when they disconnected.

"Yeah."

"Kissed Elijah yet?"

Sullivan grumbled. "She better not be even thinking about it."

"Some emotions you just can't stop. Wanting to kiss a boy is one of them."

Sullivan looked into his eyes and a bubbling panic filled Reid's sternum. He zipped his hands to the trim waist of Sullivan's jeans. "How much trouble will I get in for taking advantage of this situation?"

Sullivan jerked back. "Taking advantage?

"The *letter*."

"Right. That. It's nothing important."

"Then tell me what it is?"

Sullivan disentangled himself, scooped up the picnic blanket, and folded it into the basket. "I think you were right. We should move if we want to do anything else."

~

"If you try sneaking your hand into my pocket again, I will tie your hands to the steering wheel."

Then stop leaning forward! "But then I couldn't change gears."

"I'll change them for you. Why are you still eyeing my ass?"

That letter was tauntingly close, poking out of his pocket, and the traffic light was still red. And working Sullivan up like this . . .

He bit his lip. "I thought I'd overrode your homophobic system. Clearly that hug wasn't long enough. Let's remedy that later."

Sullivan's expression waffled between amusement and disbelief. "Do you ever hear yourself?"

"Hear what? The jokey man-loving stuff? It doesn't mean I'm angling to jump you, Sullivan. You have nothing to worry about."

Sullivan muttered under his tongue, shifted, and gazed out the passenger window. "We've seen a dozen places, enjoyed coffee at Kings, I suppose we're headed to the marina?"

"One last stop."

"Where?"

They were pulling up there now. "The library. I've been meaning to check out some of Sam Baton's books. See what all the fuss is about."

The color from Sullivan's face drained.

"You okay?" Reid asked, frowning.

"You want to read Sam Baton's books." Not a question, a statement. A worried one if Reid read Sullivan correctly.

"After you gave them such a ringing endorsement at Target, I figure I better."

"They're not . . . don't."

"What? Why not?"

"Because, I don't want you to."

Was Sullivan embarrassed about the books he loved to read? "I love romance books. It's cool if you dig them."

"Yes, but. It's these particular books . . . please don't."

"What are they, full of erotic kink you don't want me to know about?"

Sullivan paused. "Yes. Do you think you could not?"

God, Reid had never wanted to check out a romance book so badly in his life. His hand rubbed his door handle, eagerly. What on earth got Sullivan off? Whips and chains? Lapping chocolate from intimate places? Daddy play?

"Do you know what happens in the story 'Bluebeard,' Sullivan?"

Sullivan narrowed his eyes at him. "Yes, the man kills all his wives."

"Why does he kill them?"

"Because they open the door to his killing chamber."

"But *why* do they open the door to his killing chamber?"

"Because he tells them never to go in there."

"Yet they do."

Sullivan grunted. "Curiosity overtakes them."

"You see where I'm headed with this, right?"

"Don't make me kill you, Reid," Sullivan said. "I like you around."

Reid laughed. "I've never been the guy who attracted a happily ever after. Never the hero, Sullivan."

"Never the hero? What are you saying?"

"Curiosity will kill me like all those other wives. However. I could be persuaded to delay the inevitable."

Sullivan frowned, either at his pessimism or knowing Reid would check out those books. "Persuaded?" he asked eventually.

Reid lunged for Sullivan's ass.

Sullivan barked out a frustrated laugh, but didn't swat Reid away, and Reid drew the letter out.

David could handle a storm, but could he handle James?

-David
Second Time Around

Chapter Eight

Reid had never planned on opening the letter, so he couldn't explain why instead of throwing it away, he'd tucked it into his bookshelf where it sat all the way to Halloween, winking at him.

He wondered if the crest stamped in the corner was from a university.

Every time he saw it, he hesitated and fought a naughty thrill to peek inside.

What was in it?

Reid took the letter to the kitchen. Joanna was trick-or-treating and Sullivan was finishing a six-day workshop at the university.

Fighting temptation, he dropped it into the trash and pulled out ingredients for dinner.

Out came the chopping boards and knives, herbs and spices, and the letter from the trash.

He crouched, whimpering at his lack of self-control.

The whole week Sullivan kept watching Reid, as if he knew Reid would eventually succumb to curiosity.

Anticipation stretched the air between them, leaving Reid a bundle of raw nerves.

He thumbed the loosening flap.

"I'm back," came Joanna's sing-song voice.

Reid lurched to his feet. Joanna stood dressed as an angel, fit with gold-tipped wings and a white-feathered halo. Her red hair was a curly, windswept mess over her shoulders and her eyes glittered. "Whatcha doing, Reid?"

"Nothing! I mean, I'm not doing anything even remotely questionable." She glanced at the letter he absently waved about. "Er, Sullivan gave it to me. He expects it to be opened."

She dropped a cotton bag of sweets onto the counter and peered at the envelope. "Ohhh, I totally forgot about that. I can't believe you're staring at it. Open it."

"Therein lies my dilemma. It's none of my business, but I really want to know."

Light from the saloon hit Joanna from behind, making her white dress glow ethereally. "I know what's in it"—her shoulders slumped—"but I promised not to say. Guess I won't."

"You won't? *You?* Child-genius puppet master?"

"Hey, Project Anchor the Storm doesn't conflict with any promise I made to dad." She grinned. "Open it! Please? Pretty please?"

"You know the difference between a lie and an omission of truth? This is like that. Making a promise and steering me to break it for you."

"I never said I was an angel," she said cutely. "Not my problem if people assume . . ."

"Why do I suddenly fear the teachers calling us to collect you from your class trip after one night?"

Joanna batted her eyes. "Go on. Open it. You know you want to. This could be a chance to help dad."

Reid shifted keenly. "Help him?"

She drew a zipper over her mouth and exited from the saloon, leaving him hanging on that hook.

The moment she slipped out of sight, he ripped into the envelope. *How could this help Sullivan?*

He drew out a prettily-headed letter and read over the contents.

He jumped a foot at Joanna's head peering around the dividing wall. "Ah ha," she cried, delighted. "That didn't take long."

Dammit. He should have known she'd spy on him. Hopefully he'd hold out longer opening the door labeled *Sullivan's erotic kink/Sam Baton's books*. But he was doubtful.

The emblem at the top of the page said Angelwood Acadia Grammar School. "His twentieth school reunion?"

"Yeah, we'll convince him to go over dinner."

"It's in London. On February eleventh."

Joanna laughed. "Are you serious?"

Reid checked again. "Yes."

"That's the day before his birthday. Okay, now he has to go."

The day before his birthday, huh. Reid folded that information away along with the invitation. "All right, let's cook."

"Cook up a plan?"

He shook his head. Not yet. He needed to ponder it. London wasn't exactly a skip, hop, and a jump away.

Joanna approached the kitchen cautiously. "You meant actual cooking? You?"

He wagged his finger at her. "Tonight, yes. A surprise for when your dad returns."

"A Halloween surprise?"

He pinned her with a look. "We'll call that plan B."

She planted her elbows on the counter. "Can you grab me a drink? Cordial?"

"Aren't you sugared to the max?"

"I'm not eating candy until I've checked they're vegan. Please?"

Reid pulled out a bottle of homemade elderflower cordial from the cupboard, uncorked it, and poured her a glass. While she drank, he carefully cut eggplant into even strips.

Joanna watched him coyly. "How do you like living here? With us?"

"I'm liking." Reid smiled secretly toward the eggplant slices as he slipped them into the oven. "I'm really liking."

"Yay!" she cheered, throwing her hands up. "Because it's been a month, tomorrow." He was quite aware. "I think Dad is already convinced you're perfect."

"Not perfect, but I'm holding out hope he'll extend this manny gig until next summer."

"Or forever."

Reid eyed her. "You won't need me that long."

"Who said need?"

"Awww. If I ever have a kid, I want her to be exactly like you."

"An angel in disguise?" She flashed him a bright, toothy grin, hiccupped, and drained her second glass of cordial.

Reid chopped onions and fought through stinging eyes. Joanna grabbed a magazine and returned to the kitchen, stumbling the last step as the boat rocked on a wave.

She flicked to the horoscopes for November.

He chuckled. "Gonna read mine?"

"First Dad's." She scanned over it. "A lot of indecision this month. And miscommunication."

Joanna laughed, shoulders jumping loosely, face scrunched in glee.

"What's so funny?"

"I don't know. Miscommunication. Looks like a funny word. So many *mmm*s."

Reid frowned with a tentative laugh. "Okay."

He opened two cans of peeled tomatoes and stopped himself before dumping them into the pan. First he had to cook the onions until glassy.

Joanna read his horoscope. "Questions of love and romance will occupy your mind this month, Cancer, and you will also be tasked with the daunting task of convincing Sullivan Bell to let his daughter go to the movies with Elijah next Friday evening."

Reid huffed a laugh. "Why do I have to tell him?"

"Because he might lock me in my cabin and throw away the key."

"What do you think he'll do to me?"

"Please, Reid?" She hiccupped. "Pretty please? Ever since he figured out I *like* Elijah, he's been ultra-controlling."

"It's called love, Joanna."

"If you could make him love me a little less . . ."

Reid sighed. "No promises."

"I looooove you."

"Yeah, yeah."

Joanna kept reading horoscope snippets, finding them hilarious.

"Wow," she said with a groan, and poured herself another slosh of cordial. "I must be tired. The room is spinning."

Spinning?

Reid's senses prickled.

Joanna tilted the glass of cordial to her lips and an unsettling realization had him gasping.

He grabbed the glass from her.

"What are you doing?" Joanna said, and hiccupped.

Praying to all the stars that he was wrong, Reid sipped.

Not wrong.

He stared at Joanna in horror.

Oh fuck. *Fuck.*

~

SULLIVAN WOULD KILL REID FOR THIS.

Just when Reid thought he'd proven himself semi-useful in the Bells' lives, he messed up.

Joanna rolled off the couch after a half hour. He let out a panicked "stay" and Joanna giggled, insisting on using the bathroom.

Okay. Fine.

Salty breezes tunneled into the saloon along with Sullivan's familiar step.

Not fine.

Sullivan slipped out of his coat and searched the room for Reid, gaze softening when it landed on him.

It was the first time Reid had seen blatant joy on Sullivan's face, and Reid was about to ruin it.

"Reid," Sullivan said, dropping his shoulder bag onto the table.

Reid jumped up from the couch on shaky legs. "I'm innocent!"

Sullivan stiffened, and he turned to face him directly, caution in his eye. "What have you done?"

"I was thinking how nice it would be to make your favorite eggplant pasta. Exactly as you taught me. To celebrate our first-month anniversary."

"Our *what*?"

"As your manny."

Sullivan released a breath, then paused before whisking into the kitchen. "What did you burn?"

"Nothing, I haven't finished it. I was concentrating."

"Get to the point, Reid."

"Joanna was thirsty and I gave her something nice while we chatted about horoscopes."

"What happened?"

"You know I would do anything for Joanna, right? She's amazing and I want the best for her."

"Where is she?"

"DAD!" Joanna stumbled into the saloon with a giggle. Thank God Reid had removed her angel wings and they weren't jolting with every hiccup. "I'm having the funniest evening. Reid did something silly, but you can't blame him." She threw herself into her dad's arms with a hiccup. "I should have realized why the elderflower cordial tasted so different. But it was super sweet and delicious and I poured myself the second cup."

The angel burped.

Steel eyes met Reid's over her shoulder, and Reid contemplated throwing himself off the ship—without his whistle.

"You got my daughter drunk?"

"I'm sorry. I've given her a lot of water, and I called the health line and they said to keep an eye on her and wait it out."

"How on earth do you plead innocent?"

"I'm incredibly sorry."

Sullivan frowned. "Okay. Help me make her more comfortable."

Reid had been prepared for Sullivan to send him off the boat immediately. Tentative relief shimmied to his riotous stomach. "Just okay?"

A raised brow landed on him. "Prefer a different response?"

"Okay is good. Fantastic even." Reid moved quickly, before Sullivan changed his mind.

Together they settled her on the couch with Sullivan's laptop and a blanket.

She watched a movie with Reid at her side while Sullivan finished cooking dinner. Occasionally their gazes clashed across the room and Sullivan shook his head in disbelief.

Each time, Reid delivered a sheepish smile and ducked his attention back to the screen.

After dinner, Sullivan returned to Joanna's other side, hand resting on the pillows behind Reid's shoulder. His energy bore into the curve of Reid's neck.

Watching TV became impossible.

Instead, Reid battled the bubbling in his belly. He couldn't believe Sullivan didn't get more upset. Definitely not the same man who had interviewed him.

Unless this somehow qualified as providing Joanna appropriate teenage developmental experiences?

For certain Reid had left a long-lasting impression on them.

But not necessarily the way he'd wanted to.

In the semi-darkness, light from the screen lit Joanna and Sullivan's faces. Different features but they shared the same analytical expressions. Chuckled at the same jokes. Shook their head synchronously.

When the film ended, darkness streaked with milky moonlight from the hatch soaked the saloon.

"I want your opinion," Reid whispered to Joanna.

She dropped her head tiredly on the couch cushion. "On what?"

Reid caught Sullivan's eye as the man moved his laptop to the table. "Do you think your dad has forgiven me?" Or was he waiting to attack him as soon as Joanna slept?

"Forgive you for what? Getting me drunk or learning about—"

Reid stopped her from acknowledging the reunion letter. Reid needed to bring it up, but not this second. Not while recovering from this fiasco. Not with Joanna present. "The drunk thing."

"I can hear you, you know," Sullivan droned.

Joanna lowered her voice theatrically. "You don't think he's forgiven you already?" She tutted and palmed her heart.

"You're assuming he doesn't have one of these. But he does. It's huge and beats hard and when you hear it the first time, you'll wonder how you ever missed it."

"Okay, enough talking," Sullivan said, perching once more on her other side.

Reid grinned. "God, Joanna. I think your dad is blushing. Keep going."

Joanna's laughter warped into a yawn. "Will you sleep better if he's forgiven you?"

"Yeah. Because the guilt is screwing with me. Your dad and I have been getting along well lately. He's only a blunt bastard half the time."

Sullivan tossed a striped cushion and Reid caught it and stuffed it behind him. The scent of Sullivan permeated Reid's senses and he inhaled deeply.

Joanna giggled wearily. "That's what I love about Cancers."

"We have a funny side? We're good at forging friendships? We know you because we feel you?"

"You accept us at our worst as well as our best."

Reid's chest thumped on a swollen hiccup. His voice croaked, "You're always at your best, Joanna."

"Tell me a story?" Joanna pleaded on another yawn. "Don't know enough about you."

Reid gnawed his head back into the cushion. "I'm not very interesting."

Sullivan snorted.

"What was that for?"

Shadowed eyes hooked Reid's. "You're interesting." Said factually. Said firmly, like Sullivan wouldn't tolerate any argument. "Now tell us a story."

Reid bit his lip, hyper-aware of the gentle rocking of the boat, the scents from dinner, and the intimate darkness.

Between them, Joanna rung out a snore.

"She's fallen asleep," Reid said, nervous relief in his voice.

"She might be asleep," Sullivan said, still watching Reid. "I am not."

Reid felt the buzz, a tickle at the crook of his neck, where all evening Sullivan's energy had pulsed into him. Shivers fingered through him, making it hard to breathe evenly. "I was born and raised in Redwood."

"What about your parents?"

Reid slammed his eyes shut, and the memory washed over him: Reid. Thirteen. Frustrated tears hot on his cheeks because his "friend" hadn't invited him to his birthday party. All the soccer boys were attending, but Reid's interest in board games and history reenacting sidelined him.

His dad was watching TV from his armchair and asked him to quiet down. Reid had stupidly screamed into a pillow.

His dad snapped the TV off and yanked Reid to his feet. *Thirteen years. All you do is cry and whine, I'm done with it. Done. I just want peace and fucking quiet.*

Reid's throat stung, and he forced himself to shrug. "Don't know much about them. They, ah, didn't want me. Mom first, then dad. He left me with Grams."

It sounded more forlorn than he'd intended. He was older now, at peace with his past. The question *Why didn't they want me?* didn't plague him anymore—or maybe he'd grown a thicker skin. He was always being left by someone, so he'd grown accustomed to it.

He shoved to his feet, staring toward the kitchen away from Sullivan. He putted out a laugh. "I have a sudden craving for coffee. I'm even liking this oat milk."

Sullivan followed him to the machine. Large and solid before him, he clasped Reid's shoulders, making Reid look up cautiously. "I'm sorry, Reid."

Reid couldn't take the weird bouncing in his belly. He

stepped out of Sullivan's reach and leaned back against the counter. "Th-thanks."

"Your Grams must be amazing to raise you alone."

"She was."

Sullivan mirrored his position on the opposite counter. The narrow space meant Sullivan's toes were a half-inch from his. "Tell me more, Reid."

Reid bumped his big toe against Sullivan's and teased, "This is more than getting to know me a little."

Sullivan shifted, pulling his foot back as though Reid had yanked him back to reality.

"Grams was amazing," he blurted, cursing himself. "She was the reason I got a university degree. She sacrificed everything to give me the best education she could. She saw me graduate, then her health declined. I sold the house she gave me and we used the funds to travel the world before she passed away."

Sullivan tentatively sank into the conversation. "You gave up your inheritance for her?"

"Sure, who wouldn't?"

"A lot of people, Reid."

Reid shrugged it off. "Seeing her happy was all that mattered."

"That's very generous."

"She kept me."

Sullivan's brow creased and his lips turned into a concerned grimace. A funny shiver shot through Reid. It felt nice when Sullivan looked at him that way. As if he saw through him. As if he cared.

Reid flustered with the rising heat to his cheeks and blurted, "We traveled to New Zealand, Australia, Europe. Went to Hobbiton, fed koalas, visited castles in Europe. So many memories."

"Is there one that stands out?"

"The London Eye. Grams and I went up. When we were overlooking—hell, all of England—she settled her frail hand in mine and squeezed."

Then she'd asked what he wanted from his life, and he'd brushed it off. Said this trip was about her. What did *she* wish out of the time she had left? A sad smile twitched at her lips, and Reid thought she was realizing how little time that was.

But that smile carried the same worried energy that Sullivan's did. Could Grams have been thinking something else?

He pushed the thought away and cleared his throat. "A simple moment, but one I'll never forget."

"Thank you for sharing. Any other stories?"

He wanted more?

Reid fidgeted as he recounted their adventures. Sullivan watched him with quiet smiles, absorbing every word.

"She died in her sleep of heart failure the night before we were scheduled to cruise from Southampton. I think she might have thought it a service to me."

Sullivan frowned quizzically. "A service?"

"If you haven't already noticed," Reid said, leaning in, "ships and I don't do well together."

That didn't earn Reid the wry smile he was expecting. Sullivan found the offending bottle of liqueur and poured them both a small glass. "What happened?" he asked softly.

Reid sipped the sweet, syrupy liquid. "I was afraid of cruising on the ocean with no land in sight. I kept reiterating all the possible disasters that might happen aboard. I listed everything. Everything but the worst—her passing before we stepped on deck."

He swiped his eyes with his sleeve, and laughed into another sip. "I'll sleep well tonight. Nothing like a few tears to give you a good night's shut eye." Reid winked at him over his glass. "You could try it some time."

Sullivan changed subject so fast Reid got whiplash. "What about Callaghan? He's your cousin, right?"

Oh, Sullivan.

Bit by bit did it, recovering this lost soul. "On my mother's side. I don't remember mom, but Grams tried to keep ties with that side of the family for me."

"Did you spend much time with him growing up?"

Reid set his glass down, declining a refill. "Every other year. Cal taught me everything about dinosaurs. How do you know him?"

"I worked with him researching the effects of climate change on mass extinction during the Cretaceous period."

"Sounds . . . depressing."

"Motivating. When was the last time you saw each other?"

"When he married Percy. Most touching wedding I've ever attended. The ceremony was in the middle of the cul-de-sac, all neighbors and friends cheering them as they kissed. God, Cal and Percy stared at each other like they were each other's whole world. It was swoony."

Reid clasped the back of his neck and looked at Sullivan through his lashes.

Should he ask about Sullivan's? He wanted to.

He also wanted to broach the reunion letter boiling in his pocket. "What about your and Riley's wedding? What was that like?"

Sullivan absorbed the question and scrubbed his jaw. "Neither of us had family who'd celebrate our commitment. We had a few close friends as witnesses. Gael and Carlos, school mates of mine from London. Joanna. We did it at a registry office. Not a flashy affair but heartfelt."

"Heartfelt is perfect. Flashy you can do next time." Reid winced.

Sullivan stiffened. "Flashy isn't my thing."

Not Reid's either. He wanted what Callaghan and Percy

had. Close friends and family showing them they would forever have a place in their hearts.

"I should get Joanna to bed." Sullivan started for the saloon and Reid halted him. They stood facing each other, heat blasting from Sullivan in the inch separating them.

Reid stared at his hand gripping Sullivan's tight forearm, hairs soft against the pads of his fingers. "Curiosity got the better of me, Sullivan."

Sullivan's eyes flashed. "You know then?"

"I'm never the hero, remember? Temptation got the better of me, and before I knew it I was reading . . ." Reid drifted his fingers off Sullivan. "Is it that bad I know?"

Sullivan rocked on his feet, swaying forward before pulling back a step. He scored a hand through his hair. "Yes. No. I don't know." He picked up the elderflower liqueur and drank straight from the bottle. "I see how you confused this with cordial."

If that was Sullivan's attempt to avoid the conversation, he hadn't tried very hard.

Reid hauled him by the shirt onto the deck, pausing to sink their feet into boots. A frosty breeze had Reid wishing he'd also brought coats, but then, he didn't want to draw out this conversation. Maybe the weather would prompt a quicker resolution.

Reid hunkered on a slatted bench and watched Sullivan pace before the stern rail, gripping his bottle.

Reid curled a finger for Sullivan to join him. Keep him warm. "Come sit?"

Sullivan drank deeply. "I'm good here. With the distance."

A sigh left Reid and he shook his head. "What am I gonna do with a drunken skipper?"

Sullivan halted mid-swig and set the bottle down. He scrubbed his face over a laugh. "Reid. *Reid.*"

"Come on, Sullivan. Is facing your school friends that hard?"

Sullivan whipped his head in his direction, frowning. "What?"

"Your reunion." Reid awkwardly tugged the invitation from his pocket. "Why don't you want to go?"

Sullivan stared at the paper, shoulders loosening. "The damn reunion? I thought you'd read—never mind."

Sullivan collapsed onto the bench next to him and pinched the letter from his grip. The paper rustled with another frigid breeze. "I didn't want you to know about it, because I don't plan on going."

"Did you go to the last one?" Reid said, fighting chattering teeth.

Sullivan must have noticed because he angled himself toward him, blocking the brunt of the wind. "Yes. Ten years ago."

"Was that one such a big deal?"

"No, I had Riley with me."

Ah.

Sullivan folded the letter. "I can't spend an entire evening having mates remind me of the past."

Reid mulled over the conundrum, understanding Sullivan's decision.

"Or you could go and not let them remind you of the past." Reid pinched the folded letter, feeling Sullivan shiver through the paper.

Hope shimmered in Sullivan's eyes, then died. "Two questions: What magic would make that happen? And how much would I have to give up for it?"

Reid smiled sadly. "You could take someone new."

"Ah. So, everything."

"You don't want to fall in love again?"

Sullivan said nothing, transfixed by the dark, tranquil water.

"You've got your whole life," Reid said, pityingly. "You can't be a monk the rest of it."

Sullivan shot him a bewildered look. "Sex and love are two very different things, Reid. There are apps for getting off. PrEP to be physically safe."

"Oh. So—"

"I've had sex since Riley. Yes. When Joanna's not around of course. Coming is not hard."

"I haven't noticed you bringing anyone to the boat . . ."

"I haven't, since you came aboard."

Reid strayed from Sullivan's intense gaze to his wide shoulders and the muscled thighs stretching his jeans. The sensory image of Sullivan pressing that sculpted heat against him . . .

Reid shot his eyes guiltily back to Sullivan's, whose eyes seemed to have darkened. He fidgeted. "You could also take a friend. A buffer, to save you from unwanted conversation."

Reid looked away, and Sullivan hummed. "A friend. Mmm. Something to think about." He stood. "For now, let's get Joanna to bed."

Sullivan was already in bed snoring over his audiobook when Reid dragged himself to the nook.

The captain wasn't usually a snorer as far as Reid knew, but clearly alcohol wrung it out of the Bells. Sullivan and Joanna were both sleeping soundly.

Reid slipped the historical novel he'd spent the last hour reading onto the shelf where the letter had sat.

Joanna had been right. It would take considerable effort to convince Sullivan to attend his reunion, and Reid felt the need to try.

He might have left it alone after Sullivan's heart-wrenching admission about not wanting to feel like a widower, but he'd spotted a glimmer of hope.

Like Sullivan had been imaging a fun, easy night with his old friends.

Part of Sullivan wanted to go.

Reid needed to help. Because Sullivan deserved fun and easy. At the very least, one night of it. Helping Sullivan achieve that could be Reid's birthday gift to him.

Reid took a quick shower, blow-dried his hair, and climbed into bed in a pair of loose flannel pajama pants, sans shirt.

He willed himself to sleep over the rumble of Sullivan's insane snore that sounded like the guy hadn't slept for four years and was making up for it tonight.

Sleep hard, man. Sleep hard.

Reid smiled toward Sullivan's cabin and wrapped a pillow around his ears.

Two hours later, Reid's compassion faded.

How could he ever sleep with that racket, dammit?

"Stop, stop, stoooop," Reid whined, tossing onto his other side.

Was the man even getting any oxygen?

Reid threw his covers off and padded barefoot over cool flooring to Sullivan's room. His knock met no response but a snore.

He paused for a second before sneaking into the cabin. The speaker droned.

I can feel him watching me. Smell his warm, slightly salty scent. Like the ocean. I could breathe it in all day, drowning in it, in him. But when I turn to catch his eyes roving over me, he looks away.

Another day he'd pretend we're just friends.

Blue light from the speaker shimmered over the room, gently outlining Sullivan's snoring form, and Reid turned off the narration.

"Psst. Sullivan. Could you turn on your side?"

Nothing. Not even a twitch of his foot.

Reid shook his head, grinning in the dark. The snoring was insane, and while it was disturbing him right then, he was thrilled about it.

A relief to know the man was human.

At another snore, Reid bravely climbed onto the firm double bed. Sullivan lay sprawled like a starfish over sheets that had been kicked off. A wedge of comforter covered his toes.

Other than a pair of tight boxer-briefs, he was naked. Reid ran a thoroughly envious gaze over Sullivan, from his shaped calves to his muscular thighs. Reid didn't believe six packs existed in the real world, but Sullivan was set on challenging his beliefs in all areas, apparently. He was effortlessly toned under a wide treasure trail.

A treasure trail that broke at his belly button, an expanse of silky skin separating it from a thick, smooth layer of chest hair.

Reid should stop staring.

He was here to cease the monstrous sound erupting from the demigod, not have an epiphany about how much he might like to rub himself on all that.

Reid gulped and shoved the thought deep. He knelt at Sullivan's hip, slid a hand under his shoulder, and tried to turn him. Dead weight. Impossible.

He pushed again.

A strong arm curled around Reid's waist, flattening him against Sullivan's chest. Reid *oofed* out a surprised breath. The silky hair on Sullivan's chest combed Reid's pecs. Rigid abs flexed under him, warm against Reid's flat, soft stomach.

Ahhh, God.

Sullivan's eyes were shut, but his lips hitched into a lazy smile. "What are you doing?"

"Trying to roll you over," Reid whispered against Sullivan's stubble-roughened jaw.

"Like this?" Sullivan wrapped a meaty leg around Reid's thigh and rolled him onto the cool mattress.

Reid squirmed at the cool sheets against his back and stilled as Sullivan's big body settled on his, soaking him with heat from his calves to his thighs to his stomach and shoulders. Sensation exploded through Reid, waking him up like most of his life had been slumber. The heavy weight of Sullivan blanketing him felt . . . God, it felt heavenly.

He swallowed, reaching for humor to save him from the intensity rattling through his veins. "Not quite what I had in mind, Captain."

"Sullivan," came a murmured response.

"Sir."

Sullivan nuzzled his face into the crook of Reid's neck and bit lightly. A frisson of electricity shot down Reid's neck straight to his dick. Sullivan rubbed himself over Reid. Oh, hell, the man was hard.

So was Reid. Achingly so.

Sullivan's large erection burned beside Reid's, and Reid struggled to keep his mind clear. What was happening?

"You're so goddamn gorgeous." Sullivan lazily thrust and Reid couldn't help arching into it, even as his mind rang with alarm. There was something distinctly sleepy and uncontrolled about the way Sullivan mauled him.

Was the man still partly asleep? Dreaming? Breath hit his ear, eliciting a thousand-volt tremor. "Want to slide into you so fucking badly."

Reid almost came, and then reality surged through him and he stiffened. Did Sullivan think Reid was his wife?

Oh, fuck. This was bad.

This felt so good.

He had to wake Sullivan up. Reid shouldn't have come into his bedroom. Sullivan had warned him not to, and like an idiot, he had.

Reid gently gripped the sides of Sullivan's head and unlatched him from the hickey he was possibly forming on Reid's neck.

"Sullivan," he spoke normally, but it sounded loud in the small room. "I'm not Riley."

Sullivan's body tensed as he realized where they were and who he was with. Reid should scramble out from under him. Hurry back to his room and pretend this never happened. Anything but hold that dawning gaze that shot nerve-wrecking shivers through Reid.

Yet, he waited, preparing for the storm.

Sullivan's head reared back, palms pinned either side of Reid's shoulders. His eyes flickered with panic and a host of emotions. Hard emotions. Angry ones.

Reid had breached Sullivan's private space and the flimsy connection they might have forged over the last month snapped.

The heat of his body vanished as Sullivan jerked away from him. He sat up, massive shoulders bunched with fury, gaze slicing to the wall away from Reid.

Guilt pierced his chest.

There was time to dash from the bed, but Reid lay there, quivering. An apology froze on the tip of his tongue. Long breaths passed before Reid choked out, "Sullivan—"

"Don't." Reid had expected Sullivan to yell at him. To pin Reid with all his anger. But his voice was soft. Sad. Resigned. "I asked you not to come in here."

"I'm—"

"Trial's over. I can't . . . I can't hire you."

Heavy-limbed, Reid climbed out of bed. He hesitated at the door. The bedroom felt different now. Not just a cozy room with a large bed but a room Sullivan had shared with someone he loved. Someone he lost and wished he hadn't.

"I'm so sorry, Sullivan."

Sullivan's eyes didn't move from where they were fixed, even though Reid needed them to.

He sighed and slumped to his nook, throat swollen like he'd swallowed a few hornets.

No amount of crooked grinning and tossing his hair would change Sullivan's mind. This time, Reid had truly overstepped. Reid was fired, and deservedly.

He'd have to leave.

Homeless once more.

He should be used to the idea. Except . . . not this time. This time he felt numb. So sad he couldn't even grasp it. He curled up on his bed and hugged the life vest he'd thought he didn't need anymore.

He had a wide, soft, friendly look about him—beautiful. Too beautiful. Best be careful.

-James
Second Time Around

Chapter Nine

The ship was never a quiet place. Waves lapped. Wood groaned. Voices carried.

Reid was used to it. Enjoyed the familiarity of it, even.

This morning, though, other sounds invaded his sleepy, intermittent sobbing.

A low rumble vibrated around him. Water punched against the boat. A giant swell lifted the vessel and dropped it suddenly. Reid's insides took a moment to catch up.

His stomach clenched. Another storm?

One glimpse outside showed a bright blue sky with fluffy clouds racing by.

Wait. *Racing by?*

Reid blotted the sheet over his eyes, clearing them of sleep and tears.

Yep, the clouds were moving at an unnatural pace.

Ensue general panic!

Reid reluctantly untangled himself from the life vest and yanked on clothes. He shrugged into the vest and clipped up, heart hammering, stomach swirling.

He was supposed to be drowning in self-pity this morning

as he packed his belongings and left the *Aquarian*. Not possibly drowning for real.

Was Sullivan so mad at him that he wanted to first torment him on the open seas?

Reid stormed upstairs with a death grip on the handrail. The saloon was empty.

The boat rose and dipped, and his body played chase with gravity, never quite catching it. The dizzying consolation prize of nausea, though—that mistress was thoroughly fucking him.

"Sullivan? Joanna?"

Reid hugged the table and glanced at the clock. Ten! Dammit. He'd slept in? But that meant Joanna had left for her class trip.

That meant she'd left before he said goodbye.

That meant . . . he frowned. He honestly had no idea what else it meant, other than the boat was being tossed about on the open sea and Reid was still on it.

"Sullivan!"

Fuck, god. He needed . . . *Sullivan to forgive him* . . . solid ground.

The boat leaned.

LEANED.

That meant they were close to capsizing.

Reid scrambled across the saloon and up the steps. He wrestled with a strong wind as he opened the door to the sun-soaked deck.

He crawled toward the stern through light sprays of seawater.

Sullivan tinkered with metal poles and netting, decked out in sneakers, jeans, windbreaker, and sunglasses.

"Sullivan."

Sullivan startled, dropping his net, gaze yanking over to Reid, who hugged the deck, cheek pressing hard against the salty surface.

"What the hell are you still doing here?" Sullivan's legs approached and then the captain himself hunkered beside him. His surprise warred with a concerned frown.

Or was it upset?

Had Sullivan expected him to leave in the middle of the night?

"I'm sorry. I'm so, so sorry. I'll be a better person, the best. I'll *never* look up Sam Baton. Promise. Just save me."

"That minx." Sullivan settled a hand on Reid's shoulder, fingers dipping under the life vest. "You're quite safe. Up you go."

Reid groaned, and followed the instruction until he was kneeling face to face with Sullivan. A flash of last night passed between them. Sullivan glanced at the tender hickey on Reid's neck, and they both glanced toward the wide expanse of choppy ocean.

"Can you explain this abduction?" Reid asked.

"Yes. Her name is Joanna."

"What have I ever done to her?"

Sullivan chuckled, gruffly. "I was upset this morning. She asked why. I told her I fired you and asked her to check if you'd left. I couldn't bring myself to look."

Reid swallowed. "I suppose she knew your plans to leave?"

"A spur of the moment idea to blow off steam. Joanna encouraged it."

Clearly, she wanted them to figure it out. Was that even a possibility?

He dared another look at Sullivan and found the man rubbing the bridge of his nose.

At a giant dipping of the boat, Reid slammed his palm to the deck. An uneasy thought sent a shudder through him. "Who is manning the ship? Oh God, we'll capsize. Sink. Freeze to death!"

"Alanis had time off and offered to captain the yacht while I test out one of my designs."

Reid gave the netting and poles a cursory glance. "Have you finished?"

"Haven't quite begun."

"You mean I'm at the mercy of the sea until . . ."

Sullivan winced. "I hijacked Alanis for two days."

Reid trembled. "Drop me back, please?"

Sullivan curled an arm around Reid and helped him into the saloon. He settled Reid onto the couch and ran a calculating eye over him. "You okay?"

"Other than the nausea and crippling fear?"

"Of capsizing? It won't happen."

"Of capsizing. Of having ruined things with you."

Sullivan let out a slow breath. "Ah, Reid."

Another sharp dip had Reid groaning.

"Hold on a sec." Sullivan disappeared. Reid twisted into the couch until he was pressed to the back. The bulky life vest rose to cushion his neck.

Sullivan returned a little breathless. He sat next to Reid pinching a black wristband with a silver buckle on one side and a silver ball on the other.

"Give me your hand."

Reid closed his eyes against another swell and shifted his arm, hand limp in the couple of inches of space between them.

"Sorry you're ill," Sullivan murmured. His cool hands took Reid's clammy one in a refreshing grip. "I'll tell Alanis to turn us back."

Sullivan squeezed Reid's palm with a rolling pressure that felt amazing—enough for Reid to ignore the rocking boat and peek out.

Sullivan focused on Reid's hand, molding Reid's fingers

together as he slipped the band on. He tightened the buckle until the silver ball pressed into Reid's inner wrist.

"What are you . . .?"

"This is a nausea bracelet. Faux leather, made from recycled plastics and bamboo. It applies pressure to this point." Sullivan drifted a finger to the ball. "It should help the motion sickness."

Reid felt better already, thoroughly distracted by Sullivan's touch.

Reid prepared for Sullivan to drop his hand, but Sullivan gripped it more firmly, massaging between his fingers and palm.

A small moan slipped from Reid. "God that feels good."

Sullivan continued, rubbing up to the tip of each finger.

"The bracelet," Reid started.

"What about it?"

"It looks new."

Insecurity flickered briefly in Sullivan's eyes. He lowered his gaze to Reid's hand. "I bought it for you a few weeks ago."

He'd had the bracelet all this time and hadn't known how to give it to Reid?

Or hadn't he wanted Reid to misinterpret the gesture?

"Guys give other guys bracelets, you know," Reid said softly. "It doesn't have to mean anything."

The massage paused. Sullivan looked like he wanted to argue, but held his tongue.

Sullivan rose to his feet. Disappointment shot through Reid, until the captain resumed his seat on Reid's other side.

He picked up Reid's left hand and scrolled his thumb over the heel of Reid's palm, drawing out another moan.

Reid dropped his head back against the wood and absorbed every second of Sullivan's magic touch.

Sullivan cleared his throat. "I fired you."

Reid groaned and peeped at him through slit eyes. "We're back at that?"

Sullivan slid his hand up Reid's arm, firmly squeezing Reid's upper arm and the knob of his shoulder.

Reid's head snapped forward and Sullivan applied a gentle pressure.

"Reid. I owe you an apology. I let my anger take over last night. I'm sorry."

Reid shot a finger to Sullivan's warm lips and pressed. Day-old stubble bumped over his knuckles. "You told me not to go in there. I ignored your warning."

Breath fizzled to the crevices of Reid's fingers. "That may well be. But my reaction was disproportionate."

Reid dropped his fingers. "Sometimes we explode in anger, sadness, frustration with little to no warning. Feelings are messy, Sullivan. Expressing them can't always be measured."

"By that reasoning, crime of passion is a matter of fact."

"Well, don't start flinging knives around. But words, yeah, let 'em loose."

Sullivan hummed, unconvinced.

Reid pushed further. "Why do you think your reaction was over the top?"

"I said disproportionate not—"

Sullivan let his sentence drop. He released his firm grip on Reid's nape and rubbed his jaw. "I felt out of control with desire and the moment you said Riley's name . . ." He let out a breath. "I should have felt guilty, but I didn't. Ironically, that made me feel guilty."

"Guilty?" Reid asked. "You were dreaming of your wife. It's perfectly natural." Sullivan's expression tightened and Reid understood. "Oh. You were dreaming of someone else."

The intensity of the moment they'd shared in Sullivan's bed awoke Reid's senses, prickling him with awareness. He shivered.

Sullivan sighed.

Reid realized his long pause might seem condemning so he planted a comforting hand on Sullivan's thigh. "It's okay, Sullivan. Is she someone you know? Someone you're interested in?"

"Yes, and I'm afraid so. But I'm not ready to admit that to . . . her. In fact, I'm avoiding telling her at all."

Who *was* this woman? Someone from the university? Alanis?

Why was Reid scowling toward the cockpit?

He shook it off. "That's okay. Because you're such a sad man, Sullivan."

Sullivan barked a laugh. "The cheek of you. But in this case, true enough."

"Seriously. Take the time you need. Be friends first. You know what? Invite her to a Thanksgiving dinner and I'll—oh. Fired. Forgot."

"Reid," Sullivan warned. "You can't think I'd apologize and still send you packing?"

Reid fiddled with his nausea wristband, biting his lip. "When it comes to you, Sullivan, I have no idea what to expect."

"Look at me."

Reid lifted his chin and met Sullivan's steady gaze.

"Don't leave. Continue helping me be the best daddy I can be."

Heat walloped Reid's cheeks, and he chuckled nervously. "Are you sure? Will you stop trying to fire me every other day?"

Sullivan grimaced. "I am not an easy man."

"No," Reid said. "But my bet is still on *worth it.*"

Sullivan squeezed him around the bracelet and stood. "I'll tell Alanis to head back to the marina."

Reid stopped Sullivan, fingers hooking, belly chasing gravity with another drop. "Two days? You'll jump in after me if I fall overboard?"

Lips twitched, and Reid felt the affirmative answer in his bones. Holding Sullivan's gaze, he shakily unbuckled his life vest and shrugged out of it. "This is too uncomfortable, but I trust that we won't hit any icebergs."

"You've really got Titanic on the mind."

Reid lifted his brow. "Whose fault is that?"

"Tonight, when we're anchored, I'll show you how amazing all this can be."

"The very least I expect after taking my virginity like this."

Sullivan spluttered. "Your what?"

"First time on the open sea. Take care of me." Reid held up his cuffed wrist. "This is a good start."

ALL REID HAD TO DO WAS SURVIVE THE REST OF THE DAY AND one night. He could do it. He had to.

"Go do your environmental experiment," Reid urged Sullivan, who looked dubious about leaving him.

"I've totally got this." Reid wobbled to his feet. "I'll hang out with Alanis."

Sullivan was ready to protest, but Reid cut him off with a brave goodbye and arrowed for the cockpit door. "Save the world. Then we'll speak."

He left Sullivan chuckling and entered the cockpit.

Alanis jumped at the sight of him.

"Hey," Reid said. "Can I join you?"

"Didn't realize we had a stowaway." She blinked at his puffy face. "Sit, love."

Reid slung himself into the second seat next to Alanis, then reared back from accidentally touching one of the hundred buttons on the console.

She grinned. "Are you interested in learning how to pilot this boat? Or are you peeing your pants?"

The damn boat leaned again as it lifted on a wave.

Reid pressed the ball of his nausea bracelet hard, imagining Sullivan's calming hands on him. God he wanted that again.

Except, he also didn't want to be totally pathetic. He knew how much Sullivan's projects meant to him and if he had the chance to try one out, Reid would give him the space. "I'm not *un*interested in how this boat works," he said, bridling the truth.

"So you've already peed yourself. Gosh, I never knew how fun this outing would be."

Reid scowled at her before it morphed into a grin. "I wish I wasn't quite so nervous."

"You want me to put some music on?"

"A soundtrack for my internal drama?"

She shrugged. "Yeah."

He waved at her to turn it on. For an hour, Reid death-gripped the seat under him while Alanis belted out Shearwater songs. Reid understood why Sullivan might like Alanis. She was pretty and could drive a fucking yacht. She cared about distracting Reid, but she had easy wit and a wicked voice.

The water settled as they neared a bay. Alanis examined charts measuring water depth and started making calculations.

"Should be calm weather tonight, here's a good spot to anchor."

Land was a good mile in. Bobbing about on the ocean all night?

He wouldn't sleep a wink.

Sullivan popped his head into the cabin, face flushed from the fresh air. "We good here?"

Alanis nodded, and the door shut as Sullivan hiked to the front of the vessel.

Reid gnawed on his bottom lip. "What do you think of Sullivan?"

She glanced from him to Sullivan hunched at the bow, preparing the anchor, and back to him.

She cocked her head, "What do *I* think of him? Like, as a man to fall for?"

He wasn't sure he could handle the answer. It felt like chewing stones, his belly getting progressively heavier.

Yet he held his breath, waiting.

She smiled at him, a playful tilt to her lips, and his heart joined the stones in his gut. "He'd make a good partner. He'd be there for good times and bad. I think a life with him would be an adventure." She bumped his arm with her shoulder. "A good choice. A very good choice. What do you think, Reid?"

That Alanis was completely in love with him!

He rubbed his neck, the tender skin there.

If only he didn't know how *amazing* it'd felt to be under the man.

These thoughts had to be banished immediately.

He was here to be Sullivan's friend.

And help him move on with his life.

By God he would. He'd start by encouraging Alanis. "I think he's pretty damn near perfect." He winked at her. "Not to mention fucking hot, eh?"

Alanis giggled. "There is that too."

Sullivan dropped an anchor over the bow and used hand signals to tell Alanis to reverse. Starting and stopping, more power. Less. Until he gave her a wide smile and thumbs up.

Look at how well they wordlessly communicated. A good sign.

At a flicker of envy, Reid refocused his energy. "I always thought the anchor dropped from the rear of the boat."

Alanis cringed. "Not unless you fancy capsizing."

Fear wormed its way back into Reid, tensing his muscles. "Fuuuuck. I hope you won't mind me hogging Sullivan tonight. He promised to show me the fun in all this."

~

Alanis didn't mind.

In fact, she turned in after dinner.

Bundled in jackets and warm hats, Sullivan and Reid moved onto the deck.

Salty air rushed over his face, and Reid pressed the wristband tight against his skin, his pulse beating erratically.

Sullivan's hand warmed the small of Reid's back as he steered him to the bow.

Reid side-eyed him. "This feels like we're about to re-enact a certain movie. I call Rose."

"You look rather like Jack."

"Yeah, but he dies. So you can be him."

Sullivan leaned back against the railing and Reid mirrored him, sticking close, because though the water was calm, only a single anchor tethered them. Their jacket sleeves bumped as Sullivan dipped his head toward Reid's ear. "Look up."

Sullivan's velvety smile set against the sunset sky nearly toppled Reid. He grabbed the rail for support. Stars carpeted the sky. Tens of thousands of bright twinkles yanked at Reid's center of gravity, making him breathless. "I feel tiny."

"Insignificant."

"You're a right prince. But yes, life has more than proved that's true."

"What do you mean?"

Reid shrugged it off. "Nothing. Your run-of-the-mill-wounded past. Everyone has one. Mine is that I'm constantly left."

Something about Reid must be fundamentally inadequate. He was the common denominator.

Sullivan spoke softly. "I'm sorry, Reid."

Reid's throat tightened. "I should just be happy that I had Grams."

"Reid . . ."

Reid waved the sympathy off. Sullivan needed him, not the other way around. He pointed to the sky and inhaled deeply. "Do you know what we're looking at?"

Sullivan respected Reid's need to change topics. "Of course."

Reid almost tutted at the know-it-all response, but lost himself in Sullivan's impassioned lecture. These stars were Cassiopeia, those Draco, Andromeda, Aquarius, Capricornus, Pegasus. Pisces.

"Aquarius and Pisces. Apt that you and your daughter share the night sky." He gazed at Sullivan's sky-tipped face. "No Cancer?"

He shook his head. "You see Cancer in spring."

"Should've known we'd be diametric opposites."

Sullivan lowered his head, catching Reid's eye. The look made Reid squirrelly inside. He rolled his shoulders and bravely pushed off the rail, blurting, "Oh, by the way. Did Joanna mention that movie she wants to see?"

He fiddled with his bracelet, rubbing his thumb across the soft edge. He turned, facing the dark, glittery water and the darker bay in the distance.

Sullivan shifted. "What movie?"

"That classic. A reshowing. Anyway, I think she should go"—Reid modulated his voice close to a whisper—"with Elijah"—and continued normally—"and have a great time."

"That's sounds fine, but with Elijah?"

Sullivan stepped behind him and Reid used his jumpy energy to point skyward. "So those stars are Aquarius?"

Sullivan's front cushioned Reid's back as he shifted his arm, prickly jaw bumping his neck as Sullivan angled Reid's finger. "Those stars."

Reid turned his head and their misty breath mingled.

Sullivan soaked in Reid's expression carefully, then cleared his throat. "A date with Elijah?"

"A movie. It's age appropriate. The date, I mean."

"The movie too, I hope."

Reid twisted sharply and Sullivan steadied him by the hip. Oh hell, his hand practically branded him. "Let's go inside. We'll watch what they'll be watching."

"How adorably naïve that you think they'd be watching the movie."

"Come on. It'll be fine. It's not like they'll be parked somewhere under the stars."

They both glanced up. The wide expanse of the universe winked at them, and with a shiver, Reid took a giant step back, rearranging his beanie. "Let's find that classic."

Sullivan murmured quick agreement.

THEY WATCHED *FERRIS BUELLER'S DAY OFF* SLOUCHED AT opposite ends of the couch. Reid kept peeking at Sullivan and jumping when Sullivan caught him.

Sullivan was no better. But his gaze-tagging was the slow-cooked variety. Mostly because Reid didn't chase him away by acknowledging it. He simply let the looks burn into his profile while he watched Ferris Bueller belting his heart out in true eighties fashion until he couldn't take it anymore and glanced over.

Sullivan returned his concentration to the screen.

Reid's nerves knotted. It felt intense. Like quiet flirtation. Maybe Reid was misreading him. Maybe Sullivan was simply making sure Reid wasn't freaking out being on the open ocean.

Whatever the reason, Reid liked Sullivan looking.

As the movie ended, Reid realized they'd soon go to bed.

To their separate cabins. Reid would be alone as the boat clung to the sea floor with a mere anchor.

"Want to watch another one?"

Sullivan yawned, hefting his arms above him in a stretch. "I think I'm beat."

Please don't leave.

Reid picked at his bracelet, over and over as the credits rolled, until Sullivan leaned across the couch and slid his fingers across the buckle. "What's wrong, Reid?"

How did he ask? Without making this awkward? "I-know-your-bedroom-is-out-of-bounds-but-would-you-sleep-in-the-saloon-with-me?" Like that, apparently.

Sullivan's fingers drifted from his wrist. "You have a cabin."

Reid resumed picking at the leathery edge.

"Nothing will happen to you, Reid."

"So I hear you and my mind understands but my body . . ."

Sullivan cleared his throat. "There's not space enough in here for us both."

"The couch opens into a bed and is wide enough for two." Reid bit his lip and spoke his mind. "Are you worried you'll come on to me again?"

"Well, my mind gets it but my body . . ."

Reid laughed. "Tonight you *know* who you're sleeping next to. It won't happen."

Sullivan glanced at the couch, still unsure about the idea.

"Look," Reid suggested, "how about I pinch your nipples if you get too handsy?"

Sullivan slammed his eyes shut. "Please no pinching."

"Fine, I'll take the floor. Just be close."

Sullivan mumbled, disappeared, and returned in his underwear and T-shirt, blankets under his arm. Reid had undressed similarly, but kept his whistle around his neck. Sullivan smirked.

Reid started a makeshift bed on the floor but Sullivan stopped him. “We’ll share.”

“Sure?”

“Sure enough.”

They pulled out the couch and fit the sheets on. Sullivan turned off the saloon light. Energy thrummed through Reid as he climbed under the heavy blankets.

He found it hard—impossible—not to flash back to the previous night. The cool sheets at his back, Sullivan pressed hotly against him . . .

Settled in bed, Sullivan focused his stare on Reid’s jaw and Reid bit his lip as he soaked Sullivan up.

He was curled on his side, sheets at his shoulders, his neck firm and naked, with a small flat scar that glistened in the moonlight.

The urge to investigate with his lips flooded him. “N-no audiobook tonight?”

“I’ve decided to wean off them.”

“Why?”

Their gazes clashed in the darkness. “Maybe after finishing his collection, I’ll try something new.”

Reid readjusted his pillow to break the ticklish connection. “Cool, cool. Trying new things. You should do that.”

Sullivan shut his eyes. Reid didn’t want to sleep yet, though. “What’s your favorite Sam Baton book? Not the content. Just the titles. Unless they’re also sexually explicit, my kinky friend.”

Sullivan huffed, the air fanning over Reid’s forehead and combing his hair. “I love every single one.”

“Are they all made into audiobooks?”

“Except his last one.”

“Are you eagerly waiting for it?”

“He’s not releasing that in audio.”

“Pity. What’s it called? I’m holding out for *one* title here.”

Sullivan shifted the blankets higher around them against a draft. “Good night, Reid.”

Reid fought back a sigh. “Night, Sullivan.”

He closed his eyes and focused on the feel of his faux-leather bracelet, slowly drifting. Then, quietly, Sullivan spoke. “*Second Time Around.*”

Reid slept peacefully, and it had nothing to do with their arms nestled together between them, Sullivan’s hand curled warmly around his bracelet.

Watching David fix his deck was painful, cringe-worthy, distressing. He didn't need help. But *I itched to give it.*

-James
Second Time Around

Chapter Ten

Reid was in trouble.

Big freaking trouble.

He wanted to tell himself off, promise he'd never think those thoughts again, and move on to greener pastures.

But he couldn't.

Ever since waking up with Sullivan draped around his back, he hadn't stopped thinking about it. About them together. In bed. Kissing. More than kissing. Way more than kissing.

He'd drunk pounds of coffee during the week, but the buzz Sullivan gave him was more intense than the coffee.

Reid was being unprofessional and doing exactly what Sullivan feared: crushing on him.

And . . . God.

The thought of Sullivan pressing into him as he held him tightly and breathed in Reid's hair made for the best right-handed affairs of his life . . .

Reid stared at his book. He hadn't turned the page in forever. He should do that.

In front of him, Sullivan paced the saloon with an aura of

parental protectiveness. Okay. Reid had to stop finding everything an emotional turn on.

He tried to bundle all the illicit thoughts and mentally sink them to the ocean floor.

Friends. They were friends. That was what Sullivan needed.

"Waiting for my daughter to come home is torture."

Reid gave up pretending to read and shut the book. Not *Second Time Around*. He'd held up to his promise . . . so far. "Looks it."

"Just yesterday she was too scared to use the toilet alone. Now she's in a musty movie theater with a boy, whose horny teenage mind is bent on taking my daughter's innocence."

"I'm so privileged to experience this conversation."

Sullivan shot him a look.

Reid bit down on a grin as he returned the book to the cupboard. "So worked up at the possibility of a kiss."

"Kissing! That's what you think he's thinking about? Remember, we were fourteen once too. Who allowed them outside unchaperoned?"

"The theatre will be packed and Mason will be waiting outside. I don't know about you, but at fourteen, I was petrified at the idea of sex." He bit his lip. "Still am half the time."

Sullivan stalled mid-pace. "Stop being cute. It's not at all distracting me."

Pity.

Gah, those thoughts had to go!

"It's true. I'm constantly wondering if the sex is good for the woman and hoping I don't shoot too soon. That's when it's a success. Other times I have glimpses of *this feels awesome* buffered by to-do lists in my head. Random stuff I forgot to write down. One time I raced through sex, sure I left the stove on. Ended up faking it just to check."

Sullivan gaped at him.

Reid tried not to let his gaze shuffle down Sullivan. He wasn't sure he was successful. "Sometimes I wonder what it would feel like to not think. To be entirely in the moment."

Sullivan doubled the speed of his pacing, cursing skyward. "This is *torture.*"

"She'll be home any moment." Reid cuffed Sullivan's elbow, halting him. With a soothing smile, Reid contorted a reluctant Sullivan to the floor near the couch. Reid sat behind him, legs clamping around the side of Sullivan's back.

"What are you doing, Reid?"

Reid massaged Sullivan's shoulders. "Helping you stop thinking about rampant hormones on the loose."

A huff. "Not working."

"Shh. Focus on my hands gliding across your shoulders, dipping to your collarbone and squeezing with the perfect pressure."

"Really not working." Sullivan dropped his head and Reid rolled his thumbs up Sullivan's nape, into his soft hair, eliciting a grumbly moan.

Don't think about that moan at your neck, in your mouth, around your—

Reid's phone rang, thankfully slicing through his thoughts.

Sullivan grumbled. "Don't answer it."

"What if it's Joanna?"

"Damn, answer it. But more of this later."

Reid laughed nervously while rubbing Sullivan's neck, and answered his phone.

A female voice hit his ears, but not Joanna's.

Shit, he should have paid attention to the screen rather than dreamily smiling at Sullivan's head. "Toni?"

Sullivan went rigid between his legs and Reid knew he was listening in.

A moment of insecurity shivered through Reid, and then

he switched to loudspeaker. Being vulnerable went both ways, and this saved Reid from rehashing the conversation.

"How was Hawaii?"

"The most fun I've had in years."

Sullivan curled a hand around Reid's heel and rubbed supportively. Reid nodded dumbly at the phone. "Go with friends?"

Stupid high-pitched voice.

"No. With Octavio."

So that was Gym-rat's name.

"Anyway, I'm calling because your stuff is still here. Can you pick it up this weekend?"

Oh, right. "Um, yeah."

"You'll need Loretta to drive you. Too much crap for the bus."

"I'll figure it out."

"Great. Text me when you'll be here. Bye." She hung up.

Sullivan rubbed his calf. "We'll borrow Alanis's car. I'll help you."

"We borrow her car too often. Have you thought about buying your own?"

"But then I wouldn't see you zig-zag on the tandem bike on the four out of five days you run late for school."

"Damn bike." Reid dropped back against the couch, flexing his legs either side of Sullivan. "I'm serious, though."

Sullivan rested his head on Reid's inner thigh and peeked at him. "Joanna and I move around a lot. Owning a car is impractical. Plus, the environment."

Reid's heart gave an impractical downward lurch. "Buy an electric one. Stay in this marina."

Sullivan shut his eyes and breathed deeply. "I'm—"

The door slammed and Joanna stormed into the saloon and marched to her room. Whoa.

Reid caught up to her at the dividing wall. "What's wrong?"

Sullivan growled. "Where is he?"

Joanna blinked back tears and bowed her head. "Is it my stupid red hair?"

"What are you talking about?"

"He didn't kiss me."

"Oh, sweetheart." Reid drew her into a hug, glancing over her head at Sullivan. "He's just petrified."

"Or gay," Sullivan said, catching Reid's eye.

"Then why wouldn't he tell me that?" she sniffed.

Sullivan continued, "It's hard, sometimes."

"He holds my hand, though. And he's supportive of Mason."

Reid didn't think Elijah was gay. He thought Elijah was a kind boy who was equally devastated about not having the guts to kiss her as Joanna was at not being kissed. "Maybe you could make the first move. Some guys need the help."

Sullivan had difficulty clearing his throat.

Joanna pulled out of the hug, sniffing. "Really?"

"I speak truth."

"Okay. Okay, I'll invite him to the winter dance. I'll kiss him then."

The dance was in January. Reid loved how much an event the first kiss was. "It'll be perfect." He shared a delighted smile with Sullivan, whose face turned ashen.

"A dance? You're far too young. What school have I sent you to?"

"This is why I didn't want to mention it," Joanna said to Reid, glumly.

Reid tugged her precious hair. "Don't worry, Joanna. Your dad just needs me to help him through his fears."

Joanna silently pleaded with her dad. "Is there any hope Reid'll manage?"

Sullivan stilled, thoughtful. He cleared his throat. "He has a certain way about him. There's not *no* hope."

Delight swept through Reid, and Joanna slipped from his grasp, disappearing to her room. "Not no hope?" Reid lifted his hands and squiggled his fingers. "Do my magic fingers have something to do with it? Come here, I'll squeeze you some more."

Sullivan's look was almost dangerous and Reid's belly liked it. A lot.

"I changed my mind. No hope at all."

But the twitch of Sullivan's lips said Sullivan was a liar.

Reid shoved the bigger box of his belongings into Alanis's backseat. He slammed the door, aware that Sullivan was frowning at him for his stupidly strong reactions.

He couldn't deal with it.

He scooped up the smaller box and, without regarding Toni's pretty—if somewhat dilapidated—duplex, slung himself in the passenger seat.

Sullivan slid into the driver's seat with a calm that was almost choking.

Reid didn't look at him. Couldn't.

He stared glumly into the box, heavy on his lap. Books, pastels, an old scarf, and a hand-painted mug.

They drove through quaint, oak-lined suburban streets, millions of golden leaves swirling in fall breezes.

Sullivan cleared his throat. "Can you tell me the history of that mug? Was it something one of your charges made you? A gift?"

Sullivan glanced at Reid, and Reid felt it prickle against his temple.

"Or," Sullivan said, "we could talk about anything else . . ."

Reid slammed his head back against the headrest and shut his eyes behind the shades he'd worn all morning.

Sullivan's hand bumped gently against Reid's knee as he shifted gears, and they drove back home in soft, contemplative silence.

They returned the car to Alanis and continued to the *Aquarian*, Sullivan toting Reid's bigger box.

On board, Reid dropped his box at the door, not ready to go inside. He breathed in shaky lungsful of salty air and meandered around the deck, staring at the vast harbor beyond. Sullivan watched him, leaning against the rail, box at his feet.

Reid gripped the railing hard. "Oh, God. I was so embarrassed."

"At Toni's? You didn't do anything remotely embarrassing."

"I didn't expect Octavio to have his own key . . ." Reid felt himself choking up again. "It's only been six weeks. Toni and I were together five months and . . ." He never got a key. "I'm all good for a silent sob, but I didn't mean to do it in front of you all."

Sullivan joined him overlooking the harbor. In the distance, two yachts passed each other. He eyed Reid compassionately. "Are you still in love with her?"

"No. I don't think I was ever in love with her."

"Then why is this affecting you so much?"

Reid pushed his hands from the rail, frustrated. He couldn't quite pin it. He was embarrassed for Sullivan watching him pack his things and be rejected.

Something else sparked this mood, too. Octavio curling around Toni and kissing her neck as he squeezed her.

It had made Reid grip his wristband, and Sullivan had caught him doing it. Unexplained guilt and need raced through him when Sullivan had slung an arm around his shoulders and steered him outside.

"I want that," Reid answered, the words pulled from him.

He'd always been a slave to emotion, and now was no different. "I want to come home to someone who loves me, who trusts me with a key."

"I trust you with a key."

"You know what I mean. I want a partner who uses the mug I made for them, no matter how ugly it is. I want stupid arguments at Thanksgiving and cozy Christmases. I want surprises on each other's birthdays. I want marriage. I want children."

Sullivan's chest heaved and he frowned toward the horizon.

Reid laughed at himself. "But I can't even hold someone for longer than six months. I was jealous today, Sullivan. That sob was purely self-pity. I'm sorry you had to witness it."

"Sometimes we explode in anger, sadness, or self-pity with little to no warning. Feelings are messy, Reid. Expressing them can't always be controlled."

Surprised laughter wrung out of Reid and he raked his hands over his face. "Did you just quote me?"

Sullivan followed the motion. "It seemed an appropriate moment."

A spindle of curious emotions overlaid Reid's grumpy mood. "Are you telling me some of what I say is getting through to you?"

His lips were full and dark pink and he rubbed them together before admitting, "It all gets through, Reid."

Reid felt like he was being airlifted out of his shady mood. "I suppose I should use this knowledge to my advantage."

Sullivan hefted the bigger box.

"Hey, get back here. I have all sorts of things I want you to absorb."

Sullivan lifted the box to his shoulder, dug into his pocket for the key, and desperately pushed it into the lock.

Reid chased after him, stooping for the smaller box. "You are thrilled for Joanna's dance next January. It is okay if I sleep in until six thirty on weekdays. You fully accept that it is okay for guys to like guys or guys to like girls and guys, and—"

The door shut in his face.

Reid grinned.

~

"This is the worst day of my life," Joanna said bluntly.

Reid was inclined to agree.

They stared into the mirror on Joanna's dresser and sighed.

"Why did you ever decide to dye your beautiful red hair?" Reid asked, shaking his head. "Why did I try to prove it wasn't so bad by using the second box on myself?"

Joanna picked up her hair dryer. "Maybe yours will look better once it's dried."

Spoiler: it fucking didn't.

Joanna was torn between laughing, groaning, and apologizing profusely. Reid shrugged it off. Joanna's muted grey hair was worse, probably because she'd done a poor job bleaching it first.

Reid picked up a box of dye and admired the dark-haired model. He looked into the mirror again and shrieked, dropping the box to the floor.

"Again. Why, Joanna? Why?"

Joanna scooped her grey hair into a bun. Patches of violet showed at the base. She let it go and whimpered. "I want him to find me pretty. Now I gotta hope he's into older women."

Reid rang out a laugh, but oh God. Was that Sullivan stepping onto the boat? How would they explain this?

The box stared at him from the floor, a fat PERMANENT mocking him. A pang of panic swished in his gut at the thought of Sullivan seeing their new looks.

Sullivan called out, and Reid and Joanna exchanged looks.

She opened a drawer full of winter hats and scarves, and Reid nodded. "It is practically winter."

"Very, very cold for fall."

They each grabbed a hat and cavalierly sauntered into the saloon. Sullivan, spooning coffee into the machine, did a double take.

Suspicion thickened his blue gaze. Reid fingered the safety whistle in his pocket.

Sullivan muttered and shook his head. Reid peered into the dozen paper bags of Thanksgiving food Sullivan had shopped for, while Sullivan prepared coffee for them and an elderflower tea for Joanna.

Bell peppers. Oat cream. Pumpkin. Half dozen bottles of wine.

Tofurky.

"Tomorrow will be an . . . interesting feast."

"We'll do prep work tonight," Sullivan said, "while Joanna watches movies in her room."

"Why doesn't she help?"

"Because the kitchen is too small for three, and you need the instruction."

Sullivan kept eyeing his hat and Reid kept tugging it over his ears.

Coffee and tea in hand, they migrated to the couch in awkward silence.

Sullivan's long, hard gaze hit Reid's.

Joanna drummed her nails over her cup, a soft, rhythmic tinker.

They continued to sip, Sullivan to survey them.

"I can't take it anymore." Joanna sprang to her feet, planted her tea, and confessed.

Reid winced as Joanna's hat fell, spilling grey curls around her shoulders. Sullivan's expression went blank as Joanna wailed about wanting to be pretty for their Thanksgiving guests tomorrow.

For Elijah went unsaid but absolutely heard.

Sullivan gathered Joanna in his arms. "Trust me, boys are nothing but trouble." He kissed her forehead. "You are beautiful."

Joanna hugged him back. Reid took easier sips of his coffee.

Their hair might be horrendous, but at least they wouldn't have to worry about dressing up for the fall parade tomorrow. He'd drag Sullivan to the parade come hell or high water.

Maybe not high water.

Sullivan whispered into his daughter's ear. She nodded, and with a warning glance to Reid, left the room.

Reid sat up straight, sloshing hot coffee over his hoody. *Dammit.* He set the mug down and wiped at the splotch.

"Hat off," Sullivan said.

Reid held the hat firmly over his head. "I think knitted suits me."

Sullivan slid his thumbs into his belt loops and approached like a lion toward its prey. "Reid, I want you to take your hat off."

Sullivan's gravelly, firm tone pulled at Reid's skin and Reid might have to replay that in his head later. Much later.

Oh God, he was a depraved manny.

"The thing is, Sullivan," he said. "I'm feeling all kinds of vulnerable about what's underneath."

"Can you pull it off?"

Reid's breath hitched at the challenge. The warning. Hot and bothered, anyone? "Only if you tell me I'm still beautiful too."

Sullivan hunkered before him, a foot away, brow arching. Reid sucked in his salty scent.

A palm landed on his knee. "Reid."

Reid fidgeted with the hat, hoping his boner wasn't noticeable. "Okay-okay, I'll show you, but first I need you to picture a frolicking gazelle." Sullivan's other brow shot up in puzzled surprise. Reid continued, "It's an elegant, fawn-colored beauty."

"Elegant?"

Okay, maybe not elegant. "We'll agree the gazelle is pretty. Now picture your favorite vegetable, the purple of its skin glittering under the kitchen light."

Sullivan reached out to pull the hat off him and Reid lurched out of reach. "I need to mentally prepare you. Now picture that gazelle mating with the eggplant."

"What are you mentally preparing me for, exactly?"

"Don't worry. No eggplants were harmed in the making of this analogy."

Sullivan leaned all that sexiness over Reid and wrestled the hat off him. Reid was too busy absorbing Sullivan's heat to stop him.

Sullivan pulled back, fisting the woolen hat, face contorting, unreadable. "Your *hair.*"

He scrubbed the hat over his eyes like it might negate Reid's purple-haired monstrosity. He bolted from the saloon.

Reid ducked into the bathroom, readjusted himself, and checked out his reflection in the tiny mirror on the door. He sucked in a breath. Not his best look.

But he expected Sullivan to see past it.

Grumpily, Reid threw on a coat and chased after Sullivan. He found him at the rear of the vessel. The water was still, the boat barely bobbing, and the marina was on full display, lit up against a setting sky. Sullivan stood at the rail and a sob bubbled from him.

"It's not *that* bad!" Reid scowled. He pulled Sullivan by the arm, twisting him around.

The skin at Sullivan's eyes pinched; his blue eyes sparkled

as he eyed Reid's hair and buckled with a hefty laugh, throwing his head back. A glimmer of a tear—the first one Reid had ever seen from him—hovered at the corner of his eye.

Reid feigned exasperated disbelief, but he was fairly sure his smile ruined the effect.

"I'm still waiting, you know."

"What for? Oh, God. I haven't laughed so hard in forever." A glance at Reid had Sullivan struggling to rope in another laugh.

"I'm waiting for you to say 'you're still beautiful.' Those exact words."

Sullivan's smile simmered and he stared into the peachy light.

"They're just words," Reid murmured. "Words that will make me feel better about having this the next eight weeks."

"Eight weeks?"

"For it to grow out. I'd re-dye it, but it stung too bad." Reid prodded him against the chest. Sullivan had raced out without a coat, and his shirt sleeves were still bunched around his arms, showing off goose-prickled skin. "Now say—"

Reid gasped as Sullivan slid hot fingers through Reid's hair, blunt nails gently scraping his scalp. He scrunched the ends in his hand with just enough pull.

Reid's heart banged about wildly and he hoped Sullivan didn't hear it. Hoped he didn't lean into Sullivan's hold, exposing his throat—

He's just checking out your dye job.

Sullivan's amused gaze flickered from Reid's hair to his eyes.

A chuckle feathered over Reid's nose as Sullivan plunged a second hand into Reid's hair and cupped his head. Thumbs rested warmly against Reid's jaw, and their eyes met. "It's truly heinous," Sullivan uttered.

Reid's gut sank a few inches along with his chin, but Sullivan steered him back up.

A warm smile touched Sullivan's lips. "You're still beautiful."

Butterflies swamped Reid's gut. Reid liked the stories they were trying to spin. "Wow."

Sullivan's smile quivered, gaze sparkling with humor. "Wow?"

Reid nodded, going weak at the knees with Sullivan's thumbs skating along his skin.

He was in Big. Freaking. Trouble. "I mean. You really said it." He backed up with a skittish laugh. "I totally have you wrapped around my little finger."

Their gazes snagged and Sullivan spun Reid and marched him across the deck, voice in his ear. "Let's put those magic fingers to work in the galley."

"Your mouth says stay away. Your eyes say come closer. You're a personified oxymoron."
"Or just a moron."

- David and James
Second Time Around

Chapter Eleven

Footsteps thumped above, a ceaseless to and fro. Reid could distinguish Sullivan's from Joanna's by the deeper groan of the wood.

Reid was supposed to be up there too, helping set up for the Thanksgiving feast they'd have after Reid dragged Sullivan and Joanna to the Redwood Fall Parade.

Instead, it was nine and he was tangled in his sheets.

He ground his palm against an echoing thump in his forehead. Far too much wine last night.

Wine he'd drunk to stop wayward Sullivan-related thoughts.

It sucked to be so turned on by a man he could never have. A man who would distance himself physically and emotionally if he found out.

God, Reid had to be careful. Sullivan was easing out of his grief-induced social coma. He was making friends and even considering staying at the marina.

Reid needed to keep the progress rolling.

Needed to encourage Sullivan's feelings toward Alanis.

Needed Sullivan to never find out Reid was attracted to him.

His phone buzzed and Reid groped for it.

Loretta: Happy Thanksgiving!

Reid thumbed back the same and asked how life was going.

Loretta: Truth? I'm so freaking in love with Natalie it consumes me. Scares me, actually.

Reid: Scares you?

Loretta: The idea of ever losing her. I think it'd kill me.

Reid's heart swelled at the intensity of Loretta's confession. It made him all kinds of achy wondering if this was how Sullivan once felt with his wife.

Loretta: Nuff fuzzies. How's mannying Sullivan?

Reid: The UST got real.

Loretta: What'cha gonna do about it?

Reid: Take a cold shower and go upstairs. I've got stuff to do.

Loretta: Sounds like it.

Reid did as he said, dressing in tight, dark jeans and two layers of warm tops. He poked his head into Joanna's cabin and said a roughened 'Hey. Ready for the parade?' to the girl playing on her phone. She returned with a long stare, "Are you?"

Reid snorted and proceeded into the saloon, wet hair dripping onto his shoulders. It was sexier wet and he wasn't keen on it drying any time soon.

The table was set for six, and Sullivan was adding spices to a bubbling pot. The air tasted of nutmeg, cinnamon, and baked apple. Reid's stomach gurgled.

Loud enough for Sullivan to hear, apparently, because he glanced at him over his shoulder.

Reid rubbed his temples. "Morning."

"Took the word right out of my mouth," Sullivan said, sidling to the coffee machine. He handed Reid one mug and took the other.

Reid's gaze narrowed on the wide mug in Sullivan's hand. "What are you drinking from?"

"This unique mug with hearts that seem to pop out no matter how you hold it." Sullivan turned the mug inspecting it. "It's fascinating."

Reid scoffed, but a ridiculous blush crept up his throat. Sullivan was using his stupid mug.

It was only a mug.

Reid avoided direct eye contact. "Are we set for Thanksgiving lunch? We've got a parade to get to. Alanis, Elijah, and Mason are joining us."

"I don't know. I didn't taste-test any of the sauces you insisted on making. The white one looks like it might need some TLC."

"I made sauces last night?"

"I told you it wasn't a great idea the day before and after a bottle of wine. But you insisted, and I had a great time watching you flounder about."

"I vaguely recall. Oh. The ginger chutney and the vegan Béchamel sauce. Why didn't you try it?"

"You told me not to. Said it would be a surprise for today."

"Drunk me likes to take risks." Not sexual ones, he hoped. Though Sullivan was far too calm for that to be the case. "Let's try it now."

Sullivan smiled into another sip, studying him over the mug. "Before the parade?"

"Before guests arrive."

"Good plan. Wouldn't want to poison anyone."

"Especially not your special someone, eh?" Reid waggled his brows suggestively. "Are you nervous?"

"About flirting with my special someone? No. I do that on a fairly regular basis. Taking it any further? Yes."

"Don't worry, Sullivan. Throw me a look if you need me to help you out."

Reid reheated the Béchamel sauce. He hefted the pot in one hand, grabbed a spoon, and trundled to Sullivan where he sat reviewing a to-do list. **Try Reid's sauce** was underlined several times.

Reid held up a spoonful of sauce to Sullivan. "Open up."

Sullivan leaned back and parted his lips, watching Reid first blow on the liquid. The curious, amused look made Reid shiver. But that happened more often than not around Sullivan.

Reid slid the spoon over Sullivan's bottom lip. Sullivan sucked off the sauce and then his face contorted and he promptly spat it back out. The white, slimy gob landed in Sullivan's lap. "What the hell was that?"

"I told you. Béchamel sauce. Bé-cha-mel."

"Terrible. Ter-ri-ble." Sullivan stood and popped the button of his jeans. The zipper drew down and Sullivan dug his thumbs either side of the waist.

Reid stared transfixed, breathless as those jeans shimmied down hairy muscular legs, revealing black boxers that gripped his ass and his very visible package. Reid hurriedly averted his gaze. He dumped the pot onto the stove, taste testing for himself. Salty. Ocean salty. But not *that* bad.

He turned to say as much to Sullivan when Joanna entered the room with her phone and a turkey glove.

She froze. "What's going on?"

Sullivan huffed a laugh. "I got Reid's"—he glanced pointedly at Reid—"*Béchamel* sauce all over my pants."

Joanna backed out of the room. "I just remembered. I forgot something in my room."

Sullivan stared after her, then frowned, and barked out a laugh. "This is unbelievable—"

"What's unbelievable is you not being manly enough to swallow," Reid muttered.

Sullivan swung his head toward Reid whip-fast. "What?"

"If that had been your sauce, I wouldn't have spat it out."

Sullivan's eyes blazed into him, then he cast his gaze skyward. "New rule. The word sauce is forbidden. You can't hold me accountable for what I might do if I hear it again."

Aquarians! So weird the things that wound them up. "Put some pants on." Goddamn it *please*. "We're off to the parade."

~

THE PARADE WAS WELL UNDERWAY DOWN A COLD BUT SUNNY Main Street.

Reid steered their group of six through a thicket of curious tourists near ropes of turkeys stretched from the local library to Kings Café.

Elijah and Mason were dressed in their usual black attire, but Alanis was practically wearing a coat of fall leaves, a wreath in her dark hair to match. Sullivan insisted on not dressing festively and Reid had compromised by stuffing a giant rubber turkey glove over his fist.

Mason, very all-American corn-fed Mason, leaned an arm on Reid's shoulder, eyeing his hair. "Thanks for the invite. You and Joanna dye your hair for the parade?"

Reid and gray-haired Joanna made a silent agreement. "Yes we did," Reid agreed. "For the parade."

Sullivan set his mouth in a tight line, gaze drinking them in that Britishy way of his. "Let's finish this. I have a Tofurky to roast."

Mason made a face that Reid totally sympathized with. "They're selling pumpkin fries. My favorite. I gotta grab some." Mason's arm slipped off Reid's shoulder and he disappeared toward the street vendor, digging out his wallet.

"Me too," Alanis chirped, hurrying after Mason in a rustle of leaves.

Reid bumped his arm against Sullivan's and kept it there.

The rubber turkey bumped over his thigh. "This parade is a yearly tradition." He lifted Sullivan's turkey-gloved arm high. "Start enjoying it."

In front of them, Joanna and Elijah watched a pumpkin float drive past.

"You know the winter dance?" Joanna said.

"Yeah," Elijah murmured.

"Would you . . ."

"Yeah."

"Cool."

Joanna turned to Elijah with a bright smile, and Elijah returned it, blushing. She side-eyed Reid and Sullivan. "Wanna freak my dad out and let me buy you a hot chocolate at Kings?"

Elijah's gaze flickered nervously to Sullivan's. Poor boy looked like he might choke.

Sullivan stared back like he wasn't afraid to murder a kid.

Reid snuffed a laugh and stepped his foot around the inside of Sullivan's, crossing their legs, blocking him. "Go," Reid told them. "Have fun. Not too much fun. We'll pop in when you least expect it."

The boy wouldn't do anything at Kings. Not so much as brush fingers.

They raced off and Reid became aware of the heat of Sullivan's leg pressing against his. He liked it. A little too much.

Moments like these might give him away.

He hurriedly whisked around, and Sullivan's gaze thankfully followed Elijah.

Alanis popped up beside them, pumpkin fries in a cup, smirking. She stage-whispered to Reid, "Does he *ever* smile?"

Reid stole a fry and chewed. "He smiles all the time."

Mason returned to Reid's other side with a bigger cup of fries. "Who?"

"Sullivan. He smiled just before you all joined us on the bus."

Sullivan pinned his gaze on Mason. "Then you all joined us on the bus."

Alanis tapped a fry against her bottom lip thoughtfully. "You'll have to tell us what *all that* feels like smiling at you, Reid."

It was quite the rush. "You'll feel it soon, Alanis. He's nervous around you."

"Nervous?" she mused, frowning.

Mason laughed jovially and casually slung an arm across Reid's shoulders. He offered Reid a fry. "Nervous is cute. But not my style." Reid took a long thick fry and popped it into his mouth. Mason grinned. "Things have been a lot more interesting since you showed up."

The way his eyes twinkled with delight had suspicion rolling through Reid. Mason was laughing like he knew about Reid's penchant for misadventure. Like he might know about accidentally losing his cruising virginity.

Even Sullivan must have thought so, because his eyes narrowed tightly on Mason.

Reid whipped toward Alanis. "Did you tell Mason about my lack of experience?"

"I'm a horrible gossip, Reid," Alanis said, blushing as red as the leaves at her head. "Everyone at the marina wants to know about the new cutie."

Mason spoke teasingly at his ear. "Hey cutie, do you think these fries need more salt?"

"Salt?"

"Yeah," Mason chuckled. "I think they do. I love salty things."

Reid brightened with a laugh that was meant for Sullivan, addressing Mason. "Then *you* might like to try my Béchamel sauce later."

Mason's hand fell from Reid's shoulders. Reid blinked at Sullivan tugging Mason aside with a grim smile. Presumably Sullivan wanted to warn him about Joanna and Elijah being alone together.

Alanis whickered out a laugh and murmured something about being jealous.

Right, Sullivan hadn't exactly given her much attention. Probably nerves. Reid smiled apologetically. "He'll be more tolerable once he's got his Tofurky basted."

"Aye, I bet. Hope that happens soon."

Sullivan stuffed the turkey glove on Mason's hand. "Keep Alanis company." He grabbed Reid's wrist around the faux leather. "Help me check on the kids."

Sullivan led Reid through the pumpkin-spiced crowd to Kings.

The café was full, and owner Wesley handled the traffic with grace and charm and the help of his husband Lloyd. Working the counter, Lloyd kept blatantly checking out both the clock and Wesley.

Guess he was ready to shut shop and do some basting of his own.

Sullivan ordered Reid's favorite along with his own oat-milk cappuccino.

"Okay, what's up?" Reid said, gut jiggling from the pressure of Sullivan's hand enclosing his. "You've barely glanced around for Joanna and Elijah."

Sullivan let go of him. "They're by the window. That's not why I brought you in here. Mason is into you."

A surprised laugh shot from Reid. He shook his head. "Because he had his arm around my shoulders? That was one hundred percent California surfer dude-ness. Nothing gay about it."

"Oh, there was plenty gay about it."

"How would you know?"

"I know."

"You're making it up. No way he's interested."

Sullivan dipped, lowering his voice so it bubbled into his ear. "I wonder if you'd recognize flirting if it bit you on your pretty ass."

"I happen to be super intuitive, Mr. Straight Guy. And I hardly think *you*'d know what cues to look for."

Sullivan struggled not to talk back.

Could Mason be into him?

"Besides," Reid said. "If he's into me, would you have a problem with it? Don't answer yes, you homophobic prick!"

Sullivan grabbed their coffees and growled as he hoofed toward the back of the café.

Reid trotted grumpily at his side. "Thank you for the coffee. I'll pay you back at home."

"I don't want you to."

"Then I'm doubly grateful. But not any less pissed at your attitude."

God, what would Sullivan think if he knew Reid's feelings toward him?

They stopped a step from their favorite L-shaped couch, where Reid had first seen Sullivan, where Reid insisted on sitting every time they came here. The seat was occupied.

"Theo! Jamie!" Reid's frustrated look gave way to a smile.

Theo jumped up and wrapped Reid into a hug. Jamie embraced him too and gestured for Reid and Sullivan to join them.

Reid made quick introductions and whispered to Sullivan to behave himself.

"So you do exist," Sullivan exclaimed.

Perhaps Reid needed to define what he meant by behave.

Jamie's brows rose. "What's that?"

Something unreadable sparked in Sullivan's eye as he looked from Reid to Theo and Jamie. "Reid's resume came a little exaggerated. It's good to know some of it is true."

Theo laughed. "You mean the spelling bee?"

Reid took a latte and held it with his middle finger pointed toward them. "We'll be here all afternoon if you start picking apart my resume. Moving on. What are you doing here? Where are the twins?"

Reid missed the energetic two-year-olds he'd babysat a few afternoons a week since they were six months. Until Theo and Jamie moved to Minnesota.

Jamie spoke, "We just finished painting the house interior. We'll spend Thanksgiving with Theo's grandma Darla and fly back tonight."

"Mom has the boys," Theo said.

Reid playfully grimaced. "Will she manage?"

"Percy and Cal are basically doing all the grunt work," Theo said. "Good practice for when they have their own."

"If they decide to adopt," Reid said, but he had a feeling they would.

Theo took out his phone. "Want to see? Mom sent a video message."

Reid jumped at the chance and took the offered phone. Reid angled it so he and Sullivan could both see. The video showed Percy and Cal wrestling the twins into socks. Percy managed and helped Cal wrangle the second pair on Darcy.

The kids scampered into the background and Cal pulled an exhausted-looking Percy into his arms and kissed him chastely. In the meantime, Darcy had his socks off again.

Cal laughed. "This is true love."

"Running after twins all day?"

"Helping each other survive it."

"That's my favorite part," Theo said, laughing. His eyes crinkled at the edges as Jamie beheld him like Cal had taken the words from him. "They're such a ridiculous handful."

Jamie hummed. "Just like you as a kid, so your mom says."

Theo groaned. "This is the perfect case of what goes around comes back to wake your ass at four thirty in the morning." His eyes shifted toward Jamie. "Hopefully the next one will be a little you. I'd love that."

Jamie expression jolted with surprise. "You still want another one?"

Theo faced him, all traces of laughter gone. "Hell yeah. We agreed on three, remember?"

Jamie sucked in a breath. "Remember? I remember every clueless goddamn moment." He grabbed Theo by the JLM lettering of his shirt and tugged him into a kiss.

Reid slapped Sullivan's thigh, stopping him from commenting or twitching in disgust.

Sullivan flexed under Reid's palm. Reid growled up at him and found Sullivan staring at him. Staring with warmth in those sea-blue eyes.

"What?" Reid mouthed.

"Later," Sullivan mouthed back.

They finished their coffees, chatting amicably, and Reid and Sullivan begged off to find the friends they'd abandoned. Joanna and Elijah had already left the café, which had Sullivan eagerly jostling through the crowds.

"Where the hell are they?"

Reid jumped, failing to spot them over the sea of heads. Despite his height, Sullivan also struggled to survey the crowds. Too many damn props and costumes interfering.

Reid tugged on Sullivan's arm, making him stoop. His lips accidentally bumped Sullivan's cold ear. "Can I climb you?"

Blue eyes whipped to him. Reid paused at the intensity of them under Sullivan's frown.

"To spot Joanna and Mason or Alanis?" Reid explained, his stomach jumpy.

Sullivan swiveled until he was in profile. "Right. Of course."

Reid eyed Sullivan for the best nooks to grab. "Should we do this face to face? Or from behind? No, wait. Might have better leverage if you give me a boost."

Sullivan scrubbed a hand through his hair and linked his fingers together. Reid settled one foot on him and gasped at the rush as Sullivan propelled him high.

Immediately, he knew it was a mistake.

Sullivan's breath fizzled over Reid's exposed 'V' line. It tickled so hard, Reid smashed his crotch against Sullivan's face.

Oh, God. The sensation was too much. Ahhhh.

The heat of Sullivan's trapped groan worsened the effect. Reid yelped and squirmed, jerking his hips to shake off the crazy shivers.

Holy fuck. Most inappropriate time to get hard.

Was there any possibility Sullivan wouldn't notice?

Gods, if you care for me in the slightest, he won't notice . . .

Reid struggled to hide his inner panic. "Joanna and company are by the fountain. Let me down."

"Are you sure it's them?"

Every. Word. Made. Him. Want. To. Thrust.

It cost him everything not to buck his hips again. "Down, down."

Sullivan guided him gently to the ground and Reid's cheeks fucking burned.

The hurried glance Sullivan gave his crotch told Reid he'd totally noticed.

Heat throttled him close to choking.

The one thing Sullivan couldn't know, and Reid was failing to keep it from him.

What would happen now? Would he withdraw? Act differently around Reid? Stop hanging out in the evenings together on the couch? Stop taking turns massaging each other's shoulders?

Loss seared painfully up his throat.

He couldn't lose that.

"I'm easily aroused," he blurted. "The slightest shift of the sheet and I'm aching. Doesn't mean I dig sheets. Doesn't mean I dig you."

Sullivan slammed his eyes shut, murmuring for Reid to just stop. Please.

Yep. The phrase "quit while you're ahead" should have been applied thirty seconds ago.

He avoided Sullivan's gaze, taking particular interest in his shoes.

"Let's . . . go to the guys. Or you can meet them and I can head back to the marina."

Sullivan cursed under his breath. "Hey, Reid?"

"Yep?" He couldn't bring himself to make eye contact. Why couldn't he joke about his? Brush it off with a laugh?

Why did it make him so awkward?

Because he knew he was being found out.

"Reid?" Sullivan said again, softly.

Reid gritted his teeth against the tightening in his throat and forced himself to look up. His grin ached. "Guess next time we should do it from behind."

The moment the words left his lips, the sexual image sprang to life.

He stared at Sullivan in horror.

Yep, no. He would cry now.

Reid had ruined them.

He whisked away and scurried through the crowd.

Sullivan tried to catch up, but speed was one advantage Reid held over the demigod.

A throng of dancing human turkeys blocked his escape, and Sullivan caught him by the elbow and turned him around.

Sullivan let out a breath. "I know I do, but I never mean to come across as a homophobic jerk."

Reid couldn't possibly be any warmer. "I'm, ah, not into you. You don't have to worry, okay?"

Sullivan's lips twisted sadly. They both heard the lie. "Oh, I do worry. But not the way you're thinking. Reid, look—"

"There you are!" Mason declared, approaching with Alanis, Joanna, and Elijah.

Reid wasn't sure if he was happy for the reprieve or frustrated at the interruption. What had Sullivan been about to say? He admitted to worrying, but promised he wasn't homophobic.

Was he worried for Reid's sake? Worried about hurting Reid by not returning his feelings? Worried about how it might affect his post as a manny?

Sullivan was extremely relieved to see the others.

Reid could deal with that. All he needed to do was steer his feelings elsewhere. Show Sullivan there was absolutely no need for concern.

"Mason," Reid said. He crooked his finger and flashed Sullivan a *we're cool* wink. "I have a question for you . . ."

After the Tofurky had been eaten—and, surprisingly, enjoyed—their guests left, Joanna disappeared to bed, and Reid found Sullivan leaning against the rail at the bow.

Sullivan quietly surveyed the stars. His coat was zipped to the base of his throat and his jeans were scrunched around his deck boots.

A smooth breeze funneled down Reid's shirt sleeves, but the shiver came deeper than that. Cinnamon from Sullivan's apple pie stuck to Reid's clothes and the lip he nervously chewed on. Since their moment at the parade, they'd not been alone together.

Sullivan had cast him furrowed looks across the dining table as Reid pathetically tried to flirt. With Mason.

The outside light was on and the stainless-steel surface of the cockpit door reflected Reid. "Ugh!"

He matted down his horrendous hair.

Sullivan glanced at him. "Still not used to it?"

"I keep wetting it to keep it bearable, but it goes right ahead and dries."

"Tough life."

Reid leaned against the opposite rail and checked for his whistle. Still there. "The toughest. I've seen purple look hot on guys, but not on me. How will I ever score a date now?"

"You were doing perfectly fine today."

"Oh, so you thought the line *you're so clingy you'll put saran wrap out of business* was a winner?"

"Mason did look slightly offended." Sullivan's smile widened. "Might be why I liked it so much."

"You really don't like him, huh?"

"Quite the keen eye you have."

"Joanna will have a first boyfriend sometime."

"It's too soon."

"It'll always be too soon." An awkward beat passed between them. Reid stuffed his hands into his pockets and pulled them out again to grip the rail. "How'd it go with Alanis? You two were talking a lot before she raced off to her other Thanksgiving meetup."

"Talking, Reid." Sullivan rubbed his jaw. "I am not interested in Alanis."

Reid jerked, surprised. *Relieved.* "You're not?"

"No."

"Why didn't you tell me?"

Sullivan met his eye and sighed deeply. "Look, I want to tell you the truth. Everything. I feel bad about not being more transparent. But every time I try to tell you, I think of the worst that can happen, and stall. Turns out I'm a big bloody coward. I'm sorry."

"The worst that can happen?"

"The decision to date—to fall in love—feels like life-or-death. I died once, when Riley did. I don't want to again."

Reid's chest wrenched. "I'm sorry if I've been pushy. You don't have to tell me anything about who you like."

Sullivan joined Reid at his rail. Reid dropped his hands to his sides, and warm fingers hooked around his wrist below his nausea bracelet. "Is this working for you?"

"Never take it off," Reid murmured. "I love the tightness of it. Makes me feel safe."

"Good." Sullivan looked at him. "I want you to feel safe."

Yep, okay. Reid was definitely tearing up. He forced a croaky laugh. "Are you telling me you'll never throw me overboard?"

"I'm telling you that afterward, I'd dive in shark-infested waters to get you back."

A tear dampened Reid's lashes. He twisted his body and faced Sullivan. "Do you remember our trip to the cave?"

"Daily."

Reid's breath caught. "Can I hug—"

Sullivan pulled Reid against him, engulfing him into the apple-spiced heat of his body. Sullivan held him snug. Perfectly close.

God, this felt so safe. So solid. So—"Uh oh."

"What?"

"If I tell you, do you promise not to let go right away?"

Sullivan's chuckle trickled over his hair. "I can do that."

"I might have daddy issues."

Sullivan's lips smacked as he searched for the right words. "You realized that now? With my arms around you?"

"Yep?"

"Right. Shall we exorcise them?"

"Exercise them? Like, on you? If I recall, you weren't too keen on being called daddy."

Sullivan's arms shifted and Reid stilled, but Sullivan didn't pull away. He unbuttoned his coat and wrapped either side around Reid, cocooning him against his body. "Ex*or*cise."

Get rid of them. "Yes. Good plan. How?"

"You say opening up helps . . ."

Reid ground his forehead against Sullivan's shoulder. "While I'm glad things get through to you, it'd be nice if you acted on them."

Sullivan hummed deeply in his throat. "Tell me about your dad."

"You want to know?" Each word had Reid's mouth brushing against Sullivan's shirt collar. It tasted of apple and under it, him. Salty and fresh.

"Yes, Reid, if you want to share, I want to know."

Reid pulled his head back enough to search the earnestness in Sullivan's face, before sighing back into the crook of his neck. "I guess I was hard work? I wasn't sporty, so we had nothing in common. I cried too easily. Didn't listen, and still asked for help too often. He never raised his fist or anything. He just . . . said he couldn't do it anymore. He arranged everything with Grams and said a tearless goodbye."

Reid found his dad packing a sticker-choked suitcase in his room. He was supposed to be mowing the lawn, but his limbs felt heavy and he flung himself on his dad's bed like an overgrown cat. "Where are we going?"

"Not we. Me."

"Where are you going?"

His dad sighed, heavy rings under his eyes. "Away."

"For how long?"

"Grams is coming to stay with you."

"Why are you going?"

"I need a break, kid. Okay? You'll have Grams."

"You'll come back?" Silence. "Is it because of me?"

The doorbell chimed and it rang hollowly through Reid's thirteen-year-old bones.

"There she is now," Dad said, zipping his suitcase and slinging on a day pack.

Reid panicked and grabbed his elbow. "Is it me?"

Dad stared down at him, jaw flexing. "It's not you, Reid. It's me."

Reid shivered remembering those final words. Words that haunted him from relationship to relationship. Words he found impossible to share with Sullivan. "That was it. That's the whole story. I never saw him again. He never came back. I tried to find him when Grams got sick. Turned out he'd died a year earlier in a forklift accident. I didn't tell Grams—didn't want her to suffer. She always hoped one day he'd come back and make it up to me. Even if I'd already grown up."

"Reid," Sullivan uttered softly.

Emotion flurried in his stomach, spooling up his throat, down his legs. He laughed to ease the building tension. "Anyway. Guess I like feeling safe. And . . . sorry. Right now you make me feel ultra-safe."

Reid reluctantly pulled back and Sullivan crushed him to his chest. "You are safe with me."

The strong, secure hold and the fluttering in his stomach made him dizzy. He wanted more. Knew that wasn't possible.

"I tried," Reid confessed against the hollow of Sullivan's neck. "But even if Mason's interested in me—"

"He is."

"—I'm not interested in him."

"I'm glad to hear it."

"But I do think I need to put myself out there."

Sullivan was quiet for a few beats. "Between now and Christmas? Worst time to find someone."

Reid frowned. "Why?"

"Too much stress. Too much to do. To buy. To organize. People aren't at their best. You're better waiting for the New Year."

"You think?"

Sullivan cleared his throat. "Yeah. By then your hair will have grown out, so you'll stand a chance."

Reid slapped Sullivan upside the head.

They parted, laughing.

"Every time I shut my door on you, it is because I want so damn badly to open wide and let you in."

-James to David
Second Time Around

Chapter Twelve

Weeks passed. Three, four, Christmas.

New Year.

Joanna bought a gold dress for her dance. Reid busied himself in additional work bookkeeping for Alanis and the marina.

Sullivan attended a four-day environmental convention.

A convention that had ended this morning. Sullivan should be home soon.

Reid handed Joanna warmed elderflower cordial—not a drop of alcohol—and jumped back onto the couch, quickly wrapping the fleece blanket around him. On top of his jeans and three pullovers, he'd also stolen Sullivan's scarf.

Joanna, huddled in the corner wearing her fish slippers, breathed into her mug. Tendrils of steam veiled her freckles. Her hair had grown, leaving her roots bright red in a sea of gray. She slurped a sip, set it into the cupboard, and resumed scrolling her phone. "My go, my go."

"It's your game," Reid said into his own mug. "You can have all the goes."

"My questions are better anyway." She cleared her

throat. "When this sign is hurt, recovering is a long process. They can't just snap out of it. Sometimes they grow more distant."

"Aquarius."

"Spot on."

"You're trying to say something else."

"Yeah, good things take time. You've made so much progress with Dad. Don't give up."

As if Reid would do such a thing. "Another one."

"Once this sign gets attached, they're gonners!"

"Aquarius. Again. Are you capable of playing this game without the heavy-handed subtext?"

"I can try. This sign can be crying one minute and ready to whip some ass the next, while still totally loving you."

Reid slanted her a look—she knew what it meant. "No grilled cheese for you."

Joanna giggled. "This sign seems serious but is actually a riot."

Reid huffed. "I *was* serious. It's too cold to think about cooking anyway."

"You haven't thought about cooking all week."

This was true. "I miss your dad."

"Me too. He said he'd be back by six. Any minute now. Okay, another one."

"Cancer," Reid answered.

"I haven't said anything yet."

"Well, I have a fifty-fifty chance the way you play."

"You're not wrong," she admitted. "But let me ask anyway."

"Eh, may as well. Not like there's anything better to do on a frozen yacht."

Joanna glanced at her phone screen. "You never know this sign until you've walked in their footsteps—or checked their browser history."

Reid spluttered on his tea. "Oh my God. I need your dad's laptop. Now."

Joanna scoffed. "Please. You don't think I'm on top of that?"

Reid made a mental note to encourage Sullivan to delete any history unsuitable for young, impressionable masterminds. Like whatever that kink was he was into.

Damn, Reid deserved a medal for resisting Sam Baton's books. Not that it had been difficult. Every time he itched to find out more, he heard the plea in Sullivan's voice.

Reid eyed Joanna. "Discover anything I'd want to know?"

Her lips twitched. "Only that . . ."

"What?"

"He Google searched you your first week here."

"Checked my name against criminal databases, or . . .?"

"Or on Facebook, Twitter, and Snapchat."

"He knows what Snapchat is?"

"Also, he looked at, like, thirty-three different nausea bracelets before he settled on yours. Like it had to be perfect."

Reid thumbed the faux leather that had softened. "That's . . . that's something."

"That's something all right. I also learned," Joanna continued, "that our not-so-subtle attempts to lure dad to his reunion might be working. Let's keep going."

Reid shot her an inquisitive look. "Really? Think we can convince him in half a week?"

"He searched for flights to London and the cost of CO2 compensation for the trip."

He did? Did that mean Sullivan was warming to the idea of attending? "That's fantastic."

"But he didn't buy any tickets. Yet."

"*Yet*, being the operative word." He winked at her. "I have one! Don't be fooled by this sign's sweetness. They know exactly how to score what they want."

Joanna blushed. "This sign is totally in love with—"

A cold breeze swept into the saloon along with the *clomp* of Sullivan's step. Reid's skin pulled into goosebumps. He jolted to his feet, blanket pooling to the cushions, heartbeat thumping. "Sullivan."

"—his jokes. But that works too. Dad!"

Sullivan dropped his bags, gaze rushing to Reid.

Joanna ploughed into her dad. He laughed and hugged her back. "Four days and you've grown."

"It's old age, Dad. You're shrinking."

He fondly tugged her ponytail. "I've missed you." He squeezed her, gaze flickering again to Reid. "Really missed you."

Gay butterflies danced in Reid's gut and he gave them a stern, silent word to settle.

Tonight, he'd put this all-consuming energy elsewhere. He'd spent the better part of the week scouting dating sites, but hadn't reached out to anyone. He would though. He needed to. The last six weeks had proven to be romantic torture. He could only handle so many smiles before he started sucking them off Sullivan's lips.

Joanna disentangled from Sullivan and tucked herself back into the fleece blankets.

Sullivan eyed Reid's approach.

"So," Reid said, jamming hands into his pockets. Totally cool, that was him. "How much is a flight to London these days?"

Maybe he and Joanna should work on subtlety. A dos and don'ts board they could frame in glitter and bolt to their doors.

Sullivan hung his coat. The sideways look he gave Reid had his pulse tripping.

"Stalking me now, Reid?"

Joanna gave a strangled gulp from the couch, and Sullivan's gaze sliced to her.

Reid threw himself on the stake. No one could say he wasn't a good manny. "If by stalking you mean doing anything to learn about you, then yes. I'm your number one stalker."

Sullivan spent an awfully long time readjusting his coat on the hook. He shut the paneled door. "I'm considering attending the reunion."

Sullivan smelled like hotel shampoo, extra fruity. "What changed your mind?"

Sullivan mirrored him, leaning against the cupboard door. His face was less than a foot away, but it was still too far. A blue gaze anchored him, and Sullivan pinched the ends of Reid's hair, mussing it between his fingertips. "Purple is almost grown out. I'm almost sorry about it."

"You're not answering the question." *But, oh, keep touching the hair.*

Sullivan dropped his hand. "Can I have a moment to put my bags away and shower?"

"You smell good to me."

Jesus, Reid had to put himself out there.

Sullivan must have registered Reid's horror because he chuckled. "I missed you too."

Reid rolled his shoulders until his back was against the wall and Sullivan dragged his bags past.

When he'd disappeared, Reid sank his head against the wall like a love-wrecked teenager, then remembered he wasn't alone.

Joanna stared at him, ponderingly.

He pushed off the wall and slouched beside her. "Excited for your winter dance tomorrow?"

"You're just as bad as dad, with the changing of subjects."

"Ready for your first kiss?"

Joanna rolled her eyes. "You know, speaking of kissing. I'm okay with it. Happening in front of me, I mean."

"Um, what?" Had she been snooping through his laptop? Did she know he was thinking of dating?

"Just putting it out there," she said. "If you're in love, you shouldn't have to care who you kiss in front of. You and dad definitely don't have to care in front of me."

"Whoa, cool it. We haven't even been on dates yet."

"Something I hope you'll be changing. Soon."

"Well I'm ready, but your dad isn't."

"Just drag dad along with you. He'll love it."

Like double dating? Without divulging too much of Sullivan's woes, he murmured, "It's a life-or-death decision for him."

"Exactly. He needs a life."

An eerie prickle broke out at his nape, and he rolled his shoulders. Joanna stared at him, waiting for him to comprehend, and Reid did. Sullivan was too focused on the death part of falling in love again, but maybe he needed reminding of the life part.

God, he was so blind.

"You might be right," he admitted.

"Child genius, remember?"

Reid clapped his hands together with newfound purpose. "I have dates to organize."

He didn't organize, though. One step down the stairs, Sullivan banged into him with his toiletries bag and a towel, and Reid pictured stalking Sullivan in the marina showers.

"Ahhhh," Reid yelped.

Sullivan's brow shot up. "You all right?"

"I'm hungry." *For you.*

Sullivan sidled past him. "Give me ten minutes to shower and I'll meet you and Joanna at the marina restaurant?"

All thoughts of dates and nagging Sullivan about his reunion fled his mind as they ate dinner and played board games in the recreation room. Time raced and bedtime approached. They couldn't stay up too late on a Thursday night.

Reid rubbed his pocket as they stepped onto the dock and hissed at its emptiness. He stopped near the gangplank to the *Aquarian*. Sullivan and Joanna halted before him, framed by water, glittering with the lamplights from the dock, the yacht bobbing to their side.

"Where's my whistle?"

Snickering, Joanna eyed the boat. "Three steps before the gangplank." Sullivan dug out his wallet. "Give me my money."

He passed her a dollar bill.

Reid folded his arms. "You're horrible people."

"Yes," Joanna agreed. "But we are horrible people who *know* you."

Sullivan set his lips in a determined line and stared back at Joanna. "Next time, I'll win."

Reid threw his hands up, acting exasperated. "Next time?" Sullivan nodded factually, and Reid whacked him against the arm. "Whistle, now."

Sullivan drew it from his pocket by the lanyard. Reid swiped for it and Sullivan pulled it out of reach, cheek twitching with the effort not to laugh. "Want this?"

"Yes. How'd you even get it?"

"It was sticking out of your pants pocket." Sullivan pressed the whistle against his lips, teasingly.

He tried to ignore the electric thrills zapping through him.

But maybe he didn't try that hard.

Dates, dates, dates. He'd organize them as soon as he stepped aboard.

First, though . . .

He lunged for Sullivan. Not for the whistle at his lips, but for the one Reid knew he carried in his pocket. He dove a hand into Sullivan's pocket and groped for the plastic.

His fingers brushed something plump against the inner lining. He hurriedly pinched the whistle and removed his hand. Fuck, he'd fondled the captain's cock.

God.

Pretend that didn't happen.

Fuck, Joanna was watching them.

Reid flushed so hard, tossing him into the ocean might make it boil. He lifted Sullivan's whistle. "Swap whistles?"

Sullivan made a noise in his throat, calmly pressed Reid's whistle to the palm of his hand, and whisked himself on board the Aquarian.

Joanna slunk next to him and shoulder bumped him.

It was possible she didn't understand the whole transaction. Hopefully.

God, Reid had touched Sullivan's cock.

And it had been semi-hard.

Joanna's voice tore him from the thought. "This is what I mean. It's totally okay to kiss in front of me."

He felt sucker-punched.

Information slammed into him painfully. He jerked his head to her. *What?*

Did she say . . .

What?

She fanned a hand in front of his face. "You okay, Reid?"

It took him a long moment to find his voice, and when he did it came out croaky. "Why would you think it's okay for me to kiss your dad?"

"In front of me," Joanna amended. "Because you're almost dating and—"

"Not in front of you. *At all.*"

She frowned and ducked her lips under her scarf, muffling her words. "You mean, you're not into dad?"

He blinked at her. "Yes, I totally am. But he is not into me. He's straight."

"Straight?" Her eyebrows hit her hairline. "Dad was married to my father for, like, seven years."

Reid stumbled back, struggling to swallow any of the salty air whipping over him. "Riley's your father?"

Joanna hugged her chest. "Yeah. I mean." Her eyes glistened. "Shit. Am I a bad daughter that I never talk to you about him?"

Fuck. Too many emotions—and that was coming from him. King of the Cancer zodiac.

He pushed back his bubbling confusion and rested a supportive hand on her shoulder, making her look at him. "Hey, even child geniuses don't have to talk about everything."

She bubbled out a laugh. "I called him daddy, and he and dad loved each other."

Reid squeezed her shoulder as tight as his throat. "I know. That much, I know."

She let out a foggy breath. "Guess dad hasn't told you much, either."

"Missed a few crucial details, yeah."

"Should I beat him up until he tells you how very not straight he is?"

Reid laughed, but it felt tender. "No. Um, Joanna?"

"Yep?"

"Could you not tell him about this conversation?"

"This is starting to sound devious. Count me in."

"Not devious. I just don't want to spook him back into his anti-social shell."

Reid steered them up the gangplank, off balance. Shaking.

It had zero to do with waking water and everything to do with waking realization.

~

Reid could full-on tackle Sullivan for this. Maybe he should storm into the saloon, wag a finger and say *I know your secret, you blunt, infuriating Aquarian.*

Reid paced the length of the dock, scowling.

Or he could beckon Sullivan to his nanny nook and start undressing, not stopping until Sullivan showed hard evidence he liked what he saw. Then Reid could wag his finger and say *You can lie about being straight, but it won't change the fact you ship the full mast.*

The pun might undermine his bubbling anger.

Also, the hard-on he'd absolutely grow in the process.

He didn't think it was possible to be so aroused and so pissed at the same time. Trust Sullivan to yank out the conflicting emotions. He was very good at that. Had been from day one.

Jaw clenched, Reid downloaded the Grindr app and searched for Sullivan.

A curl of panic unwound in him until he saw Sullivan's profile.

Intense warm eyes stared at him from the screen, hair slightly longer than his usual crew cut, and two-day stubble.

38 years old

6'4, 180lbs

Inventor, skipper, environmentalist

It was true then. No doubts. Sullivan liked men.

Reid punched his stupidly handsome face with the pad of his finger. "Why'd you lie, you maddening dick?"

Punching wasn't enough. He screenshotted Sullivan's face and brought out the paintbrush and added a fitting pair of horns on his head. *The devil will pay.*

Maybe Joanna was right. Maybe he was devious after all.

His finger stilled on the part that read: ***No dates. No relationship. No repeats.***

Some of Reid's anger evaporated. Those words sounded so final. So stubborn and tragic.

It begged the question: Why did Sullivan lie to Reid?

A tired sigh leaked out of him and he sagged against a post knotted with rope that moored the *Aquarian*. He felt the whistles in his pocket, as tangled as his thoughts.

The spark of joy in Sullivan's eye as he'd held his whistle hadn't been a lie. None of the moments they'd shared felt fake.

But this "straight" lie cast every memory in a different light.

He slammed his eyes shut on a storm of feelings.

He needed advice. He needed Loretta.

"Reid?" Loretta answered croakily. "Do you know what time it is here?"

"No?"

"Neither do I. But late." Loretta yawned and Natalie murmured a strangled hello from the background. "What's up?"

"Everything?" The question stuck in his throat. "How are, um, your travels?"

Loretta hummed suspiciously but went along with the question. "Good. Good. Great. Well, a few unexpected detours."

Reid stared at the name of the ship, shiny in the moonlight. "Detours?"

"Bought the wrong train tickets in Germany and ended up in Thüringen with no accommodation. I left my baggage on the train." Loretta sighed. "I thought Natalie had it."

"I don't have three arms," Natalie said in the distance.

"We got stranded in Rohr, and ended up at a medieval festival, where I discovered the love-of-my-life has a phobia. It's not possible to tell you any more without crying. In laughter."

Natalie grumbled. "Don't forget the time we couldn't find a toilet . . ."

Loretta choked. "The knight in the tin helmet wasn't that funny. Why are you calling, Reid?"

Reid poured his heart out in one blubbering frenzy, barely stopping to catch his breath. "What do you think? Should I be pissed or understanding of the sad bastard?"

The little hitch in his heart gave Reid his answer. He'd called Loretta not for her advice, but to unleash his internal storm before facing Sullivan. "Fuck, that needed out. Thanks."

Loretta hummed down the line. "I wondered if the Unresolved Sullivan Tension is still strong. That answers it."

Reid huffed a laugh.

"Every relationship has ups and downs. Natalie and I have been through some challenging moments. Among them a sword-stealing panic attack in Rohr and an unfortunate *must* with an adult diaper."

"What's your point?"

"There'll be things done that you can't take back. But if you care enough, you'll work through them."

"Sound advice."

Loretta paused. "Thank you. Now, kindly fuck off and let me sleep."

"Hate you, too."

Smiling, Reid pocketed the phone and dragged in a lungful of sea-air.

He cared. He cared a lot. He cared so goddamn much he'd work through this with Sullivan.

The question was how?

Should he confront Sullivan or let the lie play out?

REID HAUNTED THE MARINA GROUNDS FOR OVER AN HOUR before he warmed himself up with a cocoa at the marina restaurant.

He sat on a firm couch and clumsily punched at his phone screen. *Sam Baton.*

Reid had wondered for months why Sullivan loved his books. Why he didn't want Reid to know about them.

Now it made sense. Sullivan didn't want Reid to learn his lie. Didn't want him to know he was gay.

Because . . .

Reid banished that breath-robbing thought, and shakily scrolled through a list of Sam Baton's books on Amazon.

He read the blurbs for every book. A few ultra-mild D/s and bondage warnings, but nothing super kinky.

Just very, very gay.

Reid bought all his books and started reading the one Sullivan had said wasn't on audio, *Second Time Around.*

He oscillated between completely absorbed to rubbing his Kindle-lit phone against his forehead, groaning. Still in shock. Still unable to absorb the magnitude of what this might mean.

At twenty-five percent in, Reid shut the Kindle app on his phone and made his way back to the *Aquarian.* He wasn't sure what he'd say, but he had to see Sullivan.

Reid fiddled with his bracelet so hard the prong of the buckle snapped. Fuck.

He weaseled the broken prong out. Thankfully the band still held, threaded through the frame.

Reid quietly shut the door behind him and slipped off his shoes. It was difficult to keep the butterflies at bay. Difficult to take off his coat without looking at Sullivan.

He held his breath and turned toward the saloon.

Sullivan sat at the head of the dining table.

His head was bowed toward the bright screen of his laptop. He pressed his lips together, nodded at some internal query, and closed the lid over the keys. The fan heater buzzed a few feet away.

Sullivan closed his eyes and leaned back. The sigh that

rumbled out of him deflated his chest, and he scrubbed his left hand over his face.

His stubble had grown long since he left for his conference. Reid imagined it was his hand brushing over the dark hairs speckled with silver. What would it feel like against his palm? His smoother jaw? His inner thighs . . .

Reid shifted, afraid the unbidden thoughts lurking near the surface would overwhelm him. He was hard enough as it was, despite his lingering frustration.

Reid felt like yelling and sighing and pulling the widowed man into a hug.

Sullivan opened his eyes and caught Reid watching. If he was surprised, he didn't show it.

Maybe he wasn't.

Maybe he'd felt Reid's presence the moment he arrived.

Maybe he liked Reid silently watching him.

Sullivan's voice came out raspy, rough. "What are you still doing out? Your alarm goes off in five hours."

Reid lounged against the wall. "My alarm, meaning you banging on my door inviting me to watch the sunrise?"

"One day you'll wake up."

Just as *one day* Sullivan might tell him the truth?

Reid chewed on his lip. "One day. Very non-committal isn't it?" He crossed the saloon.

Sullivan lifted a brow, gaze ransacking Reid, pulling his skin taut.

God, there was nothing British about it. There never had been. Unless British was a synonym for unicorn-level gay.

"Would you like to commit?" Sullivan asked, landing at Reid's eyes.

Reid spoke through a shiver. "Yes. Yes I would." He stopped a foot from Sullivan, calves warm from the heater. He couldn't hold the gaze, it cost him too much to maintain control. He glanced at the laptop. "What were you doing?"

"Wrapping up last-minute business, until my battery died. Can I use your phone?"

Reid handed it over blindly.

Sullivan scrolled and something dinged in the background. Two fingers hooked into his belt loops and pulled at Reid, stealing his attention.

Sullivan was frowning. "You okay?"

Reid's voice hopped along with his nerves. "Why? If I wasn't, would you take care of me?"

"You're bloody right I would. What's the matter?"

Why did you lie about being straight?

It was on the tip of his tongue, but he swallowed it. Reid feared he understood why he'd lied, and he couldn't take it tonight. Not while he was wading through a maelstrom of feelings about Sullivan being gay.

He shoulders sagged and he rocked away from Sullivan. "Nothing. Just tired."

"We'll do sunrise another time, then," Sullivan said.

Reid wrecked his hair with his fingers as he slunk back toward the partition. "No. Morning is good."

"Sure?"

Yeah. Yeah, he was. "Knock on my door."

Reid second-guessed his commitment when Sullivan tapped on his door five hours later. He'd much rather put off dragging himself out into the icy morning for another day.

But it was far too easy to put things off for better conditions, wasn't it?

Reid rolled out of bed and shoved some clothes on.

Sullivan didn't speak much, and Reid didn't know how to start either. They settled quietly on a park bench at the marina, sharing a thermos of steaming coffee.

Dawn approached from inland, stretching thin fingers around the buildings behind them toward the *Aquarian* and the calm harbor she slept on.

Sullivan stared toward the horizon, less at peace than Reid expected. He eyed it like the end of his story lay out there somewhere, beyond his reach.

Reid's stomach cinched. He was familiar with the look. He'd spent every relationship in the pursuit of his own happily-ever-after.

Waiting for someone to say, "You're the family I want. I choose you."

He wanted to be hopeful, even if he'd started to suspect his story was a tragedy with a flawed protagonist.

Reid studied Sullivan's profile. His voice rumbled out of him, rough from the early morning. "Which sign is intellectual, independent, humanistic, witty, generous, handsome—but also distant, contradictory, difficult, and doesn't trust me?"

Sullivan's head whipped to him. "Have I missed something?"

Reid pressed his lips.

"I trust you," Sullivan said. "You had sole responsibility for my daughter for a week."

Reid looked away. "You really, deeply trust me?"

"Yes."

"Okay." Reid passed Sullivan the thermos and pushed to his feet. "I'm setting us up for dates while Joanna's at her dance tonight."

"Dates." Said bluntly. Said like Sullivan was allergic to the word. "I told you—"

"It's about *living*, Sullivan."

Sullivan twisted the cap on the thermos, tight. Reid waited for Sullivan to sort through his bottled feelings. "I . . . I'm not sure whoever you'll set me up with will work."

"Why is that?" Reid asked and waited, expectantly.

"I haven't told you what I like in a partner."

Reid lifted a challenging brow. "Tell me now."

A flash of guilt shadowed Sullivan's expression.

Reid felt the urge to offer him a reprieve. "What should she be like?"

Sullivan studied him for a few long beats. "Funny. Nice. Good to the core. Full of adventure." He glanced to Reid's hair. "Misadventure."

Reid's heart jackhammered.

There was the truth. Right there for Reid to see. So blatant, so beautiful, so achingly tragic.

Sullivan had never been homophobic. He had pretended to be straight because he thought it shielded him. From falling in love.

With Reid.

Reid shut his eyes as a storm of emotion ripped into him and lifted him so damn high he was flying; he was in the middle of the constellation Aquarius.

"Anything else I need to know?" Reid croaked.

"Yes."

"What?"

Sullivan didn't say it.

Reid started to fall.

He opened his eyes to find Sullivan's on him, caressing his every feature, weighted with inner conflict. A pocket of wind caught under Reid.

Sullivan might be afraid, but Reid saw the fight in there too. Sullivan wanted to tell him. Badly. Reid held onto that like he did his safety whistle.

Maybe he would wind up in a sea of his own tears, but not without trying every possible strategy to help Sullivan overcome his fears.

He met Sullivan's pained blue gaze. "Date's tomorrow."

"Who are you taking?"

"Someone I discovered online."

"Who is she?"

Reid backed toward Dock J. "*He* is a guy, and a fucking beautiful one too."

Sullivan's posture stiffened. "He? You found him on Grindr?"

"Yep."

"Be careful, Reid. I don't want you getting hurt."

"There's always a risk when you put yourself out there."

"Some risks are not worth taking."

"Some are, Sullivan."

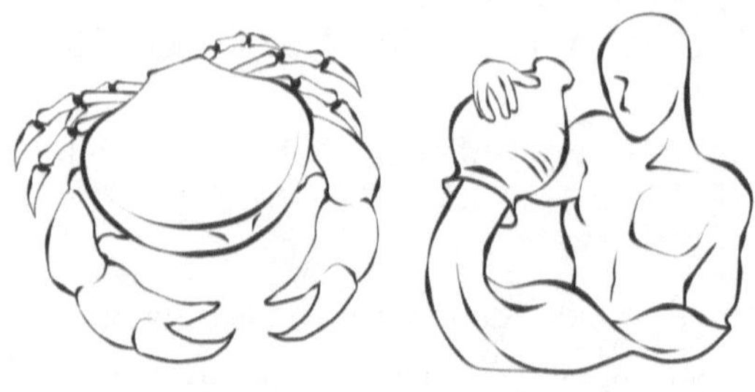

"Great love is an adventure. It means breaching comfort zones. It might even mean falling in love again."

-David to James
Second Time Around

Chapter Thirteen

By breakfast, Reid was so wired that he pulled on jogging gear and went for a run. He ran until his lungs ached and his stomach burned. He ran until his legs turned to jelly. So a good ten minutes.

After a shower, Reid walked his visceral storm to the main office. The door dinged, and Alanis glanced up from her desk, cupping her coffee mug.

"It's the great organizer." She took in his face, and paused. "Who is looking very green today."

"Didn't sleep much," Reid mumbled. "Sunrise was worth it though. Gimmie your seat."

She looked at the padded gray one next to her. "What's wrong with yours?"

"It doesn't swivel. I need to swivel."

Alanis vacated her spot, laughing. "Dare me to interfere with a swivel emergency."

Reid sank into the seat and stared at the ceiling mural of a ship negotiating rough seas.

He imagined being on that ship. Thirty-foot waves lifted and dropped him.

Lift and drop. Lift and drop. Reid was powerless against it. Could only trust in Sullivan at the helm, steering them through the storm.

Alanis's head peered over him and he gripped the plastic arms with a startled "gah."

"Oh, you need to tell me what you're thinking about."

Reid sighed. "Sullivan."

"I guessed that much. What about him?"

"He's not into you. Sorry."

Alanis sprayed a mouthful of coffee over her polo shirt. She dabbed at it with a tissue, eyeing him disbelievingly. "Do I look vaguely mannish?"

What? "No."

"Then why would that even be a possibility?"

Reid straightened, ticking points off his fingers. "We talked about how hot Sullivan is. How he makes our hearts go boom. How he'd make a great partner."

"Yes," Alanis said, vigorously nodding. "For *you*."

"You know he's gay?" Was Reid the only clueless fool who hadn't?

"He mentioned his late husband, Joanna's father, when he signed his year lease."

Reid scowled out the windows toward Dock J and the *Aquarian*. "He pretended—correction, is still pretending—he's straight."

Alanis perched her ass on the desk in front of him. "I see ideas forming in your eye. Damn, I love managing this marina."

Reid drummed his fingers over the chair arms. "Alanis. What plans do you have tonight?"

A bright blush darkened her tan cheeks and Alanis pulled out her hair tie and regathered her hair.

"Alanis?"

"Okay, fine." She dropped her hair. "I have a date with

Troy. Guy I meet at the marina shop over Christmas."

Reid blinked at her, then shook his head as he smirked. "For someone who loves to gossip, you sure kept him quiet."

She lifted her leg, planted it on the swivel chair, and pushed him away. "It's weird, okay. I like him. He's nerdy. But full of life, and he's spontaneous."

"How spontaneous?" Reid asked, swiveling.

At her arching brow, he tossed out an idea.

Alanis stared at him for a few long beats, and dug out her phone. "That spontaneous."

REID CHASED AFTER JOANNA TO FINISH PINNING IN HER HAIR. He hoped he'd done a good job of the French twist and it held for the evening. It'd help if she'd stand still long enough for him to stick this last pin in.

They weren't running *that* late.

Her puffy gold dress took up most of the saloon.

Sullivan highlighted a legal pad. He set it aside and admired his daughter. "You look . . ."

"Beautiful?" she supplied.

"Like I want to lock you up in your room and throw away the key."

Reid snuck up behind her and plucked the curly loose lock he wanted to pin.

Joanna laughed at her dad and twisted to Reid, grabbing his arms and thwarting him mid-pin. She shook him. "It's time. It's time."

"Almost. I'm thinking you'd prefer me to walk you to Elijah and Mason, to be sure you make it?" He grinned at the scowl Reid knew Sullivan was giving him. "Now stand still."

Joanna twisted and paced the space between him and her dad. "I can't kiss him!"

Sullivan was quick to answer. "You don't have to do anything you don't want to do."

"No, I *want* to. I just can't." She looked desperately at Reid for help.

He eyed her and that curl. "Nervous, eh?"

"What if I giggle? I take pride in being serious, but if I let out a high-pitched noise against his lips, he'll know I'm like any other girl in our class."

Reid halted her pacing, two hands and a pin on her shoulders. He met her gaze. "You're almost fourteen. Giggling is allowed. In fact, giggling is a requirement. If you don't giggle once, I'll fail you."

"You're grading me on my first kiss?"

"Sure." Reid pinched the curl with his left hand and tried to clip over it, but facing Joanna, it was impossible. "You love being graded."

Her tension dissipated. "This is true. Okay," she said, determined, "you can grade me."

"Good," Reid said, twisting her around and slipping that curl into place. "Remember to giggle."

"I hate you."

Joanna slipped into strappy, flat shoes that glittered, and Reid stuffed himself into a jacket.

"Don't forget this." He held open a wool coat for her. "Now, show your innocent face to your dad one last time and we'll go."

Sullivan spared Reid a reproachful look, but it melted as he kissed Joanna's cheek. "Have a fantastic time tonight, love."

"I will, Dad. What about you?"

Reid jumped and answered for him, belly jerking with anticipation. "Your dad and I will have fun too."

~

Too much fun, maybe.

Reid raised his hand and cued Alanis and Troy heading toward their table.

Alanis looked amazing in a red strapless dress that clung to her curvy waist and matching red heels. A far cry from the practical, durable clothing she wore day to day at the marina.

Troy, Alanis's date, was a small, thin man with a magician's confidence and floridly curved mouth.

He thanked his stars they'd agreed to this.

Sullivan, dressed in hot-as-fuck, ass-hugging jeans and a crisp button-up shirt, followed Reid's gaze toward their dates and muttered a satisfying "bloody hell."

Reid stifled a laugh. He wasn't sure how to play his hand during this double date—he wanted Sullivan to admit he'd lied.

No sooner had Alanis and Troy sat down, Sullivan jolted to his feet.

"Reid, we need drinks." He turned swiftly toward the bar.

Reid winked at his wine-sipping accomplices and followed Sullivan. Could getting Sullivan to admit the truth have worked that quickly?

Reid tripped on someone's extended foot.

Sullivan caught him by the elbow before Reid face-planted to the sticky floor. Reid felt every ounce of frustration in Sullivan's fingers as Sullivan steered him to the bar, and he liked it.

Reid propped himself on a stool and ordered drinks from the bartender.

Their knees bumped as Sullivan assumed a neighboring stool, and Reid noted that Sullivan left his there, a light pressure on his outer thigh.

Reid looked at him. "You look like you want to say something."

"I want to say a lot of things."

"So say them."

He glanced back at their table. "Alanis. I thought I told you I'm not . . ."

"Not what?"

Sullivan scrubbed his jaw. "Interested in her."

"Sometimes we say things we don't mean." Reid cocked his head. "I thought bringing her on this date might help you admit your true feelings."

The bartender served up two drinks, a merlot and sparkling water. Reid paid and passed the merlot to Sullivan.

Sullivan eyed the water questioningly.

Reid sipped, the fizz rushing up his nose. "I want to stay clear-headed. I intend to commit my first date with a man to memory. Every second of it."

Sullivan glanced at Troy, jaw locking. "I'll need more than wine to forget it."

Reid shrugged. "You probably don't want to drink that much. We need to be there for Joanna when she returns from her first kiss."

Sullivan jumped. "We should head back to the marina already."

Reid snickered. "We have until nine thirty. Our date's just begun."

He slipped off his stool and Sullivan's knees parted to give him room. Now the light pressure kissed either side of his thighs. He flattened his shirt, drawing Sullivan's eye, and then raked a hand through his hair. "Do I look good?"

"He doesn't deserve you."

"He's an amazing guy. Maybe one day he'll realize he does."

Sullivan flashed another seething glance at Troy. "This is your *first date*."

"We've chatted a lot, he sure knows how to make me laugh."

"So watch comedy shows."

"Encourages me to learn new things."

"So read a book."

"He's not good at showing his emotions. Although . . . I have a feeling I've been bad at reading them."

"You and your damn feelings," Sullivan muttered grumpily.

Reid enjoyed every jealous stroke. He urged Sullivan up by the arm, wine glass in hand. "Come, let's order aphrodisiacs and start flirting."

Sullivan stood and Reid fizzled with a million tiny shivers. He hid a tremble in a long sip of water before gazing up into Sullivan's brooding face. Reid hoped his voice didn't break. "You look damn great, by the way."

"I hope Alanis doesn't think so."

"What about her doesn't work for you? She has a vibrant charismatic personality and loves adventure."

Sullivan plucked Reid's nausea bracelet. "The problem is, she's . . . she's—"

"Sorry to butt in," Troy said. "I spilled my wine. Would you mind passing me a bunch of napkins?"

Reid gritted his teeth on a cry. He had suggested Troy interrupt them to keep the tension high, but now he wished he hadn't. Sullivan had been so close to spitting it out.

Reid stuffed napkins into Troy's hand. "Here. I'll be right with you."

Troy grinned, cheek dimpling. "Order the oysters?"

Sullivan glowered after him as Troy returned to their table. "*That* guy?"

Troy flirted shamelessly with Reid and Reid feared the daggers Sullivan threw would maim him. Alanis did a good job smooching up to Sullivan, too, and Reid swallowed nervous laughter.

Sullivan looked close to cracking.

"You're nice," Troy said with a daring pat to Reid's wrist.

Sullivan's eyes were pools of jealousy and frustration. He narrowed them on Troy. "He's a lot more than nice."

Troy braved on. "Tell me more about yourself, Reid."

Sullivan clutched his wineglass so hard, Reid thought it would break. Reid wanted Sullivan to cut the bullshit and take Reid's hand between the candles where no one would miss it.

He inched his fingers across the table toward the salt. Toward Sullivan.

"What do you want to know?"

Sullivan cut over him, addressing Troy. "I want to know how tall you are."

Reid's brow shot up, glad he was angled so Sullivan didn't see it.

Troy flashed a set of white teeth. "Five eight."

Sullivan harrumphed, looked at Reid, and mumbled something like, "You'd have to stoop."

Troy asked Reid if he'd ever travelled north of Brainerd in Minnesota. "Most romantic cabins around the lakes, there."

Sullivan pushed back his chair and rose. "Excuse me." He nodded stiffly at Troy and a little more kindly to Alanis. "I'm suddenly feeling unwell."

He grabbed his coat from the chair, dropped far too much money on the table for his drinks, and left with barely a goodbye glance to Reid.

Reid slumped in his chair. He'd hoped . . . what? That Sullivan would make an urgent announcement that he's gay and publicly claim him?

Alanis swirled her drink, sharing a smirk with Troy. Reid gulped Sullivan's leftover wine, hoping the alcohol would mellow the frustration.

He kept eyeing the door, wanting to chase. Not sure what to expect if he did.

Alanis murmured something to Troy. Troy laughed low, their gazes locking, and the intimacy . . .

Reid lurched to his feet.

Alanis's gaze swiveled to him.

"Thanks for loaning me your Troy." Reid acknowledged Troy with a nod as he shrugged into his parka. "I've gotta . . . Enjoy your date."

"Enjoy yours."

Reid settled his bill and pushed out into the crisp night. He walked fast, foggy breaths puffing out at irregular intervals. He'd been silently amused all evening watching Sullivan fail to school his jealousy, but now he feared he'd indulged himself too long. Maybe playing Sullivan like this had been the wrong move. Maybe Reid had taken the cowardly path because he didn't know how to confess he knew.

Reid entered the marina. The restaurant glittered with fairy lights at the water's edge. He followed the brightly lit path to Dock J and the darkened *Aquarian*.

Movement to his left halted him.

On the park bench, where they'd watched the sunrise, sat a hunkered demigod, elbows on his knees, fingers speared into his hair.

Sullivan.

Reid jammed his cold hands into his pockets and slowly crossed to him.

Water sloshed gently against the wooden supporting beams and the bottom of the boat. Reid focused on the scent of waterlogged wood rather than the skin-tightening fact he and Sullivan were alone.

Reid blinked under lamplight and shivered at how exposed he felt.

Sullivan had to see him now.

Reid swallowed and turned.

Sullivan had lifted his head, elbows still on his knees, but his hands clasped in the space between his legs. He was startled to see Reid. Maybe relieved.

That relief pulled at him.

"You're back already?" Sullivan asked, shifting over to make space on the bench.

Reid didn't sit. Lamplight stretched to the bench, enough to give a slight glow to Sullivan's face. His eyes kept scrolling Reid's for a clue what he was thinking.

"Not the date you hoped it would be?" Sullivan asked.

"I don't know. I expected a different ending." Reid shrugged. "Maybe I was too hopeful."

"Hopeful?" Sullivan deflated. "You really like him?"

"Yep."

Sullivan scowled.

Reid chuckled and craned his head to take in the starry sky. Cassiopeia, Pegasus, Aquarius. He breathed in their magic, like it might help him continue.

He looked down at Sullivan, and quoted him. "'You'd have to stoop?'"

Sullivan grimaced. "It's true, and a neck cramp will zap you, but I won't be there to massage you better."

"You realize, demigod that you are, ninety percent of the time, you have to be stooping too."

"Yes, but I can also lift my partner up."

Partner was getting closer. But not close enough.

"You're heightist," Reid said.

"I am not."

"Well, from where I'm standing, it's heightist or homophobic."

"Heightism doesn't exist."

"Sure it does. You're a big guy who looks down on little ones."

"Ridiculous. I just don't think you should be stooping to Troy."

"You don't know anything about him."

"I don't want to. More than that, I don't want *you* to."

A cool breeze fluttered through Reid's hair and over his eyelashes. His breath plumed in the air. His stomach was a hot soup of butterflies and his cheeks were flushed.

"Why did you leave the bar, Sullivan?" he asked quietly.

"Why did you follow?"

Reid stared at him.

Understanding flickered in Sullivan's eye. His mouth curved in surrender, and he cursed under his breath.

Sullivan dropped back against the bench and shut his eyes. "You never believed I was interested in Alanis."

"Not tonight at any rate."

A huffed laugh escaped him. "She was there to help me admit my true feelings." His eyes shot open. "And Troy?"

"What do you think?"

"Encourage me to commit murder?" Sullivan's twitching jaw cleaved the words into a growl.

Reid bit his grinning lip. He leaned forward, bracing a hand on the bench beside Sullivan's shoulder. His other hand jerkily caressed Sullivan's cheek. The scratch of his stubble sent electricity up Reid's arm. "My date might have ended the way I hoped after all."

Their gazes melded.

"That's what you wanted?" Sullivan asked, voice barely above a whisper. "Admitting I'm gay? Admitting I pretended otherwise because I'm terrifyingly attracted to you?"

Reid shut his eyes at the rush of Sullivan's words. His elbow buckled involuntarily and he dropped an inch closer to Sullivan.

Sullivan clasped Reid's wrist at his cheek, and lightly pressed the metal ball of his bracelet.

"Say it again?" Reid said, opening his eyes.

Sullivan's brow furrowed like he was fighting the storm inside, pushing through savage gales to get to Reid. "Terrifyingly." Sullivan squeezed Reid's nape and pulled him close, until their noses bumped. His words tingled over his lips, "Christ, do you know what it does when you look at me like that?"

Sullivan kissed him.

Reid tasted wine and warmth and need. He wanted to travel back in time and re-watch every one of their interactions. Wanted to spot all the signs, because this kiss felt like it had been building for months.

He trembled.

"You okay?" Sullivan asked.

Yes. No. Absolutely. Hell no. Was he setting himself up for the worst fall of his life?

Reid couldn't care. "Can't help but notice, I'm stooping."

Sullivan's lips twitched against Reid's. "I was wrong. It looks fucking great on you."

A hot palm gripped his hip under the hem of his jacket, and Sullivan steered Reid onto his thighs.

Reid sagged onto Sullivan, lips soldered together.

Sullivan darted his tongue along the seam of Reid's mouth, and Reid's synapses fried. He moaned into Sullivan, parting his lips for more.

The slide of tongues, the rasp of stubble against chins, the pressure of splayed fingers at his waist and nape. Reid was all sensation.

Sullivan made a deep noise in his throat and Reid's stomach flurried. Never had a kiss felt like this. Not once had a person reduced him to a whimpering puddle that kept repeating "please, please."

Please what? Reid didn't know.

Please stop the sweet torture?

Please go on forever?

Please don't regret this.

Reid cupped Sullivan's head and poured his wish into their kiss, hot, deep, needy. Emotional.

Sullivan drank it in, steady and solid under him.

Reid needed to breathe but was afraid to.

Sullivan captained the kiss though. Gently, he steered Reid back and pressed their warm foreheads together, Sullivan's slightly warmer than his own.

What did that mean? "Sullivan?"

Sullivan's phone burst to life, vibrating against Reid's thigh, at the head of his restrained hard-on. He let out an undignified moan and slipped off Sullivan's lap.

Sullivan drew out his phone. "Mason," Sullivan answered.

Reid stiffened.

Sullivan hummed. "Okay, we'll get them." He looked at Reid. "Mason's car broke down."

Reid called Alanis for the favor and rummaged for her spare car key in her desk drawer.

Sullivan stood in the main office, right under the mural of the ship, and frowned. "How is it you have a key for the office?"

"Look around," Reid said, making a mental note to organize this drawer next week. "Notice anything different?"

Sullivan took in the space. "It's cleaner."

"Bingo. I couldn't handle the creative keeping of paperwork. Especially receipts and bills. I took charge."

"She should pay you for it."

"She wanted me to check if the marina has the budget for it. It does." Reid found the key and snapped it up. "Ah ha!"

Reid drove them to Joanna's school, hyper-aware of Sullivan.

He pulled up outside the school gates, squeezing into a tight spot between other anxious parents. He kept the engine running to keep the heater blasting. Not that he strictly needed it, but it helped disguise the persistent flush on Reid's neck.

Reid snatched Sullivan's gaze. "What?"

"Do you have enough time to help me as well as Alanis?"

Really, Sullivan? "Absolutely."

He hummed. "As long as you're not overworking yourself."

Reid wanted to rest his hand on Sullivan's knee but couldn't unglue his hands from the wheel. He held Sullivan's eyes. "My time on the *Aquarian* is never work."

Sullivan nodded silently and gazed out the windshield.

Girls in pretty dresses and guys in tuxedos streamed out from the school, searching for their parents.

"Ask me if I'm going to my reunion," Sullivan said.

Reid got whiplash from turning his head so fast. Was Reid's incessant encouragement working? If Sullivan could change his mind about this, what else could he change his mind about?

He gnawed his lip. It still tasted of their kiss. "Are you going to your reunion?"

Sullivan watched him. "On one condition."

His heart thumped. "What's that?"

"You come with me."

Reid didn't hesitate. "Yes."

"Good. I bought our tickets last night."

That's what he'd been doing at the laptop last night? "Bit presumptuous."

It was Sullivan's turn not to hesitate. "No. This was your idea."

Which idea was he talking about? The idea to take a date? Or the idea to take a friend? Reid wanted to ask. "When do we leave? Who'll look after Joanna? How much do I owe you?"

"Three days. Alanis owes me big time after tonight. Nothing."

"Come on, I have to pay something."

"Sure. Pay for lunch on my birthday."

As if Reid wouldn't anyway. But this was clearly a fight for another time. He wanted to soak up the good feelings of being invited. Reid wanted to know what he was dressing as, but he didn't know how to ask, and Joanna and Elijah stole his next breath.

They'd stopped at the sprawling oak tree just behind the school gates. Joanna glittered in her gold gown and the flashes of headlights. Elijah stood like a solid shadow.

On impulse, Reid grabbed Sullivan's hand, excitedly. He squeezed as Joanna leaned, and Sullivan squeezed back. "Her first kiss!"

Sullivan grunted.

Joanna set chaste lips on Elijah's and Elijah seemed to be pressing back. It was so awkward and totally adorable. A+ all the way.

He rubbed his thumb over Sullivan's veined hand. "I bet it felt perfect." Sullivan shifted. Those waves inside lifted him higher and higher. "I bet she can't wait for more."

Sullivan's tremor rippled up Reid's arm, and Sullivan pulled his hand away. "With me as her apprehensive dad, she might need to."

Reid didn't look at him, but he understood. He waved at Joanna, who seemed to be searching for Mason's car. She spotted them, and pulled Elijah toward them.

Reid wrung the steering wheel and glanced at Sullivan. "What was tonight, Sullivan? What's London?"

Blue eyes met his. "Two steps forward."

Reid swallowed an anxious buzz that sounded a lot like *one step back.*

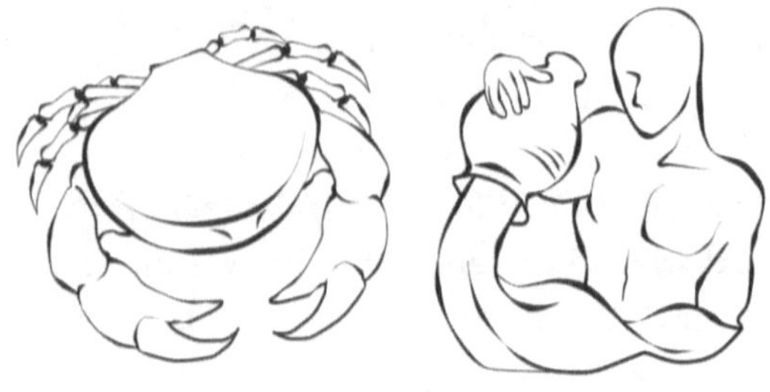

David was a lighthouse in the darkness. He was so bright, I thought I could sail safely again. But . . . what if his light went out?

-James
Second Time Around

Chapter Fourteen

Reid loved flying. Something about the experience was effortless. Even turbulence didn't bother him.

Sullivan, on the other hand, did not love flying. The majority of the long-haul flight to London he gripped the arms of his seat and stared straight ahead. God forbid anyone pass him to shimmy to the bathroom.

Reid shut his Kindle app and leaned toward Sullivan. "For an air sign like Aquarius, you sure are freaked out being in the air."

"For a Cancer, you sure are scared of the sea." Sullivan didn't look at him. Turning his head might affect the balance of the plane. "A pair we make."

A pair indeed. But what kind?

Since their passionate kiss last Friday, they hadn't kissed again. Hell, they'd barely touched.

True, they'd been busy organizing themselves and Joanna for this trip, but there had been chances. They'd stared at each other on the cusp of something thrilling, only for the moment to break.

Now, here they were, alone for the next three days, and Reid wanted to know the deal. What kind of pair were they?

Could they fucking kiss again already?

Reid would ask.

Sullivan groaned at a shudder of turbulence.

Reid would ask later.

They arrived at their hotel suite and awkwardly each claimed a queen bed. Reid had seen the view of the city with the London Eye and known Sullivan booked it thinking of him and the good memories he'd shared with Grams.

He showered and, mostly dressed, stood at the suite windows, absorbing the glittering view of London.

Gram's question simmered to the surface of his mind. *What do you want from your life, Reid?*

He glanced at Sullivan, fiddled with his bracelet, tightening, tightening, tightening.

He couldn't take the head-pounding question anymore. They were due at Sullivan's old school in less than thirty minutes, and Reid had to know before then.

He moved to the full-length mirror and fiddled a tie around his collar.

No matter how hard he tried, he couldn't knot the damn thing like Sullivan's. He eyed Sullivan's reflection. He was standing in the glow of the bedside lamp, staring at the comforter. His suit framed him with slick elegance, and his tie lay perfectly in a double Windsor knot.

Reid gave up on his own and turned around. "Could you tie me up?"

Blue eyes hit Reid with a punch of heat that Reid would definitely ask him about. Soon.

Sullivan's gaze sank to the blue mess at Reid's throat and desire simmered down to amusement. In three long strides, Sullivan crossed over to him.

God, he was tall. And handsome. And the smirk on his lips begged Reid to lick it.

Sullivan tugged his tie, freeing it from Reid's neck with a *whick*. He tossed the tie onto the bed, carefully removed his own, still perfectly knotted, and pulled it over Reid's head. He pushed the knot snug against Reid's throat and his fingers bumped along his skin as he folded the collar.

Reid was glad for the restricting briefs he'd put on, because Sullivan's deft hands were doing things to him.

Sullivan looked into Reid's eyes. "That's a good knot on you."

Reid never wanted to take it off. "I get it."

"Get what?"

"Why you're okay on fifteen-foot swells but frozen with fear in a sturdy plane."

Sullivan plucked Reid's tie off the bed and worked it around his neck. He glanced at Reid. "Finish your thought."

Reid shivered, cock pulsing. "You like to be in control."

Maybe it was why unleashing his inner storm was so difficult. Why Sullivan had overreacted finding Reid under him in his bed . . .

Sullivan picked up Reid's dinner jacket and helped him slip into it. His arms snaked around Reid's front and worked the buttons. Breath trickled down his collar and Reid watched them in the mirror with a shaky smile. He liked this. He liked this so goddamn much.

Sullivan's eyes flickered to his. "Let's move."

Reid agreed entirely.

Angelwood Acadia Grammar School was large and imposing, much like its former student Sullivan Bell.

Reid followed Sullivan up the path toward stately stairs

leading to open doors. Sullivan slowed his step and breathed in frosty air tinged with the scent of dirt.

"Hard to believe it's been twenty years since I was messing around with my mates at school."

Reid halted, and Sullivan turned to him, questioningly. "Wow. My mind went places, Sullivan."

Sullivan barked a laugh. "Not much of *that* sort. Nothing more than swapping hands in dark movie theaters."

Reid resumed walking. "Your concern about dates at movie theatres now makes sense."

It also explained why every time in the past months they had watched something, Sullivan had sat as far from Reid as possible.

Another movie night was in the forecast. And soon.

Sullivan absorbed the façade of the main school building, lips pressing together, as if remembering the last time he was here and who he was with.

The weight of the evening settled heavily on Reid's shoulders.

Sullivan eyed him. "You're suddenly looking how I feel."

"How do you feel?"

"Like I'm in a plane."

Out of control. Reid sucked in his lips and nodded. "I'm also nervous."

"Nervous?" Sullivan asked. Reid ground the heel of his dress shoe against the asphalt path. "Is this about us?"

Reid clasped his nape and forced himself to look up at Sullivan through his lashes. "Is there an us?"

Sullivan shifted. A group of five men swept past them singing something about Angelwood Acadia.

Reid didn't let them distract him from hearing Sullivan's answer. He stepped forward, close to an embrace.

"You want a label," Sullivan said.

Yes. "I want a label that works for you. I want to know what we're telling your mates in there."

"I don't know."

Reid chuckled over his disappointment. "I thought you knew everything?"

"Best friends," Sullivan said.

"Best friends," Reid repeated, testing out the phrase. He loved it because it was true. He hated it because it wasn't true enough.

Two men raced down the stairs and tackled Sullivan. One had long black hair lobbed into a man bun and the other wore a waistcoat and bowtie. "Sully! We've been waiting for you."

Sullivan cuffed their necks with his arms. "Gael. Carlos."

Carlos—Bowtie—slapped Sullivan's shoulder and pulled back. "The clubs and recreation room's been turned into a history classroom. Can you believe it?"

History? Reid perked up.

Sullivan addressed his mates. "That's bad." Reid's posture showed eagerness. "I'm sorry, *very* bad."

The reference from Reid's nanny interview was not lost on him, and Reid enjoyed the spark in Sullivan's eye at the shared private joke.

Gael—Man Bun—giggled. "Total tragedy, mate. I feel for students these days. Actually have to study."

Carlos sent Gael a withering look. "This might be why you work in a shopping center."

"*Manager* of a shopping center." Man Bun scowled and refocused on Sullivan. "So where's R—"

Carlos cut over him. "We're at the same table after a little creative swapping of placeholders." Carlos smiled at Reid. "You must be the friend Sullivan emailed about. You're seated next to my wife. Start talking about arachnoids if she pries too much. Love the woman to pieces, as much as she loves knowing everyone else to pieces."

Gael and Carlos trotted ahead, Carlos whispering intently into Gael's ear, and Sullivan and Reid followed behind.

Reid side-eyed his *best friend*, who must have felt the look, because he sighed. "What, Reid?"

"Sully?"

"*Sullivan.*"

Reid snickered. "Yes, sir."

DOZENS OF ROUND TABLES FILLED AN ELEGANTLY DECORATED gym.

Over dinner, Carlos and Gael fondly engaged in stories of their past. Reid committed each detail to memory, fleshing out the picture he was making of ol' Sully.

Carlos's wife chatted with Gael's girlfriend, who had swapped chairs with Carlos almost immediately, then turned her brightly painted lips on him. She was attractive, tall, and elegant with a prying spark in her eye. "What's Sullivan doing these days?"

Sullivan tensed beside him.

Reid slipped a hand under the table and squeezed Sullivan's thigh. In Reid's world, best friends didn't give a damn about touching one another. Although this was a little higher up than necessary.

He was only human. Sue him. "Oh you know," Reid answered, "Your average superhero stuff. Saving the world one invention at a time."

"Yes," she pressed, "but how's he holding up?"

A hot palm landed on his. Calloused fingers slid between his, and Reid hopped in his seat.

Carlos's wife frowned. "Are you okay?"

Reid quickly recovered. "Tables have been in storage a long time. Probably a spider racing down my leg."

She drew sharply back from the table. "Excuse me. I need the ladies."

Reid didn't know which was making his heart thump more, that sliding pressure between his fingers or Sullivan's words pebbling at his ear. "You're amazing."

"Just your average superhero stuff. Saving Sullivan one spider at a time."

Sullivan let go of his hand and answered some inane question Gael threw at him. "Want a tour of the school?"

"And learn all your filthy boys' school stories?"

Reid was already standing.

Sullivan laughed, pushing in their chairs. "It's history. You love history. It deepens one's connection to a place. And"—Sullivan met his eye—"to a person."

If Sullivan kept quoting him, Reid would have a problem.

Forget that. He already had a problem.

The doors to the gym shut behind them and they had a giant, oak-dominated corridor to themselves.

The school motto ran in gold cursive along one wall: *Your future starts here.*

Reid decided it was an excellent place to make a point.

He caught Sullivan's hand, turning him. Sullivan's brow hitched in query.

Reid tried to steady himself, concentrating on the stone floor beneath his feet, the cool air seeping through his shirt, the giant clock above the drinking fountain ticking soundly. The taste of bread pudding on his tongue.

His voice broke with nerves. "Shove me up against this wall."

"Oh, Christ," Sullivan muttered, gaze turning molten, making Reid's heart pound.

"Please—"

Sullivan pushed him against the cool wall, covered Reid in the warm heat of his body, and slammed their lips together.

Reid sucked in a breath and Sullivan pushed his tongue inside.

God. Finally. He'd dreamed of this all week.

A door squealed and concern flickered through Reid. Would Sullivan rip himself away?

Sullivan cupped Reid's face and pressed against him, like he wanted to drown in Reid.

Reid relaxed, folding into the kiss, lost in the tingles racing from his fingers, to his nipples, to his crotch.

It felt perfect. Tight, safe, like anything could happen and Reid would be okay.

He didn't want to live another week without this.

Reid pushed Sullivan's chest and Sullivan rocked back. "You okay?" Sullivan asked, balling Reid's tie around his fist, a wonderful pressure at his neck.

Reid calmed his breath. Met Sullivan's attentive gaze. "What about 'best friends with benefits'?"

Sullivan tugged Reid and their mouths collided. Their hard dicks, too.

Reid whimpered at the light, torturous friction and Sullivan's smile tasted delighted.

Never stop.

The choir in the gym erupted into song, pulling them apart.

Reid adjusted himself and swept a hand through his hair, but his shirt was a mess, tie definitely wonky, and his cheeks burned fiercely.

Sullivan looked as slick as ever. He had to adjust himself too, though.

Reid watched him blatantly until Sullivan crooked a finger under his chin and steered his face up. "Let me show you my old form room—homeroom."

Sullivan told him stories of his past and Reid listened,

committing every fact to memory. Two sets of stairs and a long hallway, and they arrived at Sullivan's homeroom.

Reid peered through the glass pane of the door and halted Sullivan. "I think some of your classmates think they're in a darkened movie theatre."

Sullivan dragged his gaze off Reid and peered inside. "Good lord." A long, awkwardly aroused beat passed. "Why are you still looking?"

Reid scoffed. "It's been four and a half months . . . why are *you* still looking?"

"It's been four and a half years."

Reid chuckled, and leaned against the wall. "You win. Wait. I thought you'd had sex since then?"

Sullivan mirrored him on the door's other side. "Not publicly. Not with the lights on."

Because he pretended his hookups were Riley?

"—and only blow and hand jobs. Anything else is too . . . intimate."

Oh. Reid rubbed his nape.

Were Sullivan's words a warning about what Reid should expect with him?

Was it so bad if that was all Sullivan could give?

Reid stepped up to Sullivan, right at the glass pane. "You know the analogy of the tortoise and the hare?"

Sullivan smirked. Like he expected this kind of response from Reid. Like he *liked* it. "The hare takes naps and the tortoise wins."

"Not the whole story." He touched Sullivan's chest. "The tortoise eventually crosses the line"—he tapped his own—"and then the hare hops over after him. Because the hare always knew the tortoise had to cross first."

"Not the story I remember," Sullivan mused.

"The point is I can take as many naps as you need."

"I might like this version better." Eyes beheld Reid with an intensity that ravished him from head to toe. "Ironically, all this talk of napping makes me want to go to bed. But not to nap."

The fire in Sullivan's eyes lit up Reid's gut. "At the cost of skipping out of here early?" Reid tutted. "We flew a long way for this."

"I don't care."

"Another hour with your mates, then I'll come down with a horrible case of stomach cramps, and you'll sweep in—the sigh-worthy superhero—and insist on leaving to take care of your best friend."

"An hour?" Sullivan didn't look impressed.

"Yes."

"Okay, but then," Sullivan said, grabbing Reid by the untucked hem of his shirt and pulling him in until their faces hovered an inch apart. Fingers slowly tucked his shirt into the waistband of his suit pants, and Reid was so fucking hard he wanted to take back the hour comment. "Then I will carry you out of here and lay you on our hotel bed, where I will show you how very gay I am. And how very much I love it."

Reid dramatically clutched his stomach. "Who needs old school friends? Let's cut and run."

THEY ENDED UP SPENDING ANOTHER COUPLE OF HOURS AT THE reunion before Sullivan lived up to his promise, fire-armed Reid over his shoulder and raced Reid's squirmy, laughing ass out of Angelwood Acadia.

They returned to their hotel room, the door barely closing before they kicked off their shoes and shrugged out of their coats.

Sullivan washed his hands in the bathroom, and Reid snuck in and did the same.

The bathroom was larger than his nanny nook, but it felt

just as constricted with the millions of horny, excited, anxious nerve-endings sparking between them.

They studied each other in the mirror. Sullivan probably fixated on the purple tips of Reid's hair, his unkempt suit, and the rawness of the lip Reid had been chewing since their walk back.

Reid, for his part, couldn't decide which part of Sullivan to focus on.

Those wide shoulders or the hard angles of his jaw or those glittering eyes that couldn't stop taking Reid in . . .

Their gazes snagged, and Reid's knees wobbled.

Through a crack in the curtains, dim light seeped in from the light-spangled city below. They stood beside the bed, and Reid heard every shift of Sullivan's clothes, felt the heat of his body, smelled the scent of vanilla soap and under it, Sullivan.

Reid licked his lip, trembling at what they were about to do. Waiting for it to happen.

Sullivan pinched Reid's tie and drew if off him slowly, keeping the knot in place.

"Sullivan?" Reid watched Sullivan set the tie carefully on the bed beside their pillows. "This is my first time with a man."

Sullivan plucked gently at his buttons. His words tickled over Reid's nose. "I bet you're wondering what I'll do with you. How it will feel."

Yes.

Firm fingers skated under the shirt, over Reid's shoulders, and his shirt slid down both arms. Sullivan pulled the material free from his wrists, sucking in Reid's scent at the crook of his neck. "The way you smell drives me crazy."

He sucked Reid's neck, and Reid moaned. "Forget my inexperience. Do anything to me. Everything." Reid gasped as Sullivan popped his button and drew the zipper over his aching cock. "Whatever floats your boat."

Sullivan's lips twitched against the soft bit of skin under Reid's ear.

"It's okay to be nervous." In his ear, "Talk. I like your voice."

"I like yours," Reid said, like the total sex-God he was.

"Let's see if you like it better around your cock."

Reid shivered.

Sullivan pulled down Reid's pants and his cock sprang free, hard and heavy. "W-what do you like doing to your . . . best friends with benefits?"

Pants and socks removed, Reid stood naked in the dark, his anklebones ticklish. The rest of him, achingly vulnerable.

Sullivan pressed close, his shirt removed, the heat of his torso kissing Reid's. "I like a lot of things. I love making you feel good."

Reid had read a few passionate love scenes from Sam Baton's books. If they were an indicator of what Sullivan liked, then—

Reid's lust spiraled to unexplored places. Places he very much wanted to travel. Especially if they were tight places he didn't have to think, where Sullivan could take control and do anything with him he liked. "Do you like bondage?"

"On special occasions."

"Tomorrow's your birthday," Reid said way too enthusiastically. *Calm, Reid.* "I mean, I want to be tied down with you. *By* you."

Sullivan's hands skated down the planes of his back, landing with a squeeze on his ass. "One day."

Reid hoped it was a 'one day' that was inevitable and not a 'one day' that pushed the topic aside.

Sullivan kissed Reid's jaw to the corner of his mouth. "There'd have to be more discussion about it."

Were they talking about the leather restraints or the other type of tied down? Or both?

"I'm the hare that naps, remember."

"Speaking of hair, I like yours."

"Are you changing the subject?"

Sullivan growled and hefted Reid up, steering his thighs around his hips. "Yes."

Reid straddled hot skin and the smooth weave of Sullivan's pants. His cock rubbed up against a damn fine stomach.

"Want to know what I love more than restraints?" Sullivan said.

"What?"

Sullivan squeezed the globes of Reid's ass. "Bossing you around the bedroom."

Oh hell yes. Reid bit his lip, and Sullivan eyed it.

"Stoop to me, Reid."

Reid dropped a kiss on Sullivan's lips.

They were going to do this.

A jittery breath escaped him, and the world tipped; air rushed around him until his bare back and ass hit the weave of the comforter.

Sullivan landed on him, arms caging him either side.

Reid searched the dark for Sullivan's expression. It was too damn difficult to read but the harsh quality of his breath suggested Sullivan was deeply aroused.

Sullivan kissed him and there was something extremely wanton and dirty about it. Raw and primal. He fucked his tongue into Reid's mouth like he was twenty—like he owned the whole world.

Like he wanted to own him.

It was so demanding, Reid envisioned restraints holding him in place—strapping him with perfect unyielding pressure.

He'd never felt so turned on.

He could cry.

Probably shouldn't do that.

Unless . . . "Would it help you connect with your emotional side if I started sobbing?"

Sullivan gently pulled back an inch. "Have you not noticed how I escape the room every time someone gets teary?"

"Good thing the lights are out. This would be an unfortunate time for you to escape." Reid arched his hips, sliding his cock along Sullivan's hot skin.

A laugh rumbled out of Sullivan, and he flattened his large hand over Reid's chest. Every splayed finger felt like it branded him.

Did Sullivan feel how rapidly his heart thumped?

Sullivan's lips bumped over Reid's nipple and Reid inhaled sharply.

With a groan, Sullivan sucked it into his mouth, fingers wrapping around Reid's hard cock. "I want you so bad."

Reid squirmed at the perfect pressure on his dick.

"But let me show, not tell." Sullivan skimmed his lips and nose over the side of his ribs, to his armpit. He bit lightly, right where Reid's goosebumps concentrated.

Reid's arms jerked and he fisted the blanket under him. Should he touch Sullivan back?

How did he do it without seeming clumsy?

As if reading his mind, Sullivan sat and stretched Reid's arms between the pillows above his head. His thumb picked at Reid's nausea bracelet and Reid liked Sullivan touching it as he kissed his chest. Like a constant reminder Sullivan knew exactly who he was with.

Calloused fingers trailed over his arms and chest, pricking him with shivers as Sullivan kissed his way south. The leaking head of Reid's cock bumped against Sullivan's chin and Reid gulped at the rasp, hands jumping up.

Sullivan tightened his hold. He spoke, positioned so every time his jaw opened it tapped him. "Keep your wrists together. Or I'll help you."

Hot and bothered took on a swoony new meaning. "We're on land. Why do I feel so spine-tinglingly dizzy?"

"Sounds like a cry for help."

"Moor me."

Sullivan moved, and cool air shifted over Reid's torso. The lightest touch of material drifted over his face and up one arm, and holy shit, yes. Sullivan looped that tie around his wrists and cinched them tight together.

He threaded the lengths of tie into Reid's palm. "Grip that."

Reid could move his arms and free himself if he needed to. This was a symbolic bond, not a functional one. But even that hurtled him close to the edge.

Sullivan levied his weight onto Reid, warm and solid, his thighs sliding on the outside of Reid's legs. His hands looped around Reid's elbows, massaging against a pressure point. Sullivan's erection was hard next to his but too frustratingly covered for Reid to feel the silky hardness of him.

Sullivan must have thought the same thing, because he rolled off Reid, ditched his pants, and resumed his position. His legs blazed heat around Reid's and their heavy cocks rubbed.

Reid wriggled under him and bit his lip on a moan.

Sullivan's cool nose hit the shell of his ear, lips pressed on the soft skin below. "You feel so fucking hot under me."

Reid wasn't sure how to breathe anymore.

Sullivan sucked on his neck and Reid gripped the tie in his hand, his cock so fucking hard it seemed impossible. Sullivan ground against him, in long, slow slides. His mouth sucked Reid's neck, drawing indecipherable pleas from him.

Sullivan's thrusts picked up their tempo, his thick length rubbing his shaft with delicious friction, his teeth teasing his neck.

God, Reid hoped he left a mark. Hoped it lasted until they returned to the *Aquarian*.

Hoped everyone would see it.

"Fuck, Sullivan. I'm going to combust. My dick is *burning*."

Sullivan gripped his hips and shuffled down his legs, locking them in place. "Guess I better put it in my mouth. A little sucking does wonders for relief."

Hot breath fluttered over his cock and Sullivan flicked his tongue against his slit.

"Quote me again and I'll come," Reid warned.

"Let's test that theory out. Soon."

Sullivan sank his mouth down Reid's length, tongue sliding slickly around him. Reid gasped, ass clenching as he fought not to buck into the depths of Sullivan's hot throat. He gripped his tie, pulling it tighter.

Sullivan squeezed the base of his cock and plunged, until Reid felt the slippery paddedness of Sullivan's throat.

Reid's body rippled with shivers at the intensity. Sullivan worked him with controlled sucking until Reid was a slave to feeling. He barely knew what he was uttering.

Sullivan continued with fevered intensity, the head of Reid's cock banging his soft throat.

Fingers massaged his balls and traced over his asshole. It felt so damn good. Because it felt like another 'one day.' Felt like Sullivan was saying he'd like to drive his pole up there.

Sullivan's cock leaked against the inner side of Reid's knee and Reid *needed*. "What about you?" he panted. "Swivel around and we can do this Cancerian-style."

Sullivan pulled off him. "Cancerian style?"

"Like the symbol, a sideways 69."

"Three things." Sullivan crawled up him and blanketed Reid's arousal-dampened body with his. Their lips locked in a musky kiss. "You're too close, I want to spend time in your throat, and I decide how we do this."

Reid's balls tightened.

"Something's missing." Sullivan rummaged over the side of the bed. He shook his phone and candlelight beamed from it, casting a soft glow over them.

Sullivan set it on the bed and caressed Reid's check. "Much better."

Reid's chest fucking fluttered.

Sullivan gripped their cocks in one hand, using Reid's pre-come to slicken his stroking. Reid's toes flexed against Sullivan's calves and, God, Reid couldn't hold back.

His arms came over Sullivan's head, the tie still tight at his wrists. Sullivan's muscles shifted as he worked them faster, and he whimpered into a thrusting kiss.

"Fuck," Sullivan grunted. "You're more responsive than I imagined."

Desire spiraled out of control. "You imagined?"

"Day one. At the café. Couldn't concentrate." Sullivan kissed him hard. Hand faster still. "You told your friends 'you love it most when you get to lie there.'"

Reid's arms and legs stiffened as sensation mounted—

"I imagined making it happen."

His orgasm ripped through him, and Reid gritted his teeth against the swamping sensation as his come pulsed between them. Sullivan milked him, prolonging the pleasure.

He scooped up Reid's come, cuffed his erection, and the whole bed shook with his fast and furious strokes until his hot release spilled over Reid's stomach and chest.

As if Sullivan knew he needed it, he dropped his full weight on him, embracing him tightly.

"How are you feeling?" Sullivan asked.

Reid emitted a strangled sound. He felt thoroughly done. Completed sated.

Sullivan laughed into a firm, dry kiss. "Did you think of your to-do list?"

"Mmm," Reid murmured. "But there was only one thing on it: more of this."

Sullivan's responding kiss was long. Leisurely. Their come dried between them and the tie around Reid's wrists loosened.

Sullivan unwound it from him and threaded their fingers together. Reid felt their bumping pulses and sighed. "I didn't think sex could feel like this."

Sullivan hummed into another kiss.

That small flat scar on Sullivan's neck winked at Reid, and he nipped it. "But I suppose being a day shy of thirty-eight you've had a lot of practice."

Sullivan dropped his head against Reid's shoulder. "Christ I'm old."

"Yeah."

Sullivan slapped the side of his ass. "You're feeling brave."

"No sharks here."

Sullivan tangled his fingers in Reid's hair and crushed him into a kiss. "You sure about that?"

"My heart is afraid."
"I'm no heartbreaker, James."
"What if it won't listen?"

-James and David
Second Time Around

Chapter Fifteen

Reid and Sullivan arrived back from London, late.

Joanna had fallen asleep on the couch next to Alanis. Reid stood in the saloon, sweaty from their plane ride and the thrilling frottage session he'd had with Sullivan in the hotel before they left.

He wanted to crush Alanis into a hug, but he was fairly certain he smelled of plane and sex and Sullivan—and wasn't sure how to deal with it if she made a joke.

Could he admit the truth?

Or were they keeping this to themselves?

How were he and Sullivan supposed to act around each other now?

London had been mostly free of those concerns, Reid snuggling up to Sullivan on a whim. Even out on the streets, middle of the bustling city.

Now they were back, the *Aquarian* swaying underfoot, and Reid was swaying with uncertainty.

Sullivan ditched his luggage and tenderly scooped Joanna up in his arms. He thanked Alanis and Joanna stirred, her head against his chest. He kissed her forehead and told her he was happy to be home.

Reid's chest constricted.

They were home.

God, he ached to be part of it.

Alanis left, and Reid carried their bags downstairs. Joanna murmured with her dad, their voices trailing softly to where he leaned at Sullivan's cabin door.

His body shivered at the need to open the door. His stomach knotted as he waited alongside Sullivan's things. Did it change the situation, now they were sleeping together? Would Sullivan allow him inside his room? His heart?

Was standing here putting too much pressure on Sullivan?

He was supposed to be the hare, after all.

Reid reluctantly pushed off Sullivan's door, grabbed his things, and hit the marina showers.

He returned fifteen minutes later, refreshed, smelling of soap and vanilla shampoo, a wet towel around his neck. Sullivan passed him in the quiet, kitchen-lit saloon, his own shower bag slung over a shoulder.

Their gazes met properly for the first time since returning to the *Aquarian*, and Reid's insides took a triple somersault. He pulled at his towel, damp material rubbing his nape. "Hey."

Sullivan hitched his bag more securely on his shoulder. "Hey."

Sullivan passed him with a heavy gait, motioning he needed to shower.

Reid snagged the ribbed bag strap and steered Sullivan back around. "Hold up." He gnawed his lip. "Are you reverting back to your pre-London ways?"

A surprised brow arched. "My pre-London ways?"

"Scandalously long eye contact and little follow through."

Sullivan cocked his head. His intimate gaze thoroughly raked

Reid, and it felt like Sullivan was undressing him. Not just out of his clothes, but further. He glanced away, like peeling back any more layers made him nervous. "What would you like, Reid?"

"Right now I'll settle on a kiss. Once you've showered, you can order me around."

Sullivan's gaze shot back to him, gleaming, interested. But his frown shadowed the look with wariness. "Joanna's here. I'm not sure we can . . ."

Empowered by the desire he'd glimpsed, Reid stepped up to Sullivan, close enough their hips bumped. He kept his voice low. "Joanna is in bed, and clever enough to know there's something between us."

Sullivan's face paled. "She knows?" Sullivan asked.

"Not with a hundred percent certainty, but she ships us. *Cancaquarian*."

Aquariancer?

Sullivan hesitated and pulled Reid in by his towel. "Can we leave it at shipping for now?"

Reid swallowed a flurry of disappointment. "Is that a yes to ordering me around?"

Sullivan's low rumble of laughter vibrated over Reid's lips. "That's a hell yes to a sock in your mouth."

"Sullivan!" Reid jolted with arousal and a sudden appreciation for how kinky he was. "My birthday's not until June."

Sullivan didn't invite Reid into his cabin. Not that night. Nor the next.

Nor any other night over the following weeks.

They settled into a pattern of discreet looks during the day, and delicious sex at night. Sex that happened on Reid's single bed, candlelight flickering at their side, Reid begging Sullivan to *fuck him, please, oh God, please*. Something Sullivan still had not done.

"Good night, Sullivan," Reid called extra-loudly into the darkened hall. "We'll discuss your habit of talking to yourself in the morning."

Reid shut his bedroom door, and his nape prickled with goosebumps. In the semi-darkness of his room, softly lit by his candlelight app, Sullivan braced an arm around Reid's waist and nibbled his neck.

Reid sank into the heavy supportive embrace, arching his neck for Sullivan to suck at that sensitive spot at the curve of his shoulder. "I'm not sure you give your daughter enough credit."

"Enough doubt will do. Now what did you mean we'll discuss my habit of talking to myself?"

Reid laughed and shivered when Sullivan nipped him. "When you're super concentrating, you bullet point your thoughts for everyone to hear."

Sullivan's hum danced over his skin like electricity. "I think you rather like that about me."

"Only because I find you fascinating in general. Taken on its own . . ."

Sullivan twisted Reid around, eyes glittering with humor. With hunger. Enough to evaporate the pesky mantra in Reid's head: *Would it be so bad if Joanna knew?*

Reid held on to Sullivan's hips. "I don't want to think. Can you make that happen?"

Sullivan's eyes blazed, and he backed Reid to bed. His ass hit the mattress and he teetered on falling. Sullivan yanked his shirt over his head, exposing Reid's chest, the small thatch of hair, his hard nipples.

Sullivan thumbed the one on the right, the more sensitive one, the one that felt like it had a direct link to his cock. He grazed the puckered nib. "Undress."

Reid didn't need to be told twice. Sullivan stepped back to watch him, and Reid had his jeans and boxer-briefs knotted around his ankles. He stomped out of them and his socks, dick bobbing as arousal hardened him.

"On the bed. Head tipped over the base." Sullivan's voice. The blunt demands. Holy shit, it slithered under his skin like a potent aphrodisiac.

Reid scrambled onto his mattress, stirring up the bedcover in his haste. He didn't care it folded under one shoulder. The edge of the mattress cushioned his nape, and Reid stared at Sullivan upside down.

"Spread your legs. Give yourself one good stroke. Spread your arms."

"You're bullet-pointing your orders. You must be into this."

"You have no idea." Sullivan's smirk glowed in the candle-light. He moved toward Reid and didn't stop. His thighs grazed either side of Reid's head until Reid was blinded by Sullivan's crotch. Reid's nose squished against the seam of his jeans. He breathed through his mouth, hard, wanting desperately for the layer between them to vanish.

God, Sullivan was fire between the sheets. He took what he wanted and Reid submitted to the safety and ease of obeying orders. Sex had never been so much fun.

Fingers ghosted over Reid's stomach, teased his treasure trail and dipped, tauntingly close to his pubes.

Sullivan's crotch muffled Reid's moan.

Something cold pressed at his balls. He gripped the sheets to remain spread open, but squirmed.

Firm hands pressed below his elbows. "I have something to . . . tie you down." Straps came up from the sides of the bed, and Sullivan clasped his wrists in softly-lined Velcro cuffs, the right one seated above his faux-leather bracelet. He stepped back, dark, aroused eyes meeting his. "How do they feel?"

Reid tested the give of the straps, loving the firm feeling

against his skin, loving more the heat deepening Sullivan's eye as his gaze ransacked every inch of Reid's trembling body. "Good." More than that. "Perfect."

Reid lifted his head up and Sullivan braced a supporting hand under him. Reid's nipples were hard and his cock stretched toward his chin, pre-come pearling at the tip. A bottle of lube was nestled at his balls and Reid's ass clenched at the prospect.

Sullivan knelt, voice caressing his cheek. "I'm going to undress. Strap your legs." He traced Reid's mouth with a finger. "Spend some quality time in your throat. Then," Sullivan whispered the last part in Reid's ear, and Reid's body arched off the bed, fucking air.

"There's enough slack for you to rest your head on the mattress."

Reid wriggled down. Sullivan palmed Reid's chest over his thumping heart and pressed their lips together. "You're fucking beautiful, Reid."

Tenderness and gentle neediness shimmered through Sullivan's voice.

Could he feel how his words made Reid's heart pound?

Could he feel how badly Reid wanted this forever?

Sullivan peeled out of his clothes one by one, taking his sweet time, a torturing smirk etched at his mouth.

He parted Reid's thighs, strapped his ankles with a couple of inches slack, and slid a safety ring on his finger. Press the button and it squealed—Sullivan's signal to stop. Sullivan made him test it.

"Good." He moved to the foot of the bed, dragging his fingertips along Reid's goosebumped skin. His shin, his thigh, his hip, his chest.

Anticipation and eagerness fluttered in his gut and Reid used his heels to propel his head back over the mattress. Sullivan's cock bobbed right there, so close, but not close enough.

Sullivan cupped Reid's head, thumbs stroking his cheek, his chin, fingers a steady pressure on his head. "So goddamn hot."

"My throat is also hot. You should find out."

Sullivan's eyes flashed and his grip tightened. "I know how hot it is."

Reid grinned. "What are you waiting for, then? Me to beg you?"

"When did you get so sassy in the sheets?"

"Technically, I'm not in the sheets, I'm on the—"

Sullivan angled his head, the spongy head of his hard cock rubbing over the bridge of Reid's nose. "I know you love talking, but there won't be much of that in the next few minutes."

"Few minutes, Sullivan? Not the stamina of a guy who goes at it eight times in one night."

"I'm no longer sixteen, Reid."

"Feed me, old—"

Sullivan hooked a thumb into his mouth and pressed his cock into the gap. A burst of salty flavor hit his tongue. He moaned at the taste. At the way Sullivan grunted.

Sullivan's thumb popped free and Reid stretched his lips over Sullivan's cockhead, eagerly taking him in.

"Jesus. Christ. Fuck, yes."

Sullivan slid in and out of his mouth with shallow, gentle thrusts. Reid loved how he started slow, and steadily built his pace and depth as though he felt the moment Reid's throat completely relaxed before he quickened and deepened his thrusts.

Reid's cock pulsed hard, in time with Sullivan, the bottle of lube bumping gently against his balls. God, it felt good watching Sullivan fall apart and knowing that he was the one making it happen.

"So soft, so wet," Sullivan murmured. "My dick is in you so deep." Sullivan fucked his throat, fingers pinching Reid's hard nipples. "You're a fucking champ."

He pulled out of Reid's throat, let him catch his breath, and then plunged back in, rocking hard to his release. "A really good boy."

The words ripped through Reid. He whimpered around Sullivan and felt Sullivan's cock swell.

"Oh, fuck. Fuck."

Sullivan's orgasm ripped through him and he came deep in Reid's throat. Sullivan pulled out, come trailing a faint taste over his tongue. Reid took in a gulping breath through his mouth, feeling eerily empty.

Fingers stroked Reid's face. "Are you okay?"

Reid couldn't respond, emotions tangling into a knot that jammed his throat.

Sullivan urged Reid to use the slack and settle his head on the mattress, then he swung onto the bed. He tossed the bottle of lube aside and straddled him. "Reid?"

Reid blinked at him, his eyes stinging.

Sullivan grabbed the straps—

"Don't."

"What's the matter?" Sullivan settled his hot naked weight against Reid, like a blanket. He steered Reid to look at him.

Reid swallowed, then found his voice. "It's just a few tears."

"You remembered the ring, right?"

He did. "I didn't need it."

Sullivan's body sagged a fraction in relief. "Tell me about the tears."

"I'm not sad."

"What are they for?"

"I'm not in pain, either."

Sullivan rocked up a brow.

"I'm also not repressing laughter even though I have a weird urge to giggle. At the situation, not you. Maybe at myself, but . . ." Reid cleared his throat. "They're nothing to worry about."

"What are they for?"

Reid stared up at the concern, the absolute protectiveness in Sullivan's watchful expression. He whispered, "I like this."

He loved this. The Velcro cuffs. Sullivan's eager thrusting as he came apart in Reid's throat. *Sullivan calling him a good boy.*

Reid blinked hard. The straps, the ordering . . . made him feel like he belonged to Sullivan.

Like he was something to be adored, used, kept.

Reid arched, his hard length rubbing against Sullivan like a plea. He needed to be close, needed to come.

Come home.

He bit his lip hard on the errant thought.

Sullivan eyed his lips and kissed him. His woodsy, salty scent invaded Reid's senses and Reid thrust his tongue into the kiss. Sullivan responded with eager intensity. He nipped down Reid's neck, sucking at Reid's favorite spot until Reid pleaded he was close to exploding.

Sullivan lifted his weight, caging him. Reid's cock ached for friction. The squirt of lube oozing onto Sullivan's hand had his lust spiraling. One slick grip curled around Reid's cock and a hot shiver ran through him.

Sullivan watched Reid as he jacked Reid's cock with expert pressure. It felt so damn good. The hand, the drilling intensity of his gaze, the restraints baring Reid to him. Showing him how vulnerable he was. How good it felt to have someone to be vulnerable with.

Sullivan dropped sizzling kisses down his stomach, over the curve of his thigh, and nosed under his balls. Hot breath fanned over his perineum followed by the flat, wriggling slickness of Sullivan's tongue.

Reid bucked into the sensation, his nerves fritzing. "Oh, fuck me. God."

One firm palm scooped his ass, tilting him, and Sullivan's tongue slipped over his entrance.

Reid gasped, never imagining how intense it felt to be kissed there.

The tip of Sullivan's tongue shallowly breached him and Reid swore, straining against the restraints.

Sullivan stroked him harder and plunged his tongue into him, fucking him. Reid bucked into it, meeting Sullivan's tongue, desperate for more.

Pleasure bolted to his curling toes, to the muscles in his arms and legs that strained to move, to his leaking cock.

Reid couldn't wait for when Sullivan was ready to fuck him. To unravel inside him.

He bit his lip on a groan, imagining Sullivan's cock stretching his ass, rubbing his prostate until he—

His orgasm slingshot through him. He grunted and spilled and spilled and spilled over his stomach and Sullivan's pumping hand.

He sank into the bed, breathing hard. Sullivan murmured to him as he unstrapped him. He left for the bathroom and returned with a warm washcloth and minty fresh breath. He cleaned Reid up, and massaged Reid's ankles and wrists.

"How did that feel?"

"Ngughf."

Sullivan laughed, lay down beside Reid and tucked him against his warm chest. "Anything you'd like to try differently?"

He shook his head. No. Not sexually. Not in the bedroom.

Just outside of it.

Sullivan letting the world know they were a thing. Letting Joanna know it.

Letting Reid know it.

"REID? REID. WAKE UP."

Reid cracked his eyes open. The warm cushion he'd been curled against was Sullivan.

"Oh! You slept here all night?" Reid's heart raced. He'd never woken so quickly.

"You murmured stories to me until I fell asleep," Sullivan reminded him. "Maybe I didn't tell you to stop. I'm cramped this morning, though."

"Cramped? Need a full-body massage?"

"Christ. The glint in your eye. It's tempting."

Sullivan rolled him over, kissed him senseless, and climbed out of bed. In a few quick moves, he was in his clothes.

"You know," Reid said hesitantly. "If we had a bigger bed, you wouldn't feel so cramped."

Sullivan bent down and kissed him deeply. "It's the first time on board I've missed the sunrise."

Reid kneeled and checked outside. "What would you know, the sun still rose."

Sullivan laughed and snapped a hand against his ass. "I'm working at the university today. I need to catch the bus." He towed himself to the door, and Reid called after him.

"Buy a damn car. I'll go halves with you."

Sullivan hummed and left.

So he might have changed conversation whip fast when Reid hinted at getting into Sullivan's bed. But the car thing. That hum.

Progress?

THE NEXT MORNING, REID WOKE TO SULLIVAN'S ARMS AROUND him. *Again.* Reid's heart thumped so hard, Sullivan had to feel it against the palm pressed to his pec.

This was more than a step forward. This meant something. Right?

All morning, as Reid readied himself for the day and prepared Joanna her lunch, he felt the outline of Sullivan's hand pressed against his chest.

Outside, rain slanted heavily. Reid hummed as he slipped on his helmet and slung on Joanna's backpack.

When they reached the bus stop, Joanna swung off the tandem bike and hiked both her brows at him. "You sound like you belong in a musical."

Reid passed her the backpack, grinning. "Why? Because I'm singing in the rain?"

"You usually hate tandem-biking."

"Oh, I definitely hate it. You know what? You should suggest riding this with Elijah."

"I have. But Mason likes dropping him off to school on his way to work—far too early for me to tag along. Ugh." She observed the seaside and the puddled road. "Besides, what would we do with the bike?"

"High time this thing got stolen," Reid said.

Joanna studied him in that clever way she did. "You just can't stop smiling today."

Reid gripped the slippery handlebars. God he wished she knew. "What do you want for your birthday?"

Joanna tutted. "You're leaving it to the last minute."

"It's Friday. Your birthday's Sunday. Also, nothing I find feels special enough."

"I know what I want, but . . ."

"What is it?"

She shrugged. "There's no point telling you, you won't give it to me."

"Okay, curiosity fully engaged. Tell me."

Joanna drew in a deep breath and stared out at the rain. "You and Dad admitting you're together."

Reid gripped the bike so hard that the handles bit into his skin. "What? I mean, how . . ."

Joanna pulled down her hood, strands of wet hair clinging to her cheek. She didn't respond, just looked knowingly at him. Knowingly, and her humored mood had saddened.

Reid's heart hammered guiltily. "Um . . . anything else? Something achievable?"

"Nah, just that," she said. After a pause, she looked at him. "Reid?"

"Yeah?"

"Dad uses your hideous mug every morning. The way you watch each other . . . there's so much electricity I don't know how you're both not already ash." In the distance, two schoolgirls raced through the rain. Joanna motioned for Reid to leave.

"Joanna . . ."

She shrugged. "I'm not angry you haven't told me, Reid." She waved at her peers, and side-eyed him. "Just disappointed."

Reid biked back to the marina, heavy. The rain soaked through his coat, dampening his pullover.

He locked the bike on board and stashed his helmet. He shivered, but it had little to do with the water running down his collar and sleeves, or the jerky rocking of the *Aquarian*.

He stripped off his soaked coat and shoes and left them on the outside hook. Quietly, he slipped inside the saloon.

All the lights were on, casting a warm, yellowish glow over the otherwise gray morning. Sullivan was having a late breakfast at the dining table. Beside his plate, Reid's ugly mug steamed with coffee. An audiobook played, and Sullivan's eyes were glazed as he stared out the rain-spattered window.

Had he heard Reid come in?

The narrator had a deep, compelling voice. "*In that moment, that quiet moment, eagerly waiting for his best friend to return, he knew.*"

With twitchy fingers, Reid pulled off his wet soaks and outer pullover. How did he ask Sullivan about Joanna's wish?

"Hey." He sank onto the adjacent bench cushion, knee bumping Sullivan's. Sullivan's blue eyes flickered with something soft, tender, and heart-thumping.

"*He knew,*" the narrator continued, "*he had damn well fallen in lo—*"

Sullivan shut off the story.

"Hey," Sullivan said.

"Hi," Reid waved. Why was he waving? He dropped his hand, glowering at it. "You know you don't have to turn off your books anymore right? I've read all of them."

Distinctly flustered, Sullivan scrubbed the stubble of his chin. "Right."

Just ask about Joanna's birthday.

Reid eyed Sullivan's laptop and cleared his throat. "Working up here again? I love this new tradition."

Fail, fail, fail.

Sullivan looked at Reid as if something similar flashed through his head. As if they both wanted to say something and couldn't.

Reid stole Sullivan's coffee and drank deeply. "Have you got Joanna a gift yet?"

Sullivan rolled his shoulders. "Part of it."

"We were talking." Sullivan blanched at Reid's words. Reid wondered if Joanna had already told Sullivan what she wanted. He continued hesitantly, "She told me what she wants most is—"

Sullivan stood and collected his bowl and spoon. "I'm thinking we give her an experience."

Reid frowned. What was making Sullivan so jumpy? "Huh?"

Sullivan dropped his bowl into the sink. "Maybe take her out on the boat, to Wingerham Bay, and watch the stars. It'll go perfectly with the telescope I bought her."

Reid fiddled with his loose nausea bracelet and tightened it. "That sounds . . . something. She'd also like—"

"It's spring, we should see the Cancer constellation now."

"Sullivan, are you all right?"

His blue eyes met everything but Reid. "Dandy. Fantastic. I ought to head to my studio. I have a lot to do."

"Want me to bring your coffee?" Reid lifted the mug and glanced back to Sullivan

He had already left.

Reid sipped the oaty drink and sighed. *What was that about?*

CHANGED INTO DRY CLOTHES, REID TOOK HIS DISTRACTED ASS and an umbrella toward the marina office. The rain petered to a lighter drizzle. Reid called Loretta, who was on the last leg of her journey with Natalie, visiting Natalie's parents in Seattle. Finally in the same time zone.

"It doesn't feel like a step back," Reid explained, "But it's not a step forward, either."

"From what you've told me, it sounds like you *like* not moving."

Reid tipped the umbrella to let light rain smatter on his boiling cheeks. "I like moving outside the bedroom. In life. Now, why would Sullivan be skittish?"

"You said he hid himself in his studio. Isn't that how you two began?"

"Only because he was spooked being attracted to me."

"So maybe something else spooked him?"

Reid hummed. Or he knew what Reid wanted to talk about and didn't want to re-discuss labels.

Loretta continued, "Why don't you ask the brainiac I can't wait to meet?"

"Not this time. She's disappointed in us."

A huff followed. "She's not the only one."

Waves slapped against pylons, the marina flag whipped a dozen feet ahead, metal dinged against the pole. Reid halted on the boardwalk. "What?"

"Can you blame me? You asked me for advice on how to touch his eggplant, you woke me up in the middle of the night. You're calling me when we're back tomorrow. Six months, and you still haven't figured out if you're boyfriends."

"Ugh. I hate you."

"I just want you happy, Reid."

He was happy. For the most part. It was just . . . "I'm the hare."

A puzzled silence preceded Loretta's, "Yeah, I'm not getting it."

"He lost his husband. He needs to take it slow. This is about him, what he needs—"

Reid sucked in a hard, cold breath.

He was back on the London Eye with Grams and her sad smile after brushing off her question. *What do you want from your life, Reid?* He'd wanted to focus on her. Give her what she needed.

"Loretta?"

"Yeah?"

"Do I put other people and their emotional needs before my own?"

"I think you know the answer to that."

Reid didn't need her affirmation, he was already scrolling back through every relationship he'd had, remembering every time he'd let his girlfriends' wants became priority.

He liked to be the guy who cared, who was unflinchingly loyal, but when did loving others come at the cost of loving himself?

Reid laughed hollowly. "This call isn't as fun as it usually is."

"Will you be okay?"

"Yeah, I just gotta ask myself a very important question." *What do I want from life?*

He ended their call—and it felt like an exclamation to his epiphany. God.

The bell dinged as he walked into the main office.

Alanis wrapped up a call and set her phone down with a tired *thunk*. "Hey, you're in early."

Reid shrugged.

"No Sullivan walking you?"

He gave her a sharp look, another realization slamming into him.

He'd been too heart-eyed to notice. For the last month, Sullivan had pretty much sat him in his un-swiveling chair before buying them all vegan muffins from the snack shack.

It'd become tradition.

Reid made a sound close to a hiccup.

"Oh, Reid." Alanis's smile twisted into worry. "Are you okay?"

Was he okay? He wasn't sure. He felt like a hot mess inside.

But why?

Because everyone could see it. Everyone except Sullivan, apparently.

He and Reid were not best friends with benefits.

They were boyfriends.

They. Were. Boyfriends.

His heart thundered in his ears and his hiccup turned into nervous, joyous laughter.

They were boyfriends who *lived together*. Who were a *family*.

He whipped out his phone and sank into his stationary chair.

Reid: Muffin.

Sullivan answered immediately, and that had Reid biting his grin.

Sullivan: You want one?

Reid: Or maybe you are my muffin.

Sullivan: As endearments go, I'm not sure it suits.

Reid: We could always go with the 'b' word.

Sullivan: Ah.

Reid suddenly hyperventilated. What if he was pushing too hard?

Reid: You know. Bitch.

Shit. He was afraid. He was the obstacle to his dream of belonging.

Sullivan: I think we should talk more about our hard limits.

Reid: Haha. Okay, I'm the bitch.

Sullivan: No. You're a good boy.

Weird, hopeful happiness lit through him like a flare.

Reid: Muffin Top?

Sullivan: Get back to work.

Reid: I'll be here till six today. Think you could do the shopping for us?

Reid held his breath, his foot jiggling.

Ding!

Sullivan: I can swing it.

Alanis swiveled to face him and folded her arms expectantly.

Reid didn't explain, just grinned harder. "I need to log into my bank account and the phone app sucks. Can I—?" He gestured to her laptop.

"Right now?" she asked.

"Yeah. A payment came through yesterday that I need to deal with." That Reid needed to send back.

Alanis seemed confused. "The marina should have paid you last week already."

"You did. This is from my . . . muffin top."

"Ah." Alanis nodded, eyes sparkling. "Could you tell your

muffin top I'm still waiting for the extension to his lease for next year?"

Reid jerked from the laptop. "His lease, what? I thought he had Dock J until June."

"Paperwork needs to be dealt with now. Monday, absolutely latest. We're at capacity, and a couple people have called asking if we have space in summer. If I don't get your man's signature, Sullivan will effectively be giving his three months' notice." Alanis cocked her head. "I'm surprised he hasn't told you about it. I gave him the extension weeks ago."

"Weeks ago?" Reid's stomach sank through the chair.

"I'm sure it just slipped his mind. Get him to sign it and bring it with you Monday."

Had it slipped Sullivan's mind or was this the reason Sullivan was acting so skittish?

Did Sullivan know they were at a crossroads?

Did he know it was time for them to make the right turn?

THAT AFTERNOON, WHEN SULLIVAN WENT SHOPPING, REID took fifteen to sneak on board the *Aquarian*—specifically, to sneak into Sullivan's studio. He turned on the light, sucked in the taste of metal, sweat, and salt, and rifled through Sullivan's paperwork.

It took him thirty seconds to find the two-page contract extending the lease on Dock J.

He collapsed onto the cot Sullivan took creative naps on and read over it. A signature and a date. That's all it needed.

"What are you doing?"

Reid jumped at Joanna's voice, guiltily stashing the contract behind him.

She noticed immediately, pushing fully into the room, her

hair wet and long from another downpour. She padded over to him in her fish slippers. "What are you hiding?"

A defeated sigh left him, and he flashed the contract at her. "There's no time for disappointment, Joanna," he murmured. "You're a child mastermind and I need you mastering your dad's mind."

She took the paper, read over it, and sank next to him, leaning her head against his arm. "I'm all mastered out, Reid. If what we've done hasn't worked, nothing will."

A part of him was scared she was right.

Another part reminded Reid that Sullivan was buying their weekly groceries right now. No longer a manny job, but a job they'd share between them. "Defeat is such a passive word. It doesn't look good on either of us."

Joanna lifted a bewildered brow.

"Deviousness is better," Reid continued, "but not sincere enough. Doggedness. Now, doggedness works."

"What are you saying, Reid?"

"I'm saying, we should show your dad how much we love him."

Reid stared at Sullivan's pinned blueprints, redesigns for his project to clean the ocean. Proof he cared for dolphins, whales, fish . . . *crabs*.

Joanna handed him back the unsigned lease extension, tapping it against his heart. "I have another wish for my birthday."

He nodded. "I've got to return to the main office. But Joanna? Let's make a plan later. I need this too."

THEY SNUCK OUT AFTER DINNER FOR A HOT CHOCOLATE AT THE marina bar, just Reid and Joanna. They cradled their drinks and spun off ideas in low voices.

"He'd totally sign if he knew how much you love him," Joanna said.

Reid licked his milk-moustache. "Telling him will be part of the plan. But I want to *show* him, too."

"I love that you're a Cancer! I'm so in tune with your feels right now."

Reid still didn't believe in the whole zodiac gag, but he was digging Joanna's enthusiasm.

She set down her drink and clapped her hands like she had the perfect solution. "What are your defining moments?"

"What do you mean?"

"Give me objects, physical things that represent you and him as a couple."

"Objects?"

"Things, Reid."

Reid rolled his eyes. "Like . . . the life vest?"

"Yessss. Keep going."

"Ah, my resume. The whistle. Eggplant pasta. Muffins. My stripy T-shirt. Elderflower liqueur"—Reid said that one with an apologetic wince—"My nausea bracelet. Hair dye. Coffee—God, lots of that. My mug. The cave—although that's a *place*—"

"Interesting the parts you insist on defining to a child genius."

"Restraints."

"Okay, that one you can explain."

Reid's neck started to boil. "Uh, it's more of a quality. I've exercised so much restraint from telling him—"

"Where to stick it?"

"Telling him off. *Joanna.*"

Joanna giggled. "This is all good stuff. We can make party hats out of your resume."

"Probably what it's best used for," Reid conceded.

"Whistle could be used singing 'Happy Birthday' to me.

The rest sounds perfect for a picnic in that cave. You can show restraint by not telling him what it means. He should figure it out on his own."

"He's fairly clever, so. Also, your dad wants to take you out on the boat to look at stars."

"Ohhh, nice. That can happen after the picnic." Joanna eyed him. "You should redo your hair. Purple was fun on you."

"The word you're searching for is funny."

"It only took a couple of months to grow out."

Reid grumbled. "And will forever have your dad laughing at me."

"That, Reid," Joanna said finally. "Will be the price of doggedness."

David pressed a hand against my chest. “Make it listen.”

-James
Second Time Around

Chapter Sixteen

One third done on his little project to show the vast scope of Reid's love for Sullivan.

He'd have to work all day tomorrow to finish before Sunday. But finish, he would.

Reid swiped to the next page on his Kindle app and read aloud, the audio program on his laptop recording.

There would be little time to edit, but he hoped Sullivan would be forgiving. At least he could pronounce everything. He hadn't won a spelling bee without some future advantages.

A knock came at his door, followed by Sullivan's husky Britishness. "Reid?"

Reid whacked the button to stop recording. "Just a sec."

He quickly shut his laptop, shoved his headphones and microphone into his sock drawer, and pushed up his suspended desk.

He flung open the door, flushed. "Sullivan. You good?"

He tried to casually lean against the doorframe, but he miscalculated and slid behind the wall until he hit his nose. Ow.

Sullivan let himself in and raised questioning brows.

"You've been in here for hours." He noticed Reid's rumpled bed and his burning cheeks. "What were you doing?"

That train of thought was better than giving away Reid's project. "Making myself happy."

"With your pants on?"

"Not all happy endings finish with orgasm."

"How philosophical." Sullivan slung himself across Reid's bed. "I am in the mood."

"For a happy ending?"

"To be philosophical about it."

"I never studied philosophy."

Sullivan's eyes twinkled. "But you're a history buff . . . ancient history, right?"

Reid pressed his lips together. The man might laugh at his exaggerations, but Reid did happen to know a fair bit about the Ancient Greeks. Like . . . "Aristotle!"

"I'm not sure that qualifies as an entire thought."

"Patience is bitter, but its fruit is sweet," Reid quoted the philosopher. "Or, you know, give me a sec." He turned off the light, shook his phone to candlelight, and turned on classical music.

Sullivan rolled on his back and tucked his arms behind his head. It stretched the sleeves of his dark shirt. His jeans were stretched, too, tight over his thighs and his blatant arousal. Reid set his phone atop *The Titanic*, and straddled Sullivan.

Sullivan's hands cupped his hips, steering him to his thighs.

Bracing a hand on the bed, Reid dipped toward a kiss. He stopped before their lips touched and peered into Sullivan's watchful eyes. "Aristotle suggested that goals are only intermediate goals, and we desire to fulfill them because they help to achieve bigger goals."

Sullivan's voice tickled over Reid's mouth. "What goal do you want to achieve?"

"Tonight?" Reid brushed his lips along Sullivan's jaw to his ear. "I'm shy to admit it."

The hands at Reid's hips tightened knowingly, and Reid let out a shaky breath. Sullivan might need to say no. What he wanted, Sullivan hadn't done since Riley.

Reid braced for disappointment. "I want you to make love with me."

Sullivan's chest expanded.

"We have classical music and candlelight, and Joanna's at a sleepover for the evening."

Sullivan flipped them, weight bearing down on Reid. Reid gasped with the feel of Sullivan's length blanketing him, and he squirmed needily.

Blue eyes shone down on him, the press of their arousals proof Sullivan didn't hate the idea—

"This isn't right." Sullivan swung off him and the bed. He stared at Reid, his expression tense.

Reid's spirits started to sink.

Sullivan clasped Reid's hand and tugged him off the bed. Reid stumbled against him, and Sullivan steadied him with a hand on his waist.

"What do you mean, not right—"

Sullivan cut him off with a kiss, and Reid folded into it.

"Come." With a confident pull, he steered Reid from his nook into Sullivan's cabin.

He shut the door behind them. Reid's pulse galloped as he took in the larger room with its simple wooden furnishings. Shadows laced the cabin, but it wasn't too dark. Light from the marina trickled in through the two portholes onto the made bed.

The bed Reid hadn't seen since . . .

He whirled to face Sullivan, searching his expression. "Are you sure?"

"Yes."

"Yes?"

"Absolutely."

Reid didn't know what to say. "I . . . wow . . . that's jumping a few goals."

"Is that okay?" Sullivan asked.

"More than okay. It's pretty damn perfect." Queasiness rushed through him, and he picked at his bracelet.

"Reid?"

"Now I'm afraid of fucking up."

Sullivan drew him against his chest and kissed his forehead, arms wrapped fiercely around him. "Me too."

Reid felt the shallowness of his breath. Sullivan surrounded him, all warmth and the promise of protection, and it felt more honest and raw and intimate than Reid had ever known to wish.

Sullivan had let him into his room and was guiding Reid with soft kisses onto his firm bed. The walls around them felt loaded with history—guardians that had witnessed Sullivan giving his heart away the first time, and were standing to see it happen again.

This was it.

Reid would have this night imprinted in his mind forever.

If he survived it.

And he wasn't yet sure he could. The way Sullivan's gaze tenderly riveted onto his. The electricity would fry him.

Reid breathed in the fresh, salty scent and he locked his arms around Sullivan's neck, body arching, seeking, pleading.

Shivers scuttled along Reid's skin where Sullivan pushed his hand up his T-shirt. Fingers gripped him with a cool bite and Sullivan thrust against his trapped erection. Oh, God, the way Sullivan's gaze darkened when Reid moaned. He knew he'd be a moaning mess by the end of this.

"Sullivan . . ." Reid said. "Please."

The broken 'please' snapped something inside Sullivan. In

a frenzy, he kissed Reid, deep, like he *needed* to fuse them together.

His lips were everywhere, on his mouth, his chin, his neck. His hands yanked at Reid's clothes, steered him up and down as he pulled them off Reid. First his shirt. Then his socks, his pants, his underwear.

Sullivan's hands warmed, became hot against his skin. He pushed and pulled, groped and squeezed. He growled when their lips had to part.

Sullivan yanked his T-shirt off and tossed it to the floor along with Reid's clothes. He plunged his tongue into Reid's mouth, thrusting with promise, robbing Reid of thought.

There was nothing in that moment but the two of them, and this devastating urge to be closer. As close as they possibly could.

Reid pleaded and begged and it all came out *Sullivan, Sullivan, Sullivan.*

He bit his lip and Sullivan dribbled lube on his fingers. The dark brow he lifted had heat ripping through Reid. Sullivan was so damn confident in bed. So comfortably in charge, and it was so fucking hot.

Light from the portholes shone over the thick hairs at his chest and did insane tricks to his defined stomach. Sullivan crawled between Reid's legs, opening his knees, spreading him. The jeans he wore scratched Reid's smooth inner thighs sinfully, and Reid knew he'd be begging Sullivan to do this to him again, later tonight. Tomorrow night. All the goddamn nights.

Sullivan's mouth on Reid's leaking cock was wet and slick. He sucked and pressed his wet fingers against his asshole.

Reid loved having his cock sucked. Almost as much as he liked sucking Sullivan's. Reid's favorite was Sullivan fucking his throat. *You're a fucking champ. A really good boy.*

Tenderness and heat spiraled in him like a caduceus, ratcheting up his need.

Sullivan gently fucked his ass with his fingers and torturously pulled his mouth off his cock. Reid's cock throbbed in the cool air. "You look sexy, Reid, stretched on my bed. Better than I ever imagined."

"You imagined," Reid murmured, smiling secretly at the ceiling.

Sullivan pulled his fingers from his ass and stripped off his jeans, his underwear. He crawled over Reid, his hard cock bobbing against Reid's stomach. Heavy, leaking, ready to fuse them together.

Reid's breath hitched, and Sullivan sucked it into their kiss. Their gazes locked and butterflies thrashed about in Reid's chest. In his gut.

Sullivan murmured, "I don't think we can go back, after this."

He meant being in this room, sharing this bed. It was so many steps forward, Reid *knew* Sunday would work. The picnic, getting Sullivan to sign the lease, showing Joanna proof they were boyfriends. Telling Sullivan with Reid's audio version of *Second Time Around* that Reid loved him.

Reid searched Sullivan's face. He gripped his cheeks and lifted his head off the pillow to kiss him and press their heads together. "I want a happy ending, Sullivan."

Sullivan kissed him and Reid saw the flash of deeper understanding in his eyes. And maybe, also, the faintest flash of panic.

The thought fled when Sullivan rocked against Reid's aching cock. "Let's work toward that."

Sullivan slicked lube over his cock, and positioned himself, nudging at Reid's entrance. His nerve endings were alight. Reid needed him so badly, he trembled.

Sullivan pushed against his ring. Do it. Fill him up with come.

Reid almost came right then, wanting it so badly.

A needy whimper left him.

"I got you, Reid."

Sullivan inched inside nice and slow, moving patiently, stopping to ask if Reid was okay. Reid braced through the burn, bit his lip, and nodded. He was okay. More than okay. He felt safe, taken care of. He felt incredibly powerful watching Sullivan's expression contort with pleasure.

Reid tilted his hips and whispered, *closer.*

With a groan, Sullivan pushed in to the hilt, and Reid's ass pulsed around him. So stretched. Sullivan so deep inside him.

Reid's synapses came to life, firing electricity twenty-fold with a single look. He felt it in the soles of his feet, his inner thighs, his neck, his cock. God, he felt it there.

He didn't play with his dick. Didn't need to. His muscles relaxed and his thighs spread further apart, and Reid just let go.

He'd be nothing but ash soon.

It couldn't come fast enough.

Sullivan drew out—palmed Reid's inner knee, nailing him in place—and pushed into him again.

Reid moaned and grabbed Sullivan's biceps. Pulling Sullivan toward him, pushing him. He didn't know which, just needed that friction. That unexpected intensity. God, it felt like the beginning of an orgasm. So damn overwhelming.

Hard breaths. Groans.

Garbled pleas. *More. Faster. Harder.*

You're so tight. So deep in you. How do you feel?

Like we could do this forever.

Sullivan thrust and thrust and thrust—a demi-fucking-god over Reid, all rippling muscle and primal fucking. His jaw was clenched. His body slapped against Reid's. The bed groaned and whined under them.

Holy shit, he'd never fucked like this before. He was a writhing, trembling, begging mess under Sullivan.

Reid's cock had never been so hard. He'd never needed to come so badly.

He still needed more.

Sullivan would have to gag him next time. He was noisy, needy. He begged, he whimpered, and he couldn't help it.

Sullivan pushed in deep, swiveled his hips, and kissed Reid fervently. "You're so fucking beautiful. I'm gonna do you again tonight. Tomorrow night. All the goddamn nights."

Reid moaned. He'd never felt so connected. So cherished. So perfectly used.

More.

Sullivan snapped into him wildly, rubbing hard and fast on his prostate. Reid's leaking dick slid against Sullivan's stomach, and Reid combusted.

Come shot out of him, pleasure crashing all around Reid. It kept going and going as Sullivan chased his orgasm. Ash. Ash. Ash.

Reid clasped Sullivan's back, urging him to take what he needed. Sullivan's breath grew ragged and their lips locked. Sullivan grunted heavily into Reid's mouth, thundering through Reid.

Sullivan pulsed inside him, stiffening.

His orgasm seemed to rip through him hard and long, and Sullivan squeezed his wrist, thumb pressed against his bracelet.

Sullivan's spent cock slipped out, leaving Reid vulnerably empty. As if Sullivan understood, he rolled off and pulled Reid onto his side, holding him close, face to face. Reid's come dribbled down his chest, but he didn't care. Their breaths mingled and they looked at each other, amazed at the place they'd gone together.

Sullivan grabbed Reid's leg and steered it over his hip. He cupped his nape and pressed their noses together.

"Happiness is a state of activity."

Reid vaguely recognized the Aristotle quote, and laughed. "Back to philosophizing?"

Sullivan hummed, and continued matter-of-factly, "And right now, I think we nailed it."

Reid snorted and buried his face against Sullivan's warm chest. "We definitely did that."

Reid spent all day Saturday finishing his recorded gift for Sullivan, and come Sunday, Joanna's birthday, he was a frightful, purple-haired bundle of nerves.

"What's that?" Sullivan eyed the business-sized envelope containing the lease extension on the counter next to their picnic basket.

Reid drummed his fingers over it. "This is for you."

Curiosity sparked in Sullivan's eye and he sidled nearer.

"To open *after* our outing," Reid explained. When, hopefully, it was clear how much Sullivan meant to him. The way he'd silently absorbed Reid's spray-on purple hair had hinted Sullivan might have an idea where this day was moving.

The way he'd smiled told him he liked it.

Sullivan reached for the envelope. "Or before?"

Reid blocked his hand, and his laugh rumbled nervously. His whole body felt like it was being tossed on a breeze. Exhilarating. "Definitely after."

Sullivan dipped his cold nose to his ear. "I think you've declared war."

If there was any declaring today, it would not be of war.

Reid slipped the envelope into his back pocket. "Don't even think about it."

By the gleam in Sullivan's eye, it was clear he was thinking about it.

Reid had two goals for the day. Make Sullivan understand how much he meant to Reid. And when he was sure Sullivan knew, hand over the contract.

"It's beautiful," Reid murmured.

Sullivan leaned against the counter. "What is?"

These feelings for you. "The rush of stepping off a cliff."

Sullivan's brow furrowed. "What exactly did you buy Joanna for her birthday?"

Reid felt the contract in his pocket. "You'll find out."

Sullivan glanced around them, and finding them alone, stole a spirited kiss, fingers gripping Reid's hair. "If it were just us, I'd tie you up under the stars and do pleasurably torturous things to you until you told me everything."

Reid hardened in his jeans and almost whimpered away his secrets right there. "That's playing unfair."

Sullivan clasped his erection and spoke low in his ear. "Who said war was fair?"

Joanna bounced into the room, on her phone. Reid kept his back to her until he'd settled down.

"I've invited my boyfriend on our trip, too." She said 'my boyfriend' with emphasis. Like she wanted to make a point. Maybe show Sullivan how easily it could be said. "So I have someone my own age to hang with."

The sparkle in her eye said it was all part of the plan.

Sullivan bristled. Reid hid a fond chuckle. This fatherly protectiveness made him melt. "Which trip are you talking about? I'll allow the picnic, but he is not coming on our trip to the stars."

"He's not the only one," Reid said. Sullivan squinted at him, and Reid threw up his arms. "What? You know how much the open water freaks me out."

"You have your bracelet," Sullivan said.

"It's like you've forgotten what a chicken I was when you kidnapped me."

"You were fine. You didn't even throw up."

"I was throwing up on the inside."

Joanna stared at Reid in disbelief. "I thought this day was all about showing how much you . . . love me."

How much he loved them both.

"Yes," Reid stared back at her. "Your birthday present will show that."

The challenge in her eyes melted. "Yeah, you're right. I'm sure it will. I know it will."

Reid gestured for Sullivan to pick up the picnic basket. Keep his hands busy and Reid's free to protect his pockets. "Let's start this party, people."

SO MUCH FOR THE CAVE.

Turns out it'd been cordoned off by the ranger out of safety concerns. The winter had been hard and rock had shifted. Mud and rock had blocked most of the cave's entrance. Was this a bad omen?

Despite Joanna and Elijah's adorable chatter and the sunshine warming Reid's skin, Reid felt ridiculously on edge.

"Would you look at all that . . . what's it called?" Sullivan mused, staring at the upturned earth. His eyes brightened far too much. "Solid, unmoving ground."

Reid deflated. It wasn't always awesome when Sullivan quoted him. "I guess nowhere is a hundred percent safe."

An elbow bumped into his ribs. "Does this mean you'll come with us later?"

Reid narrowed *hell no* eyes on him.

Sullivan gave him a lopsided smirk. "I hope you change your mind."

They started toward the car and Reid felt Sullivan close behind him. Too close.

He whipped around and Sullivan raised his arms, amused and frustrated. Reid patted his ass, making sure the contract was still there. It was.

He might have given it to him if Sullivan had groped his ass in front of Joanna, but as it was, she'd run ahead with Elijah to the parking lot.

Reid slapped his ass and grinned up at Sullivan. "I'm not sure you're ready for all this."

Sullivan's boot crunched on twigs and thumped on packed dirt as he closed the gap between them. He leaned down and Reid inhaled his scent. It was as if he took a part of the ocean wherever he went.

Hot breath fluttered over the top of his ear. "I sure was last night."

Reid's asshole throbbed, greedily remembering the last two nights of Sullivan absolutely wrecking him.

Sullivan nipped his throat teasingly and hiked off.

Reid swore under his breath, adjusting himself. He'd either declare his love or kill him.

THEY ARRIVED BACK ON THE *AQUARIAN* AND REID UNPACKED alongside a bubbling Joanna.

He raked an eye over Sullivan across the table, searching for any sign he understood the significance of the eggplant pasta, the muffins, the elderflower liqueur.

Sullivan scanned their feast and plucked the party hat from Reid's head.

Moisture still clung to his dark hair, and it complemented him. Fresh.

Blue eyes that earlier brimmed with arousal had softened to

fondness. His lips kicked up into a small smile, and Reid's gaze dropped to them. Dark pink and sweet. Sullivan's last kiss gave Reid a phantom tickle and he licked his lips.

It had been playful, that kiss.

It had been all kinds of hopeful.

It spoke a vision of the future. Them in twenty years, teasing and blunt and full of warm pressing lips.

Joanna grabbed a plate, piled on some muffins, and towed Elijah toward her cabin.

"Where are you going?" Sullivan demanded.

Reid knew where this was going. But he had expected she'd let them put a candle in a muffin for her to blow out first.

"I'm going to kiss my boyfriend." She stopped, and poor Elijah didn't know the web he was caught in, burning red beside her. "Unless you want us to do it out here?" she offered, smiling brightly at her dad. "Where you can see us."

For .3 seconds, Reid legitimately feared for Elijah's life. Then Sullivan shuddered and jerked a finger toward her room. "Door stays open so I know exactly what's happening."

Joanna might as well have cackled the way her eyes glittered. "Oh, trust me. The door is staying wide open."

Reid hoped she overheard everything she wanted to.

They left, and Reid didn't know how many more flutters in his stomach he could handle. Sullivan shifted, bench groaning as he settled into it. Paper rustled as he donned Reid's resume party hat. Each sound prickled more goosebumps at his nape.

He sat his weak legs down, shoveled some pasta onto his plate and scooped a piece of eggplant. He sucked it into his mouth.

Without taking his eyes off Reid, Sullivan picked up the elderflower liqueur and poured them both a half sip. "The only thing that's missing is you clutching your life vest."

Sullivan understood the meaning of the picnic, then.

Reid took the offered half shot and downed it. "And

blowing your whistle," he added. Wait. Did that sound dirty? His gaze snapped to Sullivan, who struggled not to laugh. "Oh my God," he said in hushed tones, "every time I've fiddled with my whistle, your mind has gone places, hasn't it?"

"Let's not forget the time you asked to swap whistles. I had to leave, Reid."

"I have been clueless."

"Yes."

"Very clueless."

"The clueless-est."

Energy snapped in his veins and Reid stood. Sullivan's eyebrow lifted.

"I'm not clueless anymore," Reid said, voice hitching.

Sullivan rounded the table. He planted steadying hands on Reid's shoulders, steering Reid until they faced. "Are you okay?"

The boat bobbed underfoot. Reid's heart pounded. "I have something for you."

Sullivan rubbed his thumbs along Reid's collar bone. "I'm not sure you understand how this works. It's *Joanna's* birthday."

"I sent you money."

"Should I put it in her account?"

Reid was blurting this all out wrong. "No, I mean I returned your last payment."

Sullivan's thumbs stopped moving. "What are you saying, Reid?"

"Have you ever been driving and startled to find you've reached your destination and have no idea how you got there?"

Sullivan lifted one of his hands off Reid and rubbed his nape. His voice came out soft. Defeated, almost. "Yes, while so lost in other thoughts. Other worries. The body took over and worked automatically to take me where I needed to go."

Their gazes held. No cluelessness here. "It's kind of scary and amazing, isn't it?"

"Definitely both those things."

"So, I find myself at this destination. We're both there, and neither one knows quite how we arrived. But we have. We've been standing there, pretending we're still on the road, and . . ." Reid waved a hand at the table of objects symbolizing their relationship. "I guess it's time we studied our map and see the route we've taken." He looked up at Sullivan. "It's time to sign-post where we are."

Sullivan's other hand drifted over his shoulder, running down his arm.

Reid's voice wavered, "It's not best friends with benefits. It definitely means you stop paying me a wage."

He pulled out his phone, and pulled up his audio-player app. "And because I'm a Cancer and need to show you how much I feel, I made you this. I've emailed you a copy."

Sullivan's voice was barely a whisper. "What is it?"

Reid set the phone on the table and pressed play. His voice jumped from the speaker, bringing Sam Baton's words from *Second Time Around* to life. He adjusted the volume to a low murmur, enough for Sullivan to hear, not enough for Joanna to.

"I know how insanely addicted you are to Sam Baton's books and I wanted you to have the one that wasn't on audio."

Second Time Around, a love story. Dedicated to my husband. Just in case.

Sullivan swallowed, Adam's apple bobbing. His eyes . . . God, they glistened. "You read out every word?"

Reid's pulse thundered. He nodded.

"Oh, God, Reid. *Reid.*" The thickness in Sullivan's voice robbed Reid of his next heartbeat.

Reid lifted his arms around Sullivan's neck and spoke in his ear. "The envelope in my back pocket? It contains the lease extension for Dock J."

Sullivan quaked in his arms.

Reid brushed his lips against the rough skin of Sullivan's jaw. "I want you to sign it."

Sullivan shook his head.

Frowning, Reid pulled back a few inches. "We've got one day left before Alanis gives the spot away."

"I know," Sullivan said quietly.

"If it's not clear already, I want to live here with you."

"I know. I can picture it. Us. Together. A family." Sullivan trembled again.

Reid took a careful breath. The butterflies in his belly stopped fluttering, and dread took their place. He spoke carefully, "There will never be enough time to overcome your loss, Sullivan. You will always love and miss Riley."

Devastated blue eyes held his. "But there will be all the time in the world to fear it happening again."

"Happening again—"

"With you."

"Sullivan—"

Sullivan pulled back a step, scoring a rough hand through his hair. "I thought I was a strong man. Unwaveringly sure. But look at me."

"You are strong, Sullivan. It's okay not to be, too."

"I can't lose you, Reid. I can't go there again."

"Setting off is the solution?"

"I want to protect everyone. Joanna. You. Me."

Reid gritted his teeth, saddened. "You can't control everything. Sometimes you have to let go and hope for the best."

He'd envisioned telling Sullivan he loved him a hundred times. Even though he'd feared Sullivan wouldn't respond the same way, he'd hoped Sullivan would. What they shared was so unlike any relationship Reid had experienced, he'd hoped it would end happily.

A tear glimmered in Sullivan's eye.

Sympathy lurched up Reid's throat, seizing it. Was this what unleashing Sullivan's storm looked like?

The thought flooded Reid with courage. Maybe if he category-fived now, he could truly settle. Reid pulled the envelope from his pocket and pushed it against Sullivan's chest. "Sullivan. Please. Sign the contract."

Sullivan's eyes were glazed, unfocused. He stared toward the table, where Reid's recorded voice spoke about the devastating shock of losing the love of your life.

On second thought, playing this story from the beginning wasn't the smartest idea.

Reid gave a panicked jump and punched the screen, dragging the scroll to the middle of the story.

Sullivan's hum sounded broken. He looked at Reid like he was fighting to reach him. "Riley would have chosen you. If he were here to tell me who I should move on with, he would have hated you. But he would have chosen you for me."

"He'd have hated me?"

Sullivan spoke emphatically. "Because I want you. I want you in my life desperately. I want you in my bed, and flailing about in the kitchen. I want to protect you and keep you safe. Riley would have hated you because you're so goddamn perfect for me. He would have chosen you, because you're so goddamn perfect for me."

A strangled sound escaped Sullivan's throat. "God. These feelings. They're too much." His eyes shuttered. "Turn it off."

"The story? Or your feelings?"

"Both."

Reid did neither. He braced for Sullivan's anger, dropped to his knees, and picked up the contract off the floor. He lifted his head to Sullivan and was aware how much it appeared like he was begging. Hell, he was.

Keep unleashing, Sullivan.

Then we move on.

"It's for one more year," Reid said, offering the contract. "We could try it."

"Turn it off. Turn. It. Off."

"Why?" Reid demanded, holding himself back from crying. "This is me saying I love you."

"This is you reading out my dead husband's words."

Reid felt like he'd been kicked in the sternum. "What?"

"Sam Baton is—was—my husband's pseudonym." Sullivan turned off the audio himself. The silence felt heavy. "*That* is the reason I never wanted you to open the door."

It made painful sense now.

Reid pushed to his feet shakily. "I'm sorry. I warned you I was never the hero." He hesitated. "I wish I'd known. I wouldn't have confronted you about it today." Sullivan inclined his head, accepting his words. Reid stepped closer. His whisper broke, "I would have done it months ago."

He slipped the contract into Sullivan's hands until Sullivan scrunched it in a fist.

"Reid, I'm so sorry."

There was something achingly final about Sullivan's tone. Reid had heard it before. He knew what it preceded. The words spilled from his throat like they scraped against sandpaper. "Sorry for what?"

Sullivan didn't say it.

Pain lanced through Reid. Sullivan took Reid's hand in his. "You are everything, Reid."

But this won't work.

He'd heard these starters too many times before.

Reid stumbled back, lungs barely managing to take the punch. The laugh he gave ached. "Yeah. I've gotta go."

"Wait. I meant you deserve better—" Sullivan was cut off from Joanna storming into the saloon, crying.

"That was not the birthday present I asked for!"

Sullivan chased after Reid, but Reid was already slipping into his shoes. Grabbing his coat. Wallet.

His eyes fucking burned.

"Reid—"

Reid spun around and hoped he was smiling. "When you look at the stars tonight, check if Cancer is broken."

"Fuck. Reid, listen. It's not *you*, it's me—"

The words bowled into Reid, throwing him onto the deck and off the *Aquarian*. He staggered on the dock, each failure pressing down on him. He didn't convince Sullivan to stay at the marina, didn't become the confidant he'd thought he was, didn't find Sullivan his perfect match.

Didn't save the family.

He was thirteen all over again. Devastated, hurt, confused.

He unhooked the ropes mooring the yacht and threw them on deck. Stupid restraints. They were meant to be secure. Make it safe. What a lot of good it had done.

Tears slipped down his cheeks. He fished out his safety whistle and tossed it at Sullivan, while Joanna pulled at his arm. "Good bye."

He walked out of the marina, each step cracking his heart.

"My first love was perfect. I didn't think I'd ever have a second one."

-James to David
Second Time Around

Chapter Seventeen

With blurring vision, Reid bussed to Kings Café.

He sank lengthwise onto his L-shaped couch, palms swatting tears.

Coming here was supposed to help. The bright walls, the Elvis pictures, the chatter of customers.

It had always helped before.

This time the creamy scent of coffee reminded him of Sullivan's addiction to the beverage. Reminded him of their oat-milk cappuccinos. Reminded him of Thanksgiving, and the first time they saw each other.

God, here. Right on this spot where his back met the couch, Sullivan had sat. The geeky demigod whose heavy ocean-blue gaze had ploughed into him so hard it made his nerves jump.

They hadn't stopped jumping since.

Reid shut his eyes and felt Sullivan's presence under him like a ghost. Loss sliced its sharp fingers through Reid.

Sullivan was everything Reid wanted in a person. Protective, intelligent, candid, surprising.

Even if he was also stubborn and uneasy about expressing emotion.

He showed how much he cared in other ways.

Reid felt for his nausea bracelet and stilled as his fingers met smooth skin. He bolted upright, knocking the cappuccino Wesley must have quietly delivered him, and frowned at his bare wrist. His bracelet must have fallen off. He was so lost in his hurt, he hadn't noticed. Fuck. He loved that pseudo-leather and the metal ball that pressed into his wrist.

A shiver rattled his bones.

He felt naked without it, stripped bare, vulnerable.

Reid rubbed the paler skin and sank defeated into the couch cushions, where he was reliving everything Sullivan said. Dissecting it word for word. Drowning in the aftermath of the storm.

This is me saying I love you.

This is you reading out my dead husband's words.

The snick of heels across the tile and familiar female voices had Reid jerking his head up. Loretta and Natalie moved purposefully toward him, pity in their big brown eyes.

"Wesley calling you to rescue me a tradition now?" he said, ending on a hiccup.

Natalie smiled weakly, and Loretta shook her head. "You look deep in despair."

"No, I'm dead." That's what it felt like in his chest.

Loretta slung herself to his side, Natalie perched on the other. Subtle perfume invaded his nose and the familiar hit made him crush Loretta into a hug. They hadn't seen each other for six months. Hadn't talked since her hard honesty over the phone.

She patted his back, and he jumbled out a string of words. "You helped me see the light."

Loretta pulled back, preening. "Can you say that again?" She glanced over his shoulder at Natalie. "A bit louder?"

Natalie snickered. "Oh, Loretta. You are such an attention-seeking Leo."

Loretta tossed her hair and mimed a sexy cat. "Meow."

Reid groaned. "You were supposed to be helping me feel better."

Loretta mouthed "Later" to Natalie, and nudged Reid's foot with her boot. "What happened?"

Tears prickled his eyes. "You helped me see the light; I was afraid I wouldn't be enough for him. Turns out I'm not."

Loretta frowned and clasped a manicured hand on his shoulder. She dug the nail of her thumb against the tender hickey at his neck. "Tell me precisely what happened."

Reid scrubbed his puffy face, and recounted the moment word for word. Each one tearing at his chest, until he was choking on the memory of Sullivan's last words '*It's not you, it's me.*'

Natalie rubbed his back. "I will never understand the minds of men."

Reid pulled back. "Huh?"

Loretta was nodding in agreement. "Sullivan wants you too much? That's why it's over?"

"Well . . . you heard the other parts, right?"

Loretta gestured to Reid's latte. "Take a good gulp of coffee, and tell me your story again."

Reid picked up his coffee and drank. Oat milk. Wesley had made it with oat milk because Reid had made it his go-to order whenever he came here with Sullivan. Because he didn't mind this vegan business so much, after all. Because sometime in the last months, he'd embraced it as much as he had embraced everything about the Bells.

He gripped the cup and his mind flashed to Sullivan, drinking from his ugly mug, and—

God, he was stupid. *Stupid.*

He drank the beverage until nothing was left. The coffee was cold, but warmth flurried at the pit of his stomach.

He met Loretta's eye. "Once upon a time, there was a misadventure-prone manny who fell for a widowed captain . . ." Reid bit his lip, tasting coffee and under it, Sullivan's last kiss. He sucked in an achy breath. "A widowed captain who fell for his misadventure-prone manny."

Reid grabbed his phone, fingers frantically swiping. "I have to get my happily ever after back."

Loretta and Natalie took that as their cue to give him space and left.

Reid called Sullivan's phone. "Come on, Sullivan. Pick up."

He didn't.

Reid tried Joanna.

Patrons chatted against soft Elvis music. Wesley had taken a moment off the coffee machines and was coercing Lloyd to dance with him. A burst of freshly baked cookie scent wafted around him. Everything about the café was cozy, and Reid had never felt more homesick.

Pick up. Please. Please.

Joanna's voice cut through the background noise. "Reid?"

Reid's heart lurched, momentarily gagging him.

Her voice came out strangled, like she'd been crying. He hated it. "Is this a goodbye call? Will Dad leave again?"

Reid dumbly shook his head. His tongue clicked against the roof of his mouth. "No, Joanna. No. What's Sullivan been telling you?"

"Nothing.

"Really? Nothing?"

"Dad helped Elijah off the boat and then we took off." Her

sigh tumbled down the line. "He's locked himself in the cockpit and he's listening to someone who sounds an awful lot like you. I think he's . . . sobbing, Reid."

Oh, God.

She continued, "I messed up. I never meant to hurt him. I don't know what to do."

Reid throat seized and his heart gave a painful thump. "Joanna? I need you to listen to me."

She sniffed. "I loved what we had. I don't want it to change."

"I know I ran away and I'm sorry, I shouldn't have. But your dad isn't going anywhere."

"He isn't?"

"I *know* he isn't" Reid was on his feet, murmuring his plan.

No more drowning his sorrows in coffee. He'd set out after Sullivan, or drown trying.

"I THOUGHT YOU WERE HEADING OFF WITH SULLIVAN AND Joanna?" Alanis said.

She was locking up the main office. She pivoted in his direction, revealing a figure-hugging dress that suggested she had a date tonight.

Reid jogged the last steps toward her, limbs aching from his run from the bus stop. "Alanis. Alanis," he said, out of breath. "You don't know how relieved I am to catch you."

"You have my phone number"—she squinted at his tear-streaked face—"Care to explain the mood?"

"I'm in one. An anticipative one. The most anticipative mood of my life."

"And you need me? Wait, are you getting me to flirt with Sullivan again?"

"Never."

"Because I would, you know."

Reid clasped his hands together, praying. Begging. "I need something bigger."

"Bigger?"

"Much bigger."

"How big are we talking?"

"Boat big. I need to see Sullivan. Tonight."

Alanis's eye caught on someone behind Reid and she waved her hand, signaling two minutes. "Have you called him? I'm sure he'd turn back."

"He's not answering his phone. He might not hear it—Joanna said he's . . . preoccupied."

Alanis slid the key back into the lock. "I'll radio him."

Reid stilled her hand and helped withdraw the key. "It's important *I* go to *him*."

Her brow quivered with curiosity, and she sighed. "My baby is on the hard."

That sounded vaguely familiar and he was completely lost. "I don't know what that means."

"For someone who works at a marina, you're oblivious."

"Something I will definitely work on. But not tonight. Please?"

"On the hard." Alanis pointed toward the dockyard, to the boats that had been on stilts over the winter.

Shit, this heart-pounding achiness was messing with his head. He'd had coffee with her last week and had to climb onboard via a ladder.

"Sorry, Reid. She goes back into the water next week."

Reid threw his head toward the setting sky. The same sky Sullivan might be staring out at, through clouded eyes.

God, Reid needed to be there. "Is there a motorboat or something?"

She laughed. "Oh, are you serious?"

"Alanis!"

"I can't let you near any vessel you have to drive—I can't let you near any vessel."

Reid made a choked sound of frustration, and Alanis continued, "But I have an idea who can help you."

ALANIS SAID SHE'D MAKE A CALL FOR HIM ON HER WAY TO THE movies with Troy, and Reid raced to Dock AA, and *Glinda*.

"Mason!"

Elijah's big brother was leaning against the deck railing, staring toward the still harbor, talking to someone on his phone —Alanis, Reid guessed.

Mason ended his call, swiveling toward the dock where Reid bounced anxiously on the balls of his feet. "Why, hello Reid."

Puffed, Reid's voice came out husky. "I need a favor."

Mason beckoned Reid up the gangplank.

Reid had never raced up one so fast.

Mason eyed Reid's getup. Jeans, the striped T-shirt that looked like the *Aquarian* interior, and an unzipped hoodie. The rest of him was no doubt flushed, too.

"I need a favor, Mason." Reid cleared his throat.

Mason leaned against the side of the cockpit. Reid stood in the shadows, gaze pleading.

"You're more forward than I thought," Mason said, voice low. Creamy. He curled a finger for Reid to come closer. "But I like giving favors."

Reid sighed in relief, eagerly moving toward him. "Thank God. I'm desperate!"

Mason eyed Reid up and down. "You want the favor now?"

Possibly not the best boat gear, but Reid couldn't care less. "I'll explode otherwise. Can't wait a minute more."

Mason shifted sharply. “Let me get Elijah settled in his bedroom. Then I’ll . . . take the helm.” He winked.

“Alanis told you what I need?”

Mason paused, brow furrowing. “Is she your keeper?”

“My savior. She was the one who suggested you help me out.”

Mason seemed surprised. “I totally owe her one.” His phone shrilled, and Mason answered it. “Yes, Reid just got here.”

The enthusiasm in Mason’s expression died and he slammed his eyes shut, chuckling. “Oh. That kind of favor.”

What kind of favor had he—oh. *Oh.*

Mason slipped the phone into his pocket. “Sorry, Mason. I need to get to Sullivan.”

Mason didn’t quite meet Reid’s eye. “Sullivan, eh? I guess I should have seen it.”

“There’s rampant cluelessness. Maybe it’s the marina air.”

Mason laughed and motioned Reid to follow him. “Might not be my ever-after, but I’d never begrudge anyone theirs.”

“You’re a good guy, Mason.”

“Do you have co-ordinates where to find your man?”

“Will Joanna’s tracking location work?” Reid handed over his phone with the active link Joanna had sent him. Wingerham Bay.

“An hour and a half trip,” Mason said. “You ready for this?”

Reid didn’t have his safety whistle. Didn’t have his nausea bracelet. Didn’t have Sullivan.

He sucked in a nerve-rattling breath. “Yes.”

When Reid said he was ready for this, he meant mentally. Emotionally.

Physically, he was quaking in his shoes, clutching the padded seat under him in the cockpit.

Mason had steered out of the harbor after a stalled start, Elijah sitting behind them texting Joanna non-stop, and while they'd been piloting strong the first hour, the last half hour felt slow.

The water was still, inky in the growing darkness, and boat light beamed over its surface.

Reid breathed in the salty air and the scent of his own fear.

Mason tried to distract Reid from his worries by telling him boating stories.

". . . and I once saw a couple of sharks around here. Mom and her baby, I think. Quite the sight. Nature is a miracle, truly." The yacht stalled again, and Mason tried to restart. "Ahead, Reid. There's another sight for you."

Reid's heart jumped at a familiar boat in the distance, toward the moon-crescent bay.

"Won't engage," Mason mused after a splutter and failed start. He frowned. "Could be a loose connection or low battery. I'll take a look."

Reid wasn't sure what Mason was talking about, only that the yacht wasn't moving, and he was a hundred yards from Sullivan.

"How long will it take?"

"Depends on what the problem is. You can always prepare the dinghy and row out."

Row out? With oars, in a flimsy shell of a boat? On the *open water*?

Fear churned in his gut, and his breathing turned funky. But it didn't stop him shooting up from his seat.

This was what Reid wanted. Needed. It was time to put his needs first. "Can you radio him? I need to speak with him now."

Mason used his VHF radio to hail the *Aquarian*. No dice.

That wasn't good enough. He needed to be there. He eyed the distance. Hell, if Sullivan were looking in this direction, he'd see them. "Flash your lights?"

Sullivan's voice came through the radio. Reid grabbed the transmitter off Mason. "I'm coming home."

He handed it back, stomach flipping. "Rowing is an option?"

Mason blinked. "I mean, sure. Use the dinghy. You'll have to manually row her, though."

"Okay. Okay. Okay," Reid said. "Upper arm strength. I can do this."

"Or you can wait."

"No. No, I can't." Reid moved around the deck, thanking Mason for his help as he lowered the dinghy and helped Reid into it.

The boat wobbled under him and he quickly sat, bracing his hands on the sides of the boat. Water rippled around him as black as the sky. Blacker.

His limbs shook.

Mason's brow arched, questioningly.

Reid swallowed and offered him a meek smile. He could do this. He would. He had to.

Mason gave Reid a life vest and instructed him on the best way to row. Reid shivered in the open air, the boat bobbing under him.

He beheld the warmly lit *Aquarian* and steeled his nerve. "Time to do this."

Holy fucking shit. He was on the open water. On a tiny boat that rocked with the slightest breeze.

Keep rowing.

Reid pushed a paddle into the inky-black, shark-infested

water. More sport than he thought, than he was used to. His arms were screaming.

He shouldn't have looked back. He was only a quarter through.

If he could go back ten minutes, he'd tell himself he had the arm strength of an ant, and this was an absolutely stupid thing to do.

But he'd also tell himself it had to be done nevertheless.

He could be warm and comfortable and safe later. Right now he had to lean into the fear and conquer it.

Something bumped against the boat. Driftwood?

He shut his eyes and drove his paddles forward, pulling harder. Not a shark, not a shark, not a—fuck, what if it *was* a shark?

He choked on a salty breeze and cursed the stars above. Cancer must be cracking up laughing at him. Or pulling out the *no relation* card and slinking quietly away.

Reid paddled himself forward with panicked flailing of his limbs.

Sullivan. Joanna. Reid. Sullivan. Joanna. Reid.

He pushed on. Halfway.

Someone yelled his name.

Reid glimpsed Sullivan's figure at the stern of the *Aquarian*. He stood at the rail, smack-bang in the middle of the deck.

He wore a coat and stared hard toward him. Deck light haloed his outline but darkened his features, his expression, and Reid rowed harder to see it.

As the dinghy neared, Reid's heart thumped so hard he feared it might capsize his boat. Sullivan's gaze scrolled over him.

He looked tired and worried and hopeful.

Emotion was a good look on him.

"Sullivan." Reid stopped rowing a half dozen yards away

and grinned at his boyfriend. "We're campaigning for stupidest couple of the year, huh?"

Sullivan leaned on his elbows, relief washing over his expression. He spoke with signature bluntness. "I have the strangest urge to remind you I'm a Bell. An inventor. Which is entirely irrelevant."

Reid rocked a brow. "That's what you lead with? Your emotional competence astounds me."

Sullivan tapped his chest. "I'm full of it."

"Full of it, all right."

They gazed fondly at each other, and Reid lurched to his feet. "Sullivan, I—" The boat jerked under him at his sudden move and Reid had the horrible sensation of losing hold of gravity. He flung his weight sharply to the other side. Overcorrected.

"—fuuuuck."

The boat tipped sideways and he hit the cold ocean. Salty water walloped over his head. His life vest steered him upward and he breached the surface spluttering, gasping for air.

Sullivan tossed him a rope and Reid grabbed it, clothes heavy. So. Cold.

Sullivan had him out of the water in under thirty seconds.

"Mason's dinghy . . ." Reid said, shivering as Sullivan pulled him urgently inside the saloon.

He helped yank off Reid's drenched shoes. "I don't give a fuck about his dinghy."

A different kind of shiver robbed Reid's voice of steadiness. "You and me, we've been a comedy of errors."

Sullivan pulled off Reid's soaking hoodie and it slapped wetly to the floor. "Arms up. Would we call it a comedy?"

Off came Reid's T-shirt. Purple hair coloring dripped from his hair, running in rivulets over his face and down his chest. Sullivan grabbed a dishtowel and scrubbed his hair dry, then snapped open the button of his jeans and thumbed into the waist, scrunching the wet material down.

Shock slowly subsiding, Reid spotted Joanna, mouth agape, watching from the couch.

He gulped and slanted Sullivan a panicked look. He was all about showing Joanna what they meant to each other, but getting naked seemed like taking it a step too far. "What are you doing?"

Sullivan continued shoving down his jeans. "I thought this moment was about showing growth. About becoming smarter." Sullivan steered Reid's feet out. "I'm undressing you. Joanna? Would you mind leaving me and my boyfriend alone for a few minutes?"

Joanna lunged to her feet, swiping at her eyes. Smiling through a sniff. "Sure, Dad. Is he okay?"

Sullivan stood. "I hope he will be."

Reid swallowed.

Joanna left, and Sullivan touched the elastic of the underwear icing Reid's balls. *Can I?* His eyes seemed to ask.

"You can peel back all my layers, if I can peel back yours?"

Sullivan hooked his gaze. "I'd like that."

Reid's underwear came off, and Sullivan stripped out of his shirt and pulled it over Reid. Soft warmth cushioned around his limbs and Sullivan steered him to the couch, throwing a blanket over his legs.

Sullivan settled on his knees before Reid, rolling his hands up and down Reid's numb thighs. Who knew the water could be that knife-stabbingly freezing?

Er, other than Leonardo DiCaprio.

"Still cold," Reid said, and Sullivan turned a space heater toward the couch.

Reid bit his lip. "Not quite what I meant, Sullivan."

Sullivan frowned, and then chuckled. He stripped off his pants and sat behind Reid, pulling him tight into his body heat.

Reid sank into his embrace with a sigh, placing his hands on Sullivan's forearms where they were strapped across his waist. "We made a right mess of Joanna's birthday."

"Yes. We'll have to make it up to her." Sullivan crushed Reid close, breathing him in. "I know a way."

Signing the lease extension.

Reid started to speak and stopped at Joanna's excited voice trailing from her bedroom.

"Holy crap, Elijah. You should have seen him. I've never seen my dad move so fast. One moment he's wallowing in the cockpit, the next he's yelling at the heavens to 'bloody well not let him fall overboard.' It's funny, because he used to say the opposite."

Reid angled his head. Sullivan's eyes absorbed him.

Joanna continued, ". . . the drama! Did you see it? Reid falling in the water? Dad pulled him inside. Looked like a drowned cat. Reid, that is." She paused. "Both of them, actually."

Reid sucked in a smile, and Sullivan's hand drifted to his cheek. The tender sweep of Sullivan's thumb over his skin and Sullivan's furious blinking had Reid turning his head to kiss Sullivan's palm—

Something leathery hit his mouth and he snatched Sullivan's arm.

Reid's nausea band. Sullivan had found it and clasped it on his own wrist.

He pressed Sullivan's arm against his chest, over his cantering heart.

The nausea and overwhelming fear had subsided—for the most part.

Sullivan whispered into his damp hair. "Reid. How I acted earlier, what I said—"

"No, you don't know what you said. Because that's the pain *I* keep bottling in." Reid trembled and Sullivan rubbed soothing circles at his chest. "'It's not you, it's me.' Those were the last words my dad said to me."

Sullivan stiffened. "And I used them."

"Yes," Reid croaked.

Sullivan pulled back, and Reid's chest heaved at the tears rimming his favorite blue eyes. "I hurt you. Oh, God, Reid. I'm sorry. So goddamn sorry."

Reid touched a pearling tear and let it soak into his thumb. "I know."

"Your audiobook surprised me, shocked me. It was too much for me to reason and understand at once, I—"

"*Unleashed*." Reid smiled sympathetically. "Feelings are messy, remember? You can't control everything."

Sullivan's Adam's apple jutted with a swallow. "I didn't want you to leave. Then I thought perhaps we needed space, to sort our heads. Our . . . hearts."

Reid watched another tear form in Sullivan's eye. He wasn't looking at James from *Second Time Around*, but the essence of his inner conflict was the same as Sullivan's. Almost like Riley had written it as a hypothetical story. A love letter to Sullivan telling him he wanted him to move on.

Even Riley had known it wouldn't be easy for him.

But he'd also known Sullivan would eventually figure it out.

"I promised Joanna to take her out," Sullivan explained, "and I know you hate being on the open water . . . I always intended on continuing our discussion. I *never* would have said those words if . . ."

"I know, Sullivan."

"You know?"

"Yes. I know everything."

Sullivan's lips twisted wryly. "Know everything, do you?"

Reid swiveled around and straddled Sullivan's thighs, meeting him eye to eye. Sullivan instinctively pulled him in, close, arms strong at Reid's back.

"What do you know?" Sullivan asked.

"It *is* you. Not me."

Sullivan inclined his head and opened his mouth to reply.

Reid stooped and kissed him quietly, letting his lips linger against Sullivan's warm ones. "I know three other things." He kissed Sullivan. "Riley will always be your first love." Another kiss. "You are allowed to be scared." Kiss. "I'm your second time around."

Sullivan cupped his cheeks. "I was afraid you might steal my heart, and I knew I'd give it to you."

Their kiss was soft, and tender, and Reid pulled back. "Your love is not why I chased after you tonight, though."

"Why did you row through your fears to get me then?"

"To give you mine. I love you, Sullivan. I also love me." He held Sullivan's calm blue eyes. Cuffed Sullivan's wrist with his bracelet. "This is my family. You, and Joanna, and me. I'll row after you every day of my life, I'm not letting you go."

"And that, Reid, makes you my hero."

"Whatever the price. Being with you is worth it."

-James
Second Time Around

Chapter Eighteen

JUNE, THREE MONTHS LATER

Reid curled onto his side, grabbed Sullivan's pillow, and shoved it over his head.

It didn't stop the horrendous noise coming from under the bed. "Up you get."

Reid waved a merry middle finger in the direction of his boyfriend, then snuggled into sheets that smelled of Sullivan and the sexy times they'd had last night.

Air rippled over his skin as Sullivan tugged the sheet to his legs. Reid peeked out under the edge of the pillow.

Sullivan stood, legs spread, arms crossed, eyes pinned on Reid's very naked, very lazy body. He was dressed for the day in jeans and a casual T-shirt. Both their safety whistles hung around his neck.

"Time to get up."

"When in the last three months have you ever seen me roll out of bed before sunrise?"

"Sunrise was six hours ago. Get out of bed or I'll snap my cold hand against your beautiful bare ass."

"Hmmm, so I'm no closer to getting out of bed. But I'm far more awake."

Reid clenched his ass invitingly.

Sullivan followed through with a nice cool clap on his left cheek.

Reid buried a laugh in Sullivan's pillow. "How about you get in here?"

"How about I *make* you come—"

"It *is* my birthday . . ."

"—upstairs." Sullivan crawled over him and kissed his cheek. Whistles dangled coldly over Reid's arm and he wriggled under Sullivan until he was on his back, staring up at Sullivan's smirking face. "God you're beautiful. Get up."

"I am." Reid bit back a laugh, and Sullivan wrapped a hand around his *very hard* predicament and gave him a tortuously slow pull.

"Get up, and tonight . . ." Sullivan whispered in his ear, kissed him and left, and Reid scrambled after him.

He yanked on clean clothes and no sooner had he stepped into the saloon, a head of bright hair blurred and Joanna tackled him into a hug. "Finally. We worked in stealth all morning for your surprise, and you need to see it immediately. Right, Dad?"

Sullivan inclined his head, sinking into his boots.

Joanna pulled Reid outside, where Sullivan had set up a small table with champagne and flute glasses.

Unfortunately, Joanna steered him past the table, over the gangplank.

Reid rocked up a brow and glanced at Sullivan trailing him. "We have to be on solid ground for my gift? I'm loving it already."

"Funny," Sullivan said. "I'm taking you out on the open water later."

Reid groaned, but was secretly excited for Sullivan taking him to the stars. "Did you buy us a car?"

"Like I'd buy that without you."

Joanna stopped mid-dock and let go of his hand. She bounced on her toes, sun beaming down on her freckled cheeks.

Sullivan closed the distance behind him, wrapping his arms around Reid's waist. A white envelope tapped Reid's chest.

Reid blinked at it. "What's this?"

"Hmmm, what could it be?" Sullivan mused. "Best let curiosity get the better of you."

Reid ripped into it. His eyes scanned the words. "Official boat name registration . . . what?"

Joanna looked bursting to speak.

Sullivan spoke in his ear. "Turn toward our boat."

Reid did, gaze latching onto the name of the yacht.

AQUARIANCER

Butterflies *thump-thump-thumped*. His throat was all kinds of sore as he held back a laugh, a cry, he didn't know which. "You shipped us."

He might die from all the feels he was getting. From all the love.

Joanna bubbled with information. "It might look like paint, but Dad had to notify insurers and update permits and licenses. He had to do loads of paperwork and change electronic equipment. And more than that, he had to overcome superstition."

Reid turned his head to catch Sullivan's eye. "Superstition?" he mouthed.

Joanna explained. "Apparently changing a boat name is terribly bad luck—"

"It is," Sullivan said, deathly serious.

Reid swallowed a chuckle. "What made you brave it?"

"I didn't take away the old name, I'm not disrespecting any

of its memories and adventures. I'm simply adding a second part to it." Sullivan took the envelope Reid pinched and pulled out a smaller slip of paper Reid had overlooked. "Plus, I found this."

Reid glimpsed a paragraph of text. "What is it?"

Sullivan strode back on board the ship, right to the champagne table.

Reid exchanged a curious look with Joanna, and they raced after him.

Sullivan positioned himself, facing north. He raised his arms, and his deep voice boomed around them. "Poseidon. Great and mighty ruler of the seas—"

No way.

This wasn't happening.

His logical, inventor boyfriend was not actually begging the Gods.

". . . grant this worthy vessel *Aquariancer* the safety and benefits of your deep, beautiful wildness."

So this was actually happening.

Best birthday present ever.

"Joanna," Sullivan instructed, "the bubbly. Pour a glass."

Sullivan continued, shifting positions, addressing all the gods.

Delighted tears blurred Reid's vision and choking laughter rippled up his throat, where he trapped it.

When Sullivan was done, he drained his glass, and Reid drained the one Joanna handed him too.

He slunk up to Sullivan. "So." He took Sullivan's empty glass and handed both their flutes to Joanna, who watched them with a goofy grin. "What was that all about?"

"One does not tempt the Gods of the Seas." Sullivan touched his cheeks. "I love you, and I'll do everything to keep you safe."

Reid fucking floated. "I love you too, muffin top."

"*Sullivan.*"

Reid grinned, lifted onto his toes, and kissed him. "Yes, sir."

THE END

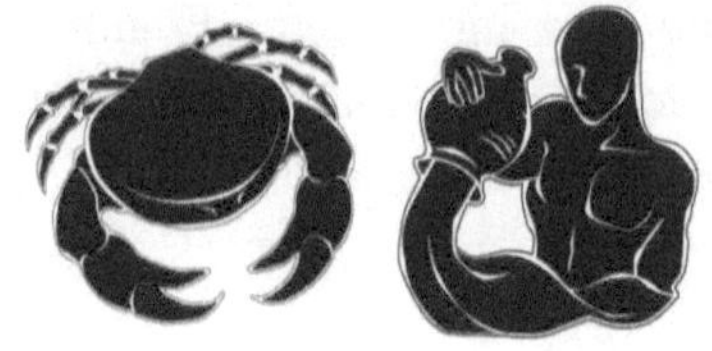

Signs of Love #5.5 - Cancer Sweetens Aquarius

Gripping a crochet hook, Reid stood barefoot in the dimly-lit saloon. Mangled wool wrapped his other hand.

Three weeks ago, everyone was happy. He'd made Sullivan speechless and Joanna snicker when he'd left home for bananas and returned home with twins. There'd been an emergency with Theo's grandma Darla and he'd swooped in to help Theo and Jamie with the toddlers.

Anyway, they were happy.

Until BAM! Their marina neighbors—Mason and Elijah—were leaving. Mason had found a new job in San Diego. Elijah and Joanna had to say goodbye.

A week later, they'd left.

Left Joanna heartbroken.

Staring at the wool cutting off the circulation in his fingers, Reid blinked back the memory of Joanna's tearful goodbye with her boyfriend. His stomach dropped with sympathy.

He squared his shoulders and used the hook to untangle himself.

"It's the middle of the night." Sullivan's sexy, sleep-croaky voice startled Reid, and he swung around to the partition where Sullivan stood in his flannel pajama pants, a tank top over his impressively toned chest. His eyes beheld Reid with concern.

Reid dropped the hook and the wool onto the couch and laughed hollowly. "I'm trying to fix this."

Sullivan pushed into the room and bent over the heater. "It's cold in here. Why don't you have this on?"

Cold floorboards bit Reid's feet as he paced between Sullivan and the couch. He gazed toward the drizzling rain and the inky sea beyond. "Maybe if . . . or . . . but . . ."

He twisted on his heel toward the couch, and Sullivan hooked strong arms around him, stilling him. Sullivan's front blazed against Reid's cool back and he sank into it.

"Hey, love," Sullivan murmured into his ear. "We'll figure it out."

Reid sighed. "I-I don't know what else to do."

Sullivan rubbed Reid's arms soothingly. "Deep breath."

"I can't. She's sad. That makes me sad."

A ticklish sigh breezed through Reid's hair. "I promise, we'll find a way to cheer her up."

Sullivan's earnestness had Reid swallowing back a tidal wave of skin-tingling, heart-pounding love. Every year, every month, every day it grew stronger. It fueled him.

And made him fiercely protective of his family. He turned and leaned his forehead against the crook of Sullivan's neck. "We've been trying since Elijah left. Two weeks, Sullivan. Two."

"I confess, I'm surprised she didn't crack a grin watching you try to crochet her slippers." Reid pulled back, following Sullivan's fond gaze to his crochet hook and wool. "You really can't crochet."

Reid laughed and forced a scowl. "The lady in the store said it was easy. Lying tart." He ran a hand through his hair. "The trip to the movies didn't work. Neither did the vegan ice cream"—he prodded a finger against Sullivan's chest—"but that's on you and your no-sugar craze."

"It's not good for you," Sullivan retorted.

"It's good when your favorite sports team loses. It's good when you've had your tonsils out. And it's good when your heart breaks."

Sullivan raised his hands in defeat. "Fine, go nuts with the sugar. Eat all the ice cream you want."

Reid pulled Sullivan with him to the couch and settled onto it. Sullivan pressed close along his side, thigh to thigh, arm to arm. Reid rested his head on the back cushion. "I just love her, you know?"

"Really? I had no clue."

Reid whacked Sullivan in the stomach, eliciting a chuckle. "She's so spirited, full of adventure and meddling awesomeness. And she makes me laugh."

Sullivan rubbed his leg, warming him through his thin

cotton pajama pants. "Joanna is turning out to be an incredible young woman."

Reid smiled at the ceiling. "Do you know the best meddlesome thing she's done?"

"I absolutely do."

"Interviewing me to be your manny."

"Running away whenever we were in a room together, hoping we'd kiss."

"Which we did," Reid murmured.

"Eventually."

Reid lifted his head and shot Sullivan a look. "Hey, that part's all on you."

Their noses were an inch from bumping. God, the man was beautiful. He leaned closer. "You were clueless."

Reid breathed in Sullivan's musky, oaky scent. "Cluelessly in love with you."

"Ah, I wanted to kiss you from the first time I saw you. It only compounded from there." A soft smile touched Sullivan's lips as he leaned in—

And bypassed Reid's lips.

Reid blinked; Sullivan bent down and pulled off his thick woolen socks. A massaging pressure at his foot had Reid moaning. Sullivan lifted his numb foot and covered it with a warm sock. The second one followed.

Reid snuggled closer against Sullivan. "I feel better."

"Warmer, anyway." Sullivan kissed Reid's forehead, lips firm and comforting. "Would you like a shot of liqueur?"

"You know that's basically sugar right?"

"That smirk is unbecoming."

"I'm sorry." Reid smiled harder.

Sullivan shook his head and padded toward the kitchen.

"So what's our plan for tomorrow?" Reid asked as Sullivan procured shot glasses.

"Seeing the sunrise with you sounds good," Sullivan said.

Reid snorted. "I love you. Good luck."

Concern softened the strong lines of Sullivan's face. "You meant about Joanna."

Reid nodded. "Yeah."

Sullivan stared at the glass bottle for a long time before twisting off the cap. "Sometimes the heart just needs time."

"She doesn't have to be over him. I'd just love to see her smile and mean it. It could be from the world's worst joke for all I care." Reid sat straight. "How about you try that one?"

That earned him a withering look. "You really know how to make a man feel special."

Sullivan handed Reid a shot glass.

Reid took it and knocked it back, throat burning. He spluttered out a cough and a firm hand patted his back.

Sullivan smoothly downed his shot and set their glasses aside. He wound an arm around Reid's shoulders and rubbed, thumb skating over the neckline of his night shirt, tickling his neck.

"So you'll attempt the dad joke?" Reid asked, a cheeky grin pulling at his lips.

Those intense blue eyes soaked up every inch of Reid's face, lingering at his mouth, his eyes. "As long as it warms your heart."

Reid squirmed, voice breathless. "It warms something. You can practice on me right now if you like."

Sullivan smiled slowly and bumped their noses together. "That was a decidedly sexy turn in conversation."

Reid groaned, and palmed his head. "You're right, how can I even think about my own fun right now?"

"If it helps, that kind of fun puts a smile on *my* face." Sullivan's laugh was husky and a flare of heat shot through Reid's body. "Any way I can sugar you up?"

"I suppose you could frost—no wait, I'm getting carried away by your sexiness." Reid pushed back against Sullivan's chest, putting a few inches between them. "Back to Joanna. We don't do anything until we have a plan."

Sullivan lunged for the nearest pen and paper. "What are we waiting for?" He scrawled PLAN in block letters at the top. "What about taking a trip to town and waking Joanna up to fresh glazed donuts?"

"I'm having a difficult time switching from sexy to sweet. Give me a sec."

Sullivan urgently crossed out the idea.

Reid peeled his eyes away from his gorgeous man. "Weren't you detailing all the antioxidant properties of cinnamon last week? What about baking cinnamon buns?"

"Maybe we should think of something else to make her smile. I work hard to keep you out of the kitchen."

Fair enough. Reid had caused enough havoc in the kitchen over the years.

His gaze dropped to the bench at the wall, and he leapt to his feet.

Sullivan snagged his hand, staring at him quizzically.

Reid grinned. "I know what to do. I'll give her the Christmas gift I got her." He pulled his hand free and headed to the hollow bench where they stashed their gifts.

Sullivan lurched in front of him, arms splayed wide, panic crossing his face.

Reid halted. "What are you doing?"

Sullivan cleared his throat. "Last week we made a pact not to look inside this bench until Christmas day."

"Yes, but that was for Joanna. Have you not wrapped your gifts yet, Sullivan?"

"No—yes. Yes! That's exactly it. I haven't had a chance to wrap mine yet."

"If you're too busy, I can do it for you and feign surprise."

Sullivan laughed drily. "No."

"Christmas is for Joanna. It doesn't matter if I know what

you got." Reid winked, and whispered, "Serious couples know everything." He tried to duck under Sullivan's arm, but Sullivan sat on the bench.

"I am serious. I seriously don't want you seeing your gift."

Reid frowned. "Fine. Pull out the palm-sized, reindeer wrapped one."

Sullivan gestured Reid to back up. Then he cracked open the bench and rummaged inside. He pulled out Reid's gift for Joanna and double-checked the lock on the bench.

He cradled the gift. "What is it?"

"Gents and gentlemen, what we have in here is a bracelet." Reid plucked it from his palm and leaned against the table. "It has stones in the shape of the Pisces constellation."

Sullivan peered down at the gift. "Sounds special."

A lump formed in Reid's throat. "She's been a part of my life for three years now. I know she's your daughter but I've found a very good friend in her."

Sullivan watched him quietly, his eyes shiny. "Sullivan?"

Sullivan stepped up to him and clasped his hands around Reid's shoulders. He swooped down and brushed his lips against Reid's, softly urgent. Tenderness surged inside of Reid and his grip on Joanna's gift doubled.

Sullivan teased his mouth open with his tongue, and they both moaned; vibrations tingled through Reid's body.

"Oh, wow." He swallowed. "Are you trying to distract me from my mission?" Sullivan's nose pressed against his, and he whispered another kiss over the bow of his lips. "Because it's almost working."

Sullivan smiled and stepped back. "No, I am one hundred percent on-board with this mission. Being the meddler is a nice change of pace."

"Do you think she'll like it?"

Sullivan gently loosened Reid's grip on the gift and inspected the neat wrapping carefully. "I think she'll love it."

"Love what?" came Joanna's sleepy voice.

Reid and Sullivan jerked toward her voice. She rested against the partition leading to the back of the boat, wearing flannel pants and what looked like one of Elijah's T-shirts. Her bright red hair tumbled wildly over her shoulders. Almost seventeen, and she was stunning. Stunning and sad.

"Sunrise has come early," Reid said.

Joanna's nose crinkled and Sullivan chuckled.

"Yeah, okay," Reid conceded. "That might be a little over the top."

"Why are you up?" Sullivan asked his daughter.

She shrugged. "There's a leak in my room."

Reid pounded into Sullivan's arms. Instinct.

Joanna rolled her eyes—was that the faintest smile on her face? "Not Titanic-type leaking. Just your regular cracks-around-the-porthole leaking."

Reid pulled away from Sullivan—but not too far—and dusted off invisible lint. "I was totally not panicking. I was testing your dad's reflexes."

"Sure. He caught you and dropped—what's this?" Joanna moved into the room and crouched, picking up her wrapped gift.

Sullivan flashed him an apologetic smile for dropping it. Hardly anything to blame when Reid had tried to vault him.

Reid grinned at Joanna. "That's for you to open."

"But it looks like a Christmas present."

"It was, but I want you to have it now."

Her eyes widened, questioning.

Sullivan cleared his throat. "Better you open it than Reid starts baking."

Reid snickered. "Big man scared of me and some cutlery."

Joanna eyed him frankly. "You really are quite frightening in there."

Reid scowled. "Will you open it?"

"Why are you so keen?"

"Just open, please. No wait—"

Joanna arched a brow. "Yes or no?"

"Get comfy. On the couch. Sullivan will make us elderflower syrup tea."

"I will?"

"Yes," Reid said, batting away his crochet attempt. He slung himself next to Joanna on the couch. "I might mix up the homemade syrup bottles with the liqueur ones—that'd make a memorable post break-up."

Joanna narrowed her eyes on him. "Break up? Is this"—she waved the gift—"you trying to make me feel better?"

Reid patted the back of her freckled hand. "Boys can cause a lot of heartbreak. We may need to start a tradition."

"I thought traditions were supposed to be fun?" She grinned but her lips quickly flattened and her shoulders slumped.

Reid pulled her into a hug. "I'm sorry it hurts."

"We'll still talk on the phone. They'll sail up here." She pulled back with a resigned sigh. "Yeah, it hurts."

Sullivan stood at the kitchen counter, teacups in hand, watching them. He looked pained. Like memories crashed together and beat out the climactic part of a symphony.

"It can rip your heart out, losing someone," Sullivan said quietly. He looked meaningfully at Reid. "*Thinking* you've lost someone." He swallowed. "Makes you want to drown."

A nervous laugh punched through Reid's nerves.

Sullivan left the kitchen and crouched in front of his daughter. "Things change with time." He squeezed her knee. "If it's possible, and it's important, you'll find a way to make it work."

Joanna threw her arms around her dad's neck.

Sullivan braced a steadying hand on Reid's thigh and hugged her with his other.

When she pulled back, she was nodding. Not smiling yet, but this was the closest Reid had come to his goal. "Like how Reid rowed over the ocean for you?"

Sullivan's chest expanded as he breathed in deeply. His gaze shifted from Joanna to Reid and held. "The most courageous thing anyone has done for me."

Reid's body thrummed with love, his feet perfectly warm in Sullivan's socks.

Sullivan continued, murmuring. "It makes me want to give you your Christmas gift early. Now."

Beside him, Joanna gasped. She started picking at the gift wrapping.

She pulled out the delicate gold bracelet and slipped it around her wrist. "It's beautiful."

She hugged and hugged and hugged him.

"Is it enough to make you smile?" Reid teased, praying it was.

She withdrew, and the old Joanna was back, a minxy twinkle lurking in her eyes. She cocked her head and eyed her dad. "You know what would make me happy?"

Sullivan seemed to read her mind, because he laughed, and pushed to his feet. He nervously rubbed his nape, glancing at Reid, and the biggest smile stretched across his face.

"What?" Reid asked, tucking his feet under him. "What would make you happy?"

She just winked at him.

Reid looked inquisitively toward Sullivan, but he was doubled over the bench, rifling through their—

Ahh. The minx wanted the Christmas gift Sullivan had gotten her too. Well, she certainly knew how to play her hand.

Sullivan returned, smile replaced by a quieter expression, a nervous tick in his jaw.

Reid had never seen Sullivan so flustered before, ever. He was always so calm. Rational, even-keeled.

Sullivan cleared his throat and knelt. Reid glimpsed a plush, square jewelry box, and laughed. Of course they both went the jewelry route for Joanna. Next year, he would insist they shop for presents together. Hopefully whatever—earrings? —he bought her matched the bracelet.

Sullivan looked at him, Adam's apple jutting. Did he want Reid's approval for giving Joanna her gift?

Reid nodded, encouraging him, and Sullivan opened the box.

Not earrings. A beautiful, white gold ring. "God that's beautiful."

Reid glanced at Joanna who gazed at her dad, tears in her eyes.

Sullivan spoke, voice cracking. "You like it, Reid?"

"Are you kidding me? It's *gorgeous*. It clashes, of course, but I'm happy to take the bracelet back and see if we can find one that will match." Reid gaped at the white-gold beauty again. "Did you check the size, because this looks like it might fall off her. Unless it's a toe ring? But this is far too nice to be covered up by a sock."

He looked up from the ring to Sullivan's flabbergasted face.

"What?"

Joanna made a weird noise in the back of her throat, like a suppressed giggle. He faced her. "Aren't you going to put it on?"

Joanna laughed. This gift truly did bring back her smile. "You want me to put it on?" Her dimples deepened as she looked at Sullivan. "What do you say, Dad? May I?"

Sullivan groaned and murmured, and Joanna plucked the ring out of its case, grabbed Reid's hand, and slipped it on him.

The smooth gold ring sank to the base of his finger and hugged his skin with perfect tightness. Reid blinked.

Heat rolled up his neck, and he swung his head to Sullivan. "You're *proposing*?"

Humor and fond exasperation beamed out of Sullivan as he took Reid's gilded hand. "Not very clearly. Let me remedy."

Sullivan's deep breath funnelled softly between Reid's fingers, around the ring. "Reid Glover, this ring is meant for you."

Reid's chest hopped with butterflies and Sullivan's outline blurred and sharpened and blurred again.

Sullivan kissed his knuckles. "Will you marry me?"

Acknowledgments

Crafting a book is no lonely process! I owe so much thanks to my beta and editing team for helping me shape Reid and Sullivan's story. Thank you to Vir, Sunne, and Heather for being involved in the developmental stage—and bearing with me as you read various incarnations of the plot. Thank you to Suki Fleet for helping me with the British aspects of the story and for your maritime expertise. Thank you to Deborah Nemeth for content editing. HJ's Editing for the fantastic line edits. Lynda for proofreading. And thank you to Vicki and Todd for final eyes reading and catching those last flubs. Maria Gandolfo, thank you for the chapter graphics of Cancer and Aquarius, and Natasha—cheers for yet another wonderful cover.

Anyta Sunday

HEART-STOPPING SLOW BURN

A bit about me: I'm a big, BIG fan of slow-burn romances. I love to read and write stories with characters who slowly fall in love.

Some of my favorite tropes to read and write are: Enemies to Lovers, Friends to Lovers, Clueless Guys, Bisexual, Pansexual, Demisexual, Oblivious MCs, Everyone (Else) Can See It, Slow Burn, Love Has No Boundaries.

I write a variety of stories, Contemporary MM Romances with a good dollop of angst, Contemporary lighthearted MM Romances, and even a splash of fantasy.
My books have been translated into German, Italian, French, Spanish, and Thai.

Contact: http://www.anytasunday.com/about-anyta/
Sign up for Anyta's newsletter and receive a free e-book:
http://www.anytasunday.com/newsletter-free-e-book/

www.ingramcontent.com/pod-product-compliance
Lightning Source LLC
LaVergne TN
LVHW091402190726
843491LV00006B/1223

* 9 7 8 3 9 4 7 9 0 9 6 4 3 *